The Anatomy of a Great Doctor

Skills, Struggles, and Success in Modern Medicine

Dr. Shahzad Younas

Dedication

My teachers, well-wishers, and patients, who helped me understand the purpose and philosophy of life.

Foreword

Providing comprehensive care has become more challenging in this era of rapid technological advancement and ever-evolving medical breakthroughs. 'The Anatomy of a Great Doctor: Skills, Struggles, and Success in Modern Medicine' is a book that serves as a guiding beacon for those who embark on the noble journey of a healer. Dr. Shahzad Younas, with the precision of a seasoned surgeon and the grace of a writer, dissects this journey with honesty and wisdom in this literary work of passion and intellect.

Expanding over 32 chapters, the volume addresses the strengths and lasting qualities of a broad spectrum of topics. As I understand it, the book creates a personal conversation with Dr. Younas as the reader goes through each page. Dr. Younas sheds light on some realities often left unsaid, truths that go beyond the limits of a clinical setting. It is a compass for those lost in the rigor of routine, a lantern for medicine students in search of illumination, and, indeed, a mirror for every healthcare practitioner. The book aims to transform readers and motivate them to reach their full potential as professionals and as role models for humanity.

Brave and provocative, yet cautious and thoughtful, Dr. Younas's insights extend beyond medicine and delve deep into the human heart. Whether you are a seasoned physician, a medical student, or a layperson intrigued by the world of healthcare, this book is a treasure trove that promises to enlighten, challenge, and inspire.

With this book in hand, let us explore the heart and spirit of medicine. So, brace yourself for a journey of profound insights and valuable lessons. Prepare to have your perspectives challenged, your well-held beliefs questioned, and your understanding deepened. After all, perfection isn't a destination; it's a journey. May we each find our path to greatness.

Dr. Adil Al Zadjali
Senior Consultant, Hepatobiliary Surgeon
Head of the Department of Surgery
Sultan Qaboos University Hospital
Muscat, Sultanate of Oman

Preface

Thank you for choosing to read this introduction. Your decision to dedicate your valuable time to this book is a testament to your commitment to personal growth and learning. I hope the words on these pages inspire you and help you achieve your goals. Allow me to provide insight into the choice of writing this book, "The Anatomy of a Great Doctor: Skills, Struggles, and Success in Modern Medicine."

Doctors are responsible for treating ailments and bringing joy and contentment to the lives of patients and their families. Sir William Osler aptly stated, "The good physician treats the disease; the great physician treats the patient who has the disease."

Medical practitioners are driven by pursuing professional growth, enhancing their public image, gaining excellence in knowledge and skills, and earning recognition. They immerse themselves in continuous learning, tireless work, and significant personal sacrifice to achieve these objectives. Unfortunately, only a few reach their desired level of recognition as great doctors, both locally and on a broader scale.

Why do only a handful achieve this excellence while many others struggle to progress professionally and lead average and unsatisfactory lives?

In today's era of scientific advancements, why do patients and doctors find themselves less content than in the past despite exceptional diagnostic and therapeutic tools?

The rising rates of burnout, anxiety, depression, and suicides among doctors globally, the surge in medical errors, malpractice, complaints, litigations, and the increasing numbers of doctors leaving the profession—all raise pertinent questions.

This book seeks answers to these questions and provides a unique platform for introspection for every medical professional. It aims to enable critical self-analysis and evaluation of their performance.

By reading this book, each doctor can identify their strengths and weaknesses, understand how to address deficiencies, and further enhance their strengths. They progress towards the apex of medical expertise by overcoming their limitations and building on their strengths.

Written in a reader-friendly and engaging style, this book is designed for every doctor to read and absorb. It encourages making notes on crucial points to facilitate personal modification and growth, ultimately striving for the satisfaction and excellence necessary to be recognized as "A Great Doctor."

I hope you find joy in reading this book. I sincerely wish that it helps reshape your thoughts and practice and ultimately aids you in achieving the esteemed recognition of being "The Great Doctor" locally, nationally, and globally.

Dr. Shahzad Younas

Table of Contents

Unveiling the Medical Profession: Expectations vs Reality

"Wear the white coat with dignity and pride; it is an honor and privilege to serve the public as a physician."

- Bill H. Warren

Overview:

We all desire a profoundly established life filled with personal success, financial stability, and robust health. Moreover, our ambition extends to making a positive contribution to the globe, serving the needs of people, and acquiring their love, gratitude, and respect. These objectives are of the utmost importance to goal-oriented and accomplished people when deciding on their career path. Prepare for a deep dive into a fundamental, life-saving profession surrounded by fascination, admiration, and a fair share of misconceptions. Though it can offer great fulfillment and satisfaction, it also presents unique and complex challenges that must be carefully considered. We aim to remove the veil of complexity often associated with the healthcare sector and offer an honest, clear-cut view of medicine. In this discourse, we draw the curtains back on the real world of medical practitioners, comparing the common assumptions and perceptions against the stark reality of this challenging profession. Those unaware of these requirements, challenges, and problems may become demoralized to the extent that they will either have to give up their dream of becoming a great doctor and settle for being an average doctor or quit the medical profession altogether. It's a must-read for aspiring medics, healthcare professionals, or anyone intrigued by this noble profession's often misunderstood dynamics. So, brace yourself as we explore this fascinating dichotomy between expectation and reality in medicine!

1: Stress-free educational journey once enrolled in Medical College:

Securing admission to medical college is arduous, involving a challenging qualifying exam that demands immense patience, determination, and student effort. Aspiring students face many educational, financial, emotional, and social challenges in preparing for the final qualifying exam. During this period, students often perceive the process as the last hurdle on their journey toward becoming a doctor. After the grueling admission process, they expect a smooth and stress-free path to fulfill their dream of becoming a doctor.

Reality:

The first few days of medical college are filled with excitement, happiness, and accomplishment. The students are confident in their decision to pursue a career in medicine. However, they quickly find themselves thrown into a new world of medical life, full of hardships, struggles, and a seemingly never-ending stream of readings. Medical students must master complex terminologies from voluminous books to excel in their exams.

Despite putting in their best efforts and showing unwavering commitment, many students who previously excelled in their academic pursuits need help to pass their exams. This is often when they compare themselves with their peers in other professions, leading to demoralization and uncertainty about their decision to pursue a medical career.

2: MBBS guarantees an enviable lifestyle:

After obtaining their MD (Doctor of Medicine) or MBBS (Bachelor of Medicine and Bachelor of Surgery) degree, young doctors feel a deep sense of pride, accomplishment, and happiness. This is a significant milestone in their life, and they feel satisfied with their hard work. They are excited to start the next phase of their lives and hope to achieve all their goals and aspirations as they embark on their medical careers.

Reality:

When interns begin training, they are usually excited and eager to apply their academic knowledge in a clinical setting. However, they soon realize that their theoretical learning has limited practical value and need guidance and supervision from experienced faculty members to apply their knowledge effectively.

During their internship, junior doctors face various challenges. These challenges may include performing repetitive and often tedious clerical tasks, responding to complex and demanding inquiries, and receiving criticism from their seniors during rounds. Additionally, they have to deal with complex patients and their families who may be demanding and uncooperative. They work long hours, often without proper compensation, and have to ignore harsh words and negative attitudes from their seniors and patients alike.

During their internship period, young doctors often face emotional challenges. They have to suppress their feelings and emotions while observing their non-medical peers move on by getting married and launching their independent careers. In addition, they must consider their future residency programs and prepare for their specialty exams. This makes it a time of impatience and frustration. As a result, many interns begin to question their decision to pursue a medical career.

3: The Residency program ensures a prosperous future:

Resident doctors who join a residency program are optimistic, believing they can complete their training without encountering significant obstacles. They are determined to excel in their preferred medical specialty and are confident they will have the opportunity to develop their skills and expertise. Their aspirations and dreams fuel their dedication to learning and excelling in their respective fields.

Reality:

The young doctors join their residency program with confidence, energy, and optimism. They are excited to learn and make a difference in the lives of their patients. However, they quickly become discouraged by their hectic schedules, heavy responsibilities, and intense competition.

Specialty residents need to enhance their theoretical knowledge and practical skills continuously. They should proactively plan elective and emergency cases and exhibit teamwork, communication skills, critical thinking, empathy, and ethical conduct while managing patients. The residency program requires a dedicated effort toward developing these core competencies, focusing on building a solid foundation for a successful medical career.

The residency program is very demanding and requires participants to work long hours, often at the expense of their sleep, leisure time, and family obligations. This can cause them to postpone essential life events such as weddings. Additionally, residents must manage their expenses while supporting their families on a modest salary. Along with challenging assignments, they must also deal with public and departmental pressure while meeting the expectations of their supervisors and senior colleagues. They also need to maintain control over their emotions and avoid outbursts.

4: Getting a fellowship degree puts you in the respected group of millionaires:

Many individuals aspire to pursue a career in the medical field because they desire financial gain and social recognition. Aspiring medical students and fellows tend to look up to their mentors, busy practitioners, and renowned doctors in their respective fields, hoping to achieve similar lifestyles and social status. Furthermore, societal pressures, such as expectations from family and peers and a feeling of social disparity, can also play a role in prioritizing financial success as a primary goal.

Reality:

The medical profession is enriching, providing both personal fulfillment and financial stability. However, achieving success in this field requires unwavering dedication, hard work, and high professional competence. It is important to note that those only interested in financial gain, without a commitment to excellence, may not find this profession suitable. On average, it takes diligent doctors between 35 and 40 years of age to attain a high level of proficiency, during which time they must learn to manage their finances with a limited income. It is common for physicians to compare their financial status with their non-medical peers, which can cause frustration despite their exceptional academic and professional achievements.

5: Recognition as Savior of life:

As individuals embark on their journey to become medical practitioners, their ultimate goal is to serve humanity by preserving the lives of the ill and dying. They aspire to be regarded as life-saving heroes, believing their vast knowledge, refined skills, and unwavering hard work can help them achieve this noble objective. The portrayal of doctors in films, TV shows, documentaries, and personal accounts of renowned, competent, and successful doctors further reinforces their convictions. It inspires them to become the best possible versions of themselves.

Reality:

Doctors play a crucial role in diagnosing, treating, and helping patients recover from illnesses and terminal conditions. However, it's essential to recognize that this is not a job only one person can do. It requires effective collaboration among the team members. Unfortunately, there are instances where team members need to work together effectively, and the doctors may overstep their boundaries. As a result, patients may receive inadequate treatment, which could lead to severe complications instead of healing.

Doctors may face various challenges during their practice, including financial and logistical limitations, peer influence, lack of patient and family education, and non-adherence to treatment. These factors can hinder the doctor's ability to provide optimal care to the patient, resulting in a potential loss of life.

These issues can leave doctors feeling disheartened, disillusioned, and infuriated. It may shatter their beliefs, aspirations, confidence, and passion, leading them to question their vocation and capacity to help others.

6: Easy to earn Unconditional Respect and trust:

Trust and respect are fundamental to establishing a successful relationship between patients and physicians. That's why the medical profession is regarded as one of the most prestigious in the world. Each doctor strives to create a sense of confidence in patients and their families, thereby confirming their position as a reliable healthcare provider.

Reality:

In recent times, medicine has become increasingly complex and challenging. The easy access to information through various media channels has helped to improve awareness and knowledge about diseases and medical practices among the general public. However, it has also led to many misconceptions and false beliefs about the profession.

The media often portrays negative aspects of the medical profession, such as errors, corruption, and incomplete information about diseases and treatments.

Unfortunately, the reputation of the medical community has been tarnished due to the actions of a few dishonest individuals. Incompetent, unqualified, or greedy practitioners have significantly harmed the public's perception of doctors, who were once revered as healers and life savers. Now, they are sometimes seen as merchants of misery who prioritize profit over patient care. This shift in perception has resulted in a notable decline in trust and respect for medical professionals and increased legal action against them globally.

The proliferation of ineffective communication, long waiting periods, short consultation sessions, and high costs of diagnostic and therapeutic procedures have eroded trust and respect for the medical community.

Strategies to balance expectations with realities:

Medical students need support, counseling, and physical care. They can overcome challenges with the right approach and attitude. Rather than being overwhelmed by the demands of their studies, they should focus on practical solutions like time management, meditation, exercise, and proper sleep. Although it's a challenging period, it's also when students learn the value of resilience, perseverance, and the importance of hard work. By prioritizing their mental and physical well-being, students can navigate the stresses of medical studies and emerge as skilled and compassionate medical professionals.

Institutions are responsible for providing fair opportunities for fresh graduates to secure paid employment and residency slots. This is essential for building a solid foundation for their future career development. Mentors and senior professionals should treat young physicians with kindness, respect, and enthusiasm. They should offer appropriate guidance based on the individual's interests and abilities.

Creating a team of competent and high-quality professionals requires a stress-free work environment. Every institution should provide a healthy, cooperative, and progressive platform free of biases for all its residents. Such an environment should facilitate learning and working with passion and efficiency. To achieve this objective, regular feedback, career counseling, communication and leadership workshops, financial support, periodic breaks, and unit get-togethers can significantly contribute to creating a positive learning and working environment. These initiatives would encourage a constructive working atmosphere, promote collaboration among residents, help them improve their skills, and achieve their professional goals.

Furthermore, the support of family, friends, and peers is crucial during this training phase to keep the young doctors motivated and satisfied. Such support plays a significant role in boosting their confidence, maintaining their interest in the medical field, and helping them overcome self-doubt and negative thoughts, enabling them to progress positively.

Regular counseling sessions, seminars, and workshops led by experienced faculty staff and guest speakers, including successful private practitioners, who can share their personal experiences, struggles, and success stories with aspiring doctors are critical in teaching the core values and practical dynamics of the medical profession to fresh graduates and residents. Apart from providing insights into the medical profession, these interactive sessions can help young doctors address their queries, doubts, and concerns.

Taking risks when confronted with logistical or financial impediments is not advisable. Instead, physicians should try to transfer the patient to a tertiary care hospital equipped with all necessary facilities after providing initial resuscitation and essential life support. Effective handling of patients and families who need to be more informed or compliant necessitates empathy, emotional intelligence, and efficient communication. Despite the challenges and obstacles that may arise, physicians must maintain hope and always strive to preserve the life of a sick or dying patient.

In contemporary healthcare, patients are more aware of their legal entitlements. Consequently, physicians must prioritize their proficiency in evidence and ethics-based medicine and effectively communicate with their patients without bias or conflicts of interest. This is the only viable approach to achieving excellence in the medical profession and establishing trust between healthcare providers and patients.

Conclusion:

The medical profession is often shrouded in misconceptions, with people believing it to be a smooth and lucrative career path. However, the reality is full of unique and complex challenges. From the stressful and demanding educational journey in medical college to the harsh realities of internships and residencies, the path to becoming a successful doctor is complex. Moreover, achieving wealth, respect, and recognition as a lifesaver may be more challenging than perceived. The profession calls for intense dedication, hard work, resilience, and professional competence, even though societal changes and media portrayals have led to a decline in trust and respect for medical professionals. However, with support and counseling, a proactive attitude, and the embracement of practical solutions, aspiring medical professionals can navigate the rigors of their profession and emerge as skilled and compassionate practitioners. Medical institutions and senior professionals create a positive and cooperative learning environment, encouraging growth and collaboration. Furthermore, ethical conduct, efficient communication, and evidence-based practice are vital to maintaining patients' trust and respect in modern healthcare.

Suggested Readings

- Jon McKenna. (2022, October 13). Infographic: Expectations vs Reality for Medical Residents. Article.

- Koshy, M. (2016). Being a doctor: Time for a reality check. In Quantitative Imaging in Medicine and Surgery (Vol. 6, Issue 2, pp. 238–239). AME Publishing Company.

- Horesh, A. (2023). Is a Medical Career Right for You? A Brutally Honest Look at the Pros and Cons.

- Adesanya, O. (2018). Medical school: expectations vs reality.

- The Medical Profession: Savior of Health and Life | by Big | Medium (2023)

- Fleming, N. (2019). Matching dreams of a career in medicine with reality.

Professional Competence In Medicine: Is it achievable?

"The practice of medicine is an art, not a trade, a calling, not a business, a calling in which your heart will be exercised equally with your head."

- William Osler

Overview:

As medicine progresses, it becomes increasingly important for healthcare professionals to be highly skilled in safeguarding public health. They are responsible for saving lives and easing the pain of those suffering from illnesses. However, there's a tendency for doctors to concentrate only on identifying and curing diseases, often overlooking the importance of emotional support. Offering comfort and hope to patients is a critical but frequently ignored part of medical care that significantly affects a patient's well-being. This discussion analyzes the essential skills needed in medicine and invites constructive conversations about abilities beyond medical treatment. It questions whether we can genuinely incorporate these skills into medical practice and prompts us to reconsider how we train, evaluate, and set standards for doctors. The goal is to continuously improve and adapt to the challenges of the medical field's complex nature.

Common miss-conception about doctor's competence:

Let's explore an interesting topic — the key traits that distinguish a competent physician or surgeon.

Physicians' competence is often associated with their ability to understand and diagnose a wide range of illnesses related to their expertise. On the other hand, surgeons' competency is usually assessed based on their proficiency in performing the relevant surgical procedures.

Here, I would like to share a famous joke about this theme.

Two men are racing to stop an elevator. One places his head in the door, while the other uses his hand. When questioned about why they would risk their body parts, the man who stuck in his head responds, "I am a surgeon, and my brain is not that vital!" The other participant replies, "I am a physician and do not need my hands either!"

This joke offers insight into the traditional views of physicians and surgeons and the perceived differences between their respective specialties.

However, a crucial question arises concerning whether the depth of a physician's knowledge or the skills of a surgeon are the only measures of their professional competence. The answer to this question is negative, but it is imperative to investigate the fundamental attributes that determine the competence of a physician or surgeon.

"Remember, competency is not a destination; it's a lifelong journey of growth and self-improvement."

Understanding the concept of professional competence:

To be recognized as a competent doctor, one must acquire the required education and skills and demonstrate professionalism, effective communication, and leadership abilities. These qualities are crucial in attaining a prominent position in the healthcare industry, and a comprehensive and evidence-based approach is necessary to become an expert in all of them.

Professionalism is a crucial aspect of the medical field that involves various values such as honesty, integrity, patient respect, and a commitment to patient-centered care. Collaborating with other healthcare professionals is also essential to promoting a culture of trust, mutual respect, and shared responsibility. By prioritizing professionalism, better patient outcomes can be achieved.

Effective communication is an essential skill that every healthcare professional must possess. It involves listening, showing empathy, and expressing oneself clearly and concisely to patients. Developing a solid and respectful bond with patients and their families is necessary to convey complex medical information, discuss various treatment options, and address their concerns while alleviating their anxiety. Effective communication is a fundamental aspect of healthcare provision, and building a reliable rapport with patients and their families is impossible without it.

Developing practical leadership skills is crucial for physicians who lead a medical team. They need to encourage, motivate, and persuade others while effectively communicating under high-pressure situations to provide uncomplicated medical care to patients and make life-saving decisions. Physicians who hone these skills excel as competent healthcare professionals, leading to outstanding patient recovery and management outcomes.

The importance of professional competence in healthcare:

The quality of patient care in the healthcare industry is closely tied to the professional competence of healthcare practitioners. Competent medical professionals are more confident, enthusiastic, and booming in their careers. Their competence allows them to achieve the highest level of patient satisfaction while also making significant contributions to the success of their healthcare organizations and institutions.

A competent, friendly, and approachable physician can create a sense of trust and comfort in their patients. This can foster a relaxing and reassuring atmosphere where patients feel comfortable discussing their concerns and asking questions. Such an environment promotes a healthy and friendly relationship between the doctor and patient, ultimately improving healthcare outcomes.

On the other hand, a lack of professional competence among medical practitioners can have severe consequences. When medical practitioners are deficient in vital skills and comprehension, patients are at risk, including severe repercussions from misjudgments in diagnosis, incorrect therapeutic approaches, and long-term suffering.

Ways to achieve professional competence:

To excel in your chosen field, you must deeply understand core concepts and skills essential to mastering your specialty. This requires a solid determination to put in long hours of hard work. Persistence and a steadfast commitment to excellence are necessary to reach your full potential and become an expert in your field. Without these qualities, you may only achieve brief and unfulfilling success.

Medical professionals need to attend educational events such as conferences, courses, workshops, and webinars to stay up-to-date with the latest advancements and breakthroughs in the medical field. By doing so, they can enhance their knowledge and skills, keep abreast of new technologies and treatments, and provide the best possible care to their patients.

To tackle the intricate aspects of patient management, such as diagnosis, communication, treatment, and surgical skills, it is often recommended to divide them into smaller, more manageable tasks. Each of these tasks must then be honed through repeated written, verbal, and practical exercises, which provide the foundation for expanding one's knowledge and enhancing technical skills. This iterative process allows for a more nuanced understanding of the subject matter and enables the development of mastery over time. By engaging in this systematic and structured approach to learning, individuals can acquire the expertise needed to address complex tasks with greater confidence and competence.

Collaboration and communication among healthcare professionals from diverse specialties are crucial for improving patient outcomes and delivering high-quality care. Appreciating and acknowledging each team member's diverse skill set and knowledge is essential. Working together as a team ensures that patients receive the best possible care, leading to better health outcomes and an improved quality of life. Effective teamwork promotes a culture of mutual respect, trust, and collaboration, which is vital for achieving success in the healthcare sector.

Reassurance from senior colleagues through feedback and guidance works wonders! Their constructively critical insights and guidance allow you to spot the chinks in your armor and polish the skills to bridge those gaps. In turn, such practices foster a positive environment of learning and team spirit, which spells good news for everyone involved in patient care.

Conclusion:

Professional competence in medicine is not solely about medical knowledge or technical expertise. It encompasses diverse skills and attributes, including professionalism, effective communication, leadership abilities, and a commitment to ongoing learning. A competent physician is confident in diagnosing and treating diseases, is empathetic and understanding towards patients, and can provide comfort and hope in challenging times. Moreover, they continually strive to enhance their knowledge and skills through continuous learning from professional events and feedback from senior colleagues. Lastly, professional competence within the medical profession is significant due to its direct correlation with the quality of patient care, patient satisfaction, and the overall success of healthcare institutions.

Suggested Readings

- Jose, A., Tortorella, G. L., Vassolo, R., Kumar, M., & Mac Cawley, A. F. (2023). Professional Competence and Its Effect on the Implementation of Healthcare 4.0 Technologies: Scoping Review and Future Research Directions. In International Journal of Environmental Research and Public Health (Vol. 20, Issue 1). MDPI.

- Khadka, M., & Kunwar, B. (2021). Ways to make medical students competent professionally: View of medical students. Journal of the Nepal Medical Association, 59(244), 1328–1330.

- Catto, G. (2003). Improving professional competence - The way ahead? In International Journal for Quality in Health Care (Vol. 15, Issue 5, pp. 375–376).

- Kirk, L. M. (2007). Professionalism in medicine: definitions and considerations for teaching. Proceedings (Baylor University. Medical Center), 20(1), 13.

- Wiese, A., Galvin, E., Korotchikova, I., & Bennett, D. (2022). Doctors' attitudes to maintenance of professional competence: A scoping review. In Medical Education (Vol. 56, Issue 4, pp. 374–386). John Wiley and Sons Inc.

- Skrinda, I., Kokina, I., & Iliško, D. (2022). Assessment of a Professional Competence of Healthcare Personnel230–237.

- Clin Med. (2004). The competent doctor.

Few Minutes Or Whole Life: What is best for doctors?

"Do not spoil the wonder with haste."

- J.R.R. Tolkien

Overview:

Medical professionals quickly juggle many patients and tough cases in our fast-paced healthcare sector. This rush can risk errors in diagnosis and treatment, raising the question: should speed trump accuracy? Investigators at Johns Hopkins, alongside the Risk Management Foundation of Harvard Medical Institutions, analyzed 15 illnesses and determined that misdiagnoses led to 371,000 deaths and permanent disabilities in 424,000 individuals across the United States. Examining the underlying causes of these undesirable events in patient care is essential. The root cause is often not a lack of knowledge or skill but rather the less time doctors spend with their patients. A doctor's expertise is useless if he doesn't realize that "Spending a few more minutes on patient management is far better than spending your whole life facing the consequences of medical mistakes."

We will delve into this principle further in our discussion to shed light on a critical yet frequently neglected component of patient care: the time taken during consultations, examinations, diagnosing, treating, and follow-up appointments. The text drives awareness about this crucial aspect, inspiring medical practitioners and health system stakeholders to consider whether an extra minute, a second look, or a double-check could save lives, prevent suffering, and assure well-being. This piece is both a call to action and a reality check, prompting healthcare professionals to take a step back and reassess how they combat the polarities of time and patient safety in their practice.

History and Physical Examination: "The Cornerstone of Diagnostic Precision."

A comprehensive and meticulously compiled medical history and a detailed physical examination are foundational elements that critically influence patient management and care outcomes. In medicine, these steps are not simply routine procedures but the cornerstone upon which a physician can make sound diagnostic decisions, personalize treatment plans, and build a meaningful therapeutic alliance with the patient. When a healthcare provider dedicates ample time and attention to collecting a patient's medical history judiciously, carries out a comprehensive physical examination with attention to subtle signs, and engages in open and empathetic communication with the patient, the benefits are multifaceted. This careful approach substantially improves the accuracy of diagnosis and the appropriateness of subsequent treatment interventions, aligning them closely with the patient's specific health issues.

On the contrary, when healthcare practitioners fall short in delving deeply during patient interviews or rush through the physical examination, they inadvertently increase the risk of medical oversights. A cursory approach may lead to the clinician missing key symptoms or ignoring potential red flags that would otherwise guide them toward an accurate diagnosis. The implications of such oversights are severe, including but not limited to increased incidences of diagnostic errors, administering inappropriate or ineffective treatments, and the escalated chance of adverse medical events. These missteps could culminate in grievous consequences for the patient, such as enduring unnecessary procedures, experiencing prolonged pain or discomfort, and losing faith in medical practitioners' ability to provide adequate care.

For example, a patient presenting with symptoms indicative of a common condition might have their underlying issue overlooked if a careful review of their medical history and a thorough examination are neglected. To illustrate, imagine a scenario where a patient consults a surgeon for atypical upper abdominal pain and, based on preliminary ultrasonography, is diagnosed with gallstones (cholelithiasis). Suppose the surgeon hastily decides to proceed with a laparoscopic cholecystectomy without delving into a thorough history-taking or conducting an all-encompassing physical examination. In that case, he might miss that the patient's symptoms could be related to a more complex condition caused by an underlying and quite likely different gastrointestinal condition, which would necessitate alternative investigative and therapeutic approaches before considering surgical options. The risk of this patient suffering from post-cholecystectomy syndrome and the surgeon facing the consequences of mismanagement is very high.

Furthermore, during the history-taking process, it is imperative for a physician to systematically consider and rule out various differential diagnoses that could present with similar symptoms to the chief complaint. Thorough history-taking involves focusing on the symptoms and methodically scrutinizing the patient's systemic inquiry results, past medical history, social history, medication history, and family history. These elements can be astonishingly revealing, sometimes unearthing diagnoses that the initial presenting symptoms might not have suggested.

Take, for instance, an elderly patient experiencing severe abdominal pain; the chief complaint alone might not provide sufficient insight into the underlying cause. However, a detailed history might reveal the patient has a history of atrial fibrillation and is on warfarin therapy, which could lead a physician to suspect acute mesenteric ischemia. This diagnosis would be supported by additional findings from a physical examination, such as an irregularly irregular pulse and the clinical signs associated with an acute abdomen. This example underscores the importance of adopting a holistic approach to medical assessment, which combines history-taking and physical examination findings to arrive at a precise diagnosis.

Ultimately, the additional time and effort devoted during the history-taking and physical examination are justifiable. When weighed against the alternative of expending valuable time, effort, and healthcare resources on unnecessary and sometimes invasive diagnostic procedures. This more deliberate approach helps avoid the longer-term consequences of misdiagnoses, incorrect treatment, and the potential for ensuing legal actions. Heightened quality in the initial stages of patient evaluation enhances clinical outcomes. It contributes to the overall satisfaction and well-being of the patient, which is the gold standard and chief priority of any dedicated medical practitioner.

Avoiding the Pitfalls of Diagnostic Dominance in Healthcare Practice:

Within the contemporary medical sphere, a practitioner manages various responsibilities, including patient care, academia, administrative duties, and personal obligations. As such, allocating sufficient time for thorough patient histories, examinations, counseling, and open lines of communication can be challenging. Furthermore, the trend towards a diagnosis-focused model, empowered by the advancements in imaging and lab testing facilities, has created a modern benchmark in clinical practice. Clinicians worldwide now rely heavily upon these investigative modalities.

It has come to light that a significant proportion of these diagnostic procedures are unnecessary. They are often prescribed as a preemptive measure in a defensive medical strategy to safeguard against potential litigation or compensate for a lack of proficiency in conducting comprehensive patient evaluations. Additionally, it is frequently observed that the results of these tests are subject to misinterpretation or oversight, leading to resource wastage, incorrect diagnoses, and failed treatments.

Therefore, to prevent unwanted complications or legal proceedings, physicians must dedicate time to carefully assessing patient histories and examination outcomes before determining the necessity of further investigations. Concurrent discussion with radiologists and collaborative team members is essential to prevent misinterpretation and the careless disregard of completed tests. Failing to do so may result in the physician's deep-seated regret and the enduring burden of justifying such errors.

The Role of Patient Counseling and Informed Consent in Mitigating Risks of Litigation:

The pivotal element in patient management involves providing thorough counseling and obtaining informed consent for treatment. Establishing a trustworthy doctor-patient relationship is critical at this moment in time. It will confer numerous benefits if the physician succeeds in fortifying this relationship. Primarily, the patient will perceive a sense of respect and safety, feel empowered to fully disclose his symptoms and concerns, collaborate during examinations, agree to necessary diagnostic investigations and procedures, and adhere to the prescribed treatment and follow-up regimen. In addition, the patient is less likely to lodge complaints or initiate legal proceedings in the event of any complications.

Furthermore, physicians must precisely delineate the indications, procedural details, potential complications, and prognosis associated with the treatment. They should also explore the spectrum of alternative therapeutic options, explaining the attendant risks and advantages. Addressing all patient inquiries is essential during the process of securing informed consent.

Effectively carrying out counseling sessions and obtaining the signed informed consent depends on the doctor investing adequate time to interact with the patient and their relatives. Failure to conduct purposeful counseling conversations and communicate the treatment process when obtaining informed consent may result in patient and family dissatisfaction. Consequently, this may lead to non-compliance with the treatment plan and an increased likelihood of litigation in the face of complications. Thus, from a medical, professional, and ethical standpoint, it is incumbent upon physicians to avoid superficial engagements and allocate the necessary time for patient counseling and informed consent to avert undesirable outcomes.

Avoidance of Haste: "The Essential Components of Effective Patient Treatment"

Following a comprehensive history, physical examination, investigative procedures, definitive diagnosis, patient counseling, and informed consent, the critical element of patient care is the implementation of an appropriate treatment modality, whether conservative or surgical.

In formulating a treatment strategy, physicians must meticulously evaluate many patient factors, including comorbid conditions, intellectual and financial status, social support systems, and familial backing. Ignoring these critical considerations could increase the likelihood of noncompliance and therapeutic failure. Such an assessment can only be conducted through thorough and dedicated communication between the physician and the patient. Should physicians neglect this duty, they may encounter adverse outcomes resulting from unsuccessful treatments.

The significance of preoperative and postoperative care in a patient's surgical management is paramount and should be regarded with the same level of importance as the surgical intervention itself. A lack of adequate patient optimization before surgery, coupled with insufficient postoperative care and follow-up, can undermine even the most flawlessly executed surgical procedure, potentially leading to increased morbidity and mortality rates. Therefore, surgeons must ensure equal attentiveness to preoperative and postoperative management and performance within the operating theater.

During the operative process, surgeons must maintain a steadfast focus on precision, quality, and adherence to the established surgical principles rather than the duration of the procedure. Rushed surgical interventions predispose patients to various avoidable complications because haste makes waste. For instance, the hurried insertion or removal of laparoscopic ports without adequate visual guidance heightens the risk of iatrogenic visceral and vascular injuries or bleeding from port site wounds. Similarly, rough and rapid operations significantly increase the possibility of iatrogenic injuries. To avoid potential drawbacks and mistakes in treatment, it is wise for a surgeon to maintain calmness and dedicate extra time to patient care during every phase of surgical procedures. Opting to expedite the operative procedure could ultimately result in spending a lifetime confronting the repercussions of such haste.

Follow-Up Plans: "The Underestimated Component in Successful Patient Management"

Follow-up plans constitute an integral yet often underestimated component of patient management. The success and outcomes of treatment depend significantly on the recommendation of post-treatment follow-up protocols and the patient's adherence to them. It is critical for the treating physician to allocate time for a comprehensive explanation of post-treatment directives, ensuring both the patient and their family fully comprehend the medication usage, necessary precautions, dietary considerations, wound care, scheduling of follow-up appointments, potential investigations, and advised levels of physical activity. Adherence to these guidelines markedly increases the likelihood of a favorable outcome, regardless of whether the treatment was conservative or surgical. For example,

i. Upon commencing insulin treatment, individuals with diabetes are encouraged to regularly check their glucose levels and implement changes in their diet and daily habits. Diligent adherence to this advice is crucial in maintaining balanced blood sugar, enhancing overall wellness, and avoiding health complications.

ii. Following open-heart surgery, it's crucial for the individual to be advised on the usage of specific anticoagulants and beta-blockers, adhere to a nutritious diet, continuously monitor blood pressure, and ensure participation in all prescribed cardiac rehab sessions. Diligently adhering to this regimen yields positive results.

iii. Patients having undergone cataract surgery should be instructed to apply prescribed eye drops, avoid certain activities that strain the eyes, and schedule regular follow-up appointments. By following these instructions, the patient reduces the risk of post-surgery complications.

iv. After gastric bypass surgery, it is recommended that a patient be counseled to follow a strict diet plan, exercise regularly, and attend follow-up visits. Compliance with these instructions will lead to successful weight loss and improvements in comorbidities like diabetes and hypertension.

v. Following prostate cancer treatment, the patient requires guidance about the need for regular PSA tests, symptom monitoring, and potential lifestyle changes. Adherence to this plan allows early detection and management of any possible recurrence.

> vi. A patient who has undergone hip replacement surgery requires advice on physiotherapy, walking aids, and medications. Following these instructions carefully leads to faster recovery and improved mobility.

Conversely, suppose a treating physician fails to offer appropriate post-treatment advice and follow-up or does so insufficiently. In that case, it significantly increases the chances that the treatment will be ineffective or complications will arise. Therefore, it is essential to acknowledge that the success of any treatment is not solely predicated on flawless evaluation, diagnosis, and treatment but equally on providing thorough follow-up advice and diligent patient monitoring. This can only be achieved through the treating physician's committed practice of dedicating time to emphasize the significance of compliance with the post-treatment regimen.

Conclusion:

The art of medicine involves more than just diagnosis and treatment. It involves a significant investment of time, careful attention, and precision. Whether it's the initial patient interview, physical examination, diagnostic procedures, treatment execution, or follow-up, every stage needs thorough attention and should never be rushed. The adage "haste makes waste" has never been more accurate or more pertinent than it is in healthcare. It is only through the diligent allocation of sufficient time to each phase of patient care - from initial consultation to surgical procedures and post-operative follow-up - that healthcare professionals can mitigate the dangers inherent in rushed medical practices. As we navigate the evolving healthcare landscape, we must keep this principle firmly ingrained in our minds: "Spending a few more minutes on patient management is far better than spending your whole life facing the consequences of medical mistakes." This approach ensures we uphold our responsibility for our patients' health, safety, and well-being.

Suggested Readings

• Cara Murez HealthDay Reporter, B., & HealthDay, B. (2023). 07-20/new-report-measures-scope-of-damage-from-medical-mistakes Recommended Videos Powered by AnyClip.

• Jaklevic MC. (2023). 'Medical errors are the third leading cause of death' and other statistics you should question. | PSNet.

• Davis, J. L., & Murray, J. F. (2016). 6 HISTORY AND PHYSICAL EXAMINATION.

• Tempdev. (2023). Understanding the Importance of History and Physical (H&P) in the Medical Field - Blog TempDev.

• Oyedokun, A., Adeloye, D., & Balogun, O. (2016). Clinical history-taking and physical examination in medical practice in Africa: Still relevant? Croatian Medical Journal, 57(6), 605–607.

• Dr Laurence Knott. (2021). History and Physical Examination information. What to expect | Patient.

• Lamichhane, P., & Agrawal, A. (2023). Precision medicine and implications in medical education. Annals of Medicine & Surgery, 85(4), 1342–1345.

• Rodziewicz, T. L., Houseman, B., & Hipskind, J. E. (2023). Medical Error Reduction and Prevention Continuing EducationActivity.

The Delicate Balance: Gaining and Applying Knowledge Efficiently

"For the things we have to learn before we can do them, we learn by doing them."

- Aristotle

Overview:

In the sophisticated and steadily evolving landscape of medical science, the pursuit and application of knowledge present a challenging equilibrium to maintain. This segment presents a comprehensive analysis of the current dynamics in medical education and practice, focusing on critical areas such as the role of medical education, the application of knowledge in medical practice, and the importance of striking a balance between theoretical knowledge and practical skills. It highlights that effective medical practice goes beyond merely accumulating extensive knowledge; it rests instead on adapting to comprehend and utilizing that information adeptly. It explores various methods and approaches designed to enhance the learning process effectively and its subsequent implementation in medicine. The ultimate aim is to equip healthcare professionals with the necessary skills and knowledge to provide holistic patient care.

The Role of Medical Education: From Theory to Practice:

Medical education encompasses a diverse range of fields that may be broadly classified into three domains: cognitive, psychomotor, and affective. The cognitive domain is concerned with acquiring knowledge and intellectual skills, while the psychomotor domain is focused on developing practical skills, agility, and coordination. Conversely, the affective domain pertains to developing attitudes and values inherent to the medical profession, such as empathy, compassion, and ethical conduct. These domains are intricately interwoven, and effective integration is crucial in producing competent and well-rounded healthcare professionals.

Integrating physical, emotional, and psychological domains in medical education is crucial for facilitating the development of a comprehensive approach to patient care by healthcare professionals. This multidisciplinary approach entails close collaboration between healthcare providers and educators, including physicians, nurses, and other allied health professionals. By integrating all three domains into the curriculum, medical education institutions can prepare and equip healthcare professionals with the necessary skills and knowledge to deliver patient-centered care that considers the whole patient.

To ensure that medical education programs are effective, they must be continuously evaluated in light of emerging healthcare technologies and evolving learning needs. Integrating new teaching methods and technologies can provide healthcare providers with the most up-to-date training, thus enhancing the quality of care they deliver to patients.

For example, a program was previously based only on textbook learning. Now, it is continuously evaluated and updated with new healthcare technologies like simulations or virtual reality for practical training. So, healthcare providers are now getting hands-on training with these advanced technologies, which ultimately enhances their ability to administer improved patient care.

Exploring the Nuances of Medical Profession: Are We Learning Right?

Exploring the nuances of the medical profession involves understanding the intricate details and subtleties that influence medical education and practice. These go beyond the typical familiarity with science and medicine, diving into the complexities of human anatomy, pathological conditions, medical procedures, healthcare systems, and ethical considerations inherent within the profession. Yet, there is a rising debate among practitioners, educators, and students over the appropriateness and effectiveness of current learning modalities in medical education. Are we learning right?

Consider the standard curriculum in most medical institutions. It primarily focuses on theoretical knowledge and developing technical skills in clinical disciplines. For instance, emerging doctors absorb an overwhelming amount of anatomy, biochemistry, physiology, microbiology, and other introductory science coursework in the early years of medical school. They learn about numerous diseases, diagnostic methods, treatment modalities, surgical procedures, etc. All these are undoubtedly important. However, the medical profession extends beyond these; it demands exceptional communication skills, empathetic patient interactions, the ability to make quick decisions, and stress management, among others. Unfortunately, these skills are often underemphasized in the conventional medical curriculum.

For example, medical simulations are essential to clinical education, helping medical students gain professional experience and enhance their critical thinking capabilities. By placing students in a simulated clinical environment with mannequins exhibiting symptoms of diseases, instructors can provide dynamic, interactive, and risk-free training. Despite its benefits, the use of simulation in teaching is not as widespread as you might expect. The core reason for this lack of widespread use could be the significant expense of setting up simulation laboratories and training educators to use them effectively. This leads to an important question: are we investing adequately in the right areas of medical education?

The ultimate goal of medical education is to develop proficient and empathetic medical practitioners capable of offering comprehensive and compassionate care to their patients. It is imperative to delve into the intricacies of the medical profession and address them effectively to ensure that the next generation of healthcare professionals is equipped to meet society's constantly evolving healthcare needs. In doing so, we can ensure patients receive optimal care from a well-rounded and competent healthcare workforce.

Interplay of Knowledge and Skills: Striking the Right Balance:

Acquiring knowledge can originate from multiple sources, such as formal education, experience, and exposure to different situations. It entails an individual's comprehension of concepts, theories, and principles. Conversely, skills are acquired through practice, repetition, and application in real-life situations. They denote the practical abilities to perform tasks and solve problems, which are fundamental for success in any field.

While acquiring knowledge is crucial in professional development, it does not necessarily translate into skill. For instance, an individual with theoretical programming knowledge may encounter difficulties coding practical applications that require a more hands-on approach. Similarly, a medical practitioner with extensive medical knowledge may not necessarily possess the surgical skills to save a life. Therefore, it is essential to understand that a balance between knowledge and skills is critical for professional success and to make a significant impact in one's chosen field.

The acquisition of knowledge is a vital component of professional success, but it is equally essential to develop and refine skills that enable individuals to excel in their chosen fields. This can be facilitated through experiential learning opportunities, such as internships, residency, and fellowship training, which allow individuals to apply their theoretical knowledge in practical settings and foster the development of critical skills. By engaging in such opportunities, professionals can enhance their knowledge and skills and gain a competitive edge in their specialties.

The Impact of Effective Knowledge Application in Medical Practice:

The influence of appropriate knowledge utilization in the medical field plays a significant role in enhancing patient care, improving diagnostic accuracy, and boosting treatment outcomes. This concept pertains to applying updated, evidence-based medical information to clinical scenarios, which is pivotal in ensuring accurate diagnoses and effective treatment plans. A physician's ability to aptly apply their knowledge can significantly affect a patient's recovery, survival, and overall health. Moreover, using practical knowledge in medical practice also leads to advancements in medical technology and pharmaceuticals, laying a solid foundation for clinical research and trials. Consequently, healthcare facilities investing in continuous education, research, and skill development of their medical professionals contribute significantly to the broader goal of health improvements in society. Thus, the impact of practical knowledge application in medical practice is undeniably crucial and beneficial for both individuals and the community.

For instance,

1. The development of COVID-19 vaccine stands as a shining example of practical knowledge application. The tireless efforts of our medical scientists, applying their most contemporary knowledge, led to the speedy and successful creation of this life-saving vaccine. This achievement is a testament to the dedication and expertise of our profession.

2. Implementing value-based care in many healthcare systems is also an example of applying adequate knowledge in medicine. Through technology and research, clinicians can now measure health outcomes and make evidence-based decisions that improve patient experience, reduce healthcare costs, and boost societal health.

3. A classic example is the introduction of Telemedicine. By applying the knowledge of digital health technology, doctors are now providing healthcare services remotely, helping

patients receive expert advice without leaving their homes, especially during the pandemic.

4. A recent study reported that oncologists who consistently updated their knowledge and applied it in practice showed a noticeable improvement in their patient's survival rates compared with those who remained stagnant with traditional protocols.

Transforming Information to Action: The Importance of Brainstorming in Medicine:

Providing high-quality healthcare services is a complex process that necessitates transforming substantial information into practical and effective action plans. To accomplish this task, medical professionals must engage in collaborative brainstorming sessions that allow them to generate innovative solutions to multifaceted problems.

Brainstorming is a potent tool that can encourage innovative thinking while promoting teamwork and collaboration. It is a process that brings together individuals from diverse backgrounds and areas of expertise, enabling them to share their unique perspectives and integrate them into a cohesive strategy. This method helps reinforce the resulting plan and engenders a sense of shared ownership and accountability over the process and outcomes.

Brainstorming is a valuable technique that offers significant advantages to professionals in the medical sector. By enabling individuals to move beyond their comfort zones, brainstorming sessions encourage exploration beyond conventional treatment methods and facilitate the discovery of new possibilities. Through brainstorming, medical professionals can challenge assumptions, question established practices, and explore alternative approaches that may enhance patient outcomes. This, in turn, fosters a culture of creative and critical thinking, which is essential for effective and efficient healthcare delivery. Overall, brainstorming is a powerful tool that supports medical professionals in pursuing innovative solutions and improved patient care.

Brainstorming sessions are vital to practical problem-solving in organizations. However, to generate optimal results, it is necessary to establish an environment that fosters openness, inclusivity, and non-judgmentalism. The medical field presents a challenge in creating such an atmosphere because of its hierarchical structure. Nevertheless, when all ideas are given equal weightage, and participants are encouraged to contribute, solutions are rooted in a comprehensive understanding of the issues under consideration. This democratic approach guarantees that all viewpoints are heard, leading to more effective and inclusive solutions.

Conclusion:

The continuous process of gaining and implementing knowledge effectively in a constantly evolving domain such as medicine holds significant importance. It's critical to ensure an integrative, patient-centered approach in medical education that elevates knowledge acquisition beyond just theoretical comprehension, fostering the development of practical, empathetic, and ethical healthcare professionals. The right balance between theoretical knowledge and practical skills in medicine should be struck, and the value of experience and hands-on training to refine these skills must be balanced. Concurrently, innovative practices such as brainstorming and medical simulations should be harnessed more effectively to promote creativity, critical thinking, and teamwork and positively impact patient care. Furthermore, given the current crucial medical training evaluation, we must redirect our focus and develop a more comprehensive educational program emphasizing the significance of medical knowledge and interpersonal skills. This approach will better equip the new generation of healthcare workers to meet the growing health-related needs of the population.

Suggested Readings

- Kirch, S. A., & Sadofsky, M. J. (2021). Medical Education from a Theory–Practice–Philosophy Perspective. Academic Pathology, 8.
- Greig, P. R., & Darbyshire, J. L. (2019). Medical educational theory in practice. In BJA Education (Vol. 19, Issue 2).
- Said Elshama, S. (2020). How to Apply Problem-Based Learning in Medical Education? A Critical Review. IBEROAMERICAN JOURNAL OF MEDICINE, 01, 14–18.
- Clinical Excellence et at., 2021 Brainstorming - Clinical Excellence Commission. (n.d.).
- Poola, V. P., Suh, B., Parr, T., Boehler, M., Han, H., & Mellinger, J. (2021). Medical students' reflections on surgical educators' professionalism: Contextual nuances in the hidden curriculum. American Journal of Surgery, 221(2).
- Grassini, S. (2023). Shaping the Future of Education: Exploring the Potential and Consequences of AI and ChatGPT in Educational Settings. In Education Sciences (Vol. 13, Issue 7).

- Harder, N. (2023). Advancing Healthcare Simulation Through Artificial Intelligence and Machine Learning: Exploring Innovations. In Clinical Simulation in Nursing (Vol. 83).

The Multi-Hat Challenge: Doctors Beyond Their Medical Role

"Trust yourself. You know more than you think you do."

- Benjamin Spock

Overview:

The evolving landscape of healthcare has brought a paradigm shift in the roles and responsibilities of physicians, expanding far beyond traditional medical practice. This segment dives into the diverse and dynamic responsibilities of modern-day doctors, unpacking the complexities and challenges that physicians face as they strive to balance their primary duty of patient care with a range of additional roles. It will shed light on how doctors transform into educators, researchers, policymakers, and leaders, adding a more profound understanding of their pivotal role in society. Ultimately, this exploration underscores the versatility, adaptability, and resilience required in today's healthcare landscape, where a doctor's role often goes beyond the treatment room. These multifaceted roles, while challenging, offer significant professional fulfillment and potential for growth. Embracing these new roles is essential in providing superior healthcare and fostering medical advancements.

Understanding the Multifaceted Role of a Doctor:

The healthcare sector is transforming, requiring physicians to assume a multifaceted role. In addition to their conventional duties of diagnosing and treating patients, physicians are now expected to engage in various activities beyond the examination room. These responsibilities may include managing electronic health records, collaborating with other healthcare providers, developing population health strategies, and advocating for policy changes that benefit patients.

The transformation in the role of physicians is motivated by a shift towards value-based healthcare, prioritizing delivering high-quality, patient-centered care that results in favorable health outcomes. To realize this objective, physicians need to engage in a broad spectrum of activities beyond the conventional limits of medical practice.

Currently, a significant number of physicians prioritize not only providing healthcare services to their patients but also actively participating in healthcare policy and advocacy endeavors. These initiatives may encompass lobbying for policy changes in reimbursement to ensure that healthcare services receive an appropriate valuation, advocating for increased funding for medical research and public health initiatives, or partnering with local and state officials to design and implement healthcare reforms that enhance patient outcomes while benefiting healthcare providers.

Doctor as a Leader: Skillfully Leading the charge:

Leadership is crucial to every profession; the medical field is no exception. Doctors must demonstrate exceptional leadership skills, given their responsibility for the well-being and safety of their patients. The medical field presents physicians with complex scenarios that require them to exercise informed decision-making in the best interest of their patients. To accomplish this, physicians must rely on their clinical expertise and apply sound judgment when faced with medical challenges.

They must inspire and motivate their colleagues, delegate tasks efficiently, and provide constructive feedback. An individual who exhibits outstanding leadership skills in the medical field can facilitate an environment that fosters collaboration, innovation, and the delivery of high-quality care.

Medical practitioners have a crucial role in the healthcare system, extending beyond their immediate responsibilities. They must remain up-to-date with the latest developments in research and technology that can enhance patient outcomes. By actively contributing to the advancement of medical science, doctors can positively impact society as a whole.

Additionally, they must advocate for policies that promote universal access to quality healthcare for all.

Doctor as Educator: Cultivating Health Awareness:

Physicians are entrusted with a pivotal role as medical professionals and educators in healthcare. Patients rely on their physicians as authoritative sources of knowledge for managing their health and well-being. Therefore, it is paramount for physicians to instill health awareness in their patients by providing them with relevant information and guidance.

Effective communication between physicians and patients is fundamental to improving health outcomes and treatment adherence. The successful delivery of a positive and empathetic approach can encourage patients to take a proactive role in managing their health, leading to improved outcomes and reducing the risk of chronic illnesses. This underscores the critical importance of effective doctor-patient communication and reinforces the concept of physicians as educators.

Physicians can inspire patients to adopt healthy lifestyle changes that can improve health outcomes. By providing evidence-based recommendations and elucidating the benefits of healthy behaviors, physicians can help patients mitigate the risk of chronic illnesses. These healthy behaviors include increasing physical activity, managing stress, maintaining a balanced diet, and quitting smoking and alcohol. Such interventions, backed by scientific evidence, can potentially improve patient health and reduce the prevalence of chronic illnesses.

Medical practitioners can educate patients about preventive healthcare measures, including routine check-ups, vaccinations, and cancer screenings. By promoting preventive healthcare, physicians can effectively assist patients in identifying and addressing health issues early on, thereby minimizing the risk and severity of chronic diseases. Hence, physicians can play an essential role in promoting overall good health and preventing illnesses by serving as educators in addition to their medical professional roles.

Doctor as Researcher: The Pursuit of Medical Progress:

Medical research represents a continuously evolving field, with doctors playing a crucial role in advancing healthcare treatments and provisions. As researchers, physicians engage in rigorous scientific inquiries to develop novel strategies and approaches to enhance patient outcomes and quality of life. Their research efforts primarily focus on two key areas: developing new therapies and medications and studying healthcare delivery and practices. Through these pursuits, doctors strive to achieve better healthcare outcomes and improve the overall quality of patient care.

Medical practitioners delve into the intricate biological processes underlying various diseases and conditions to identify potential targets for drug therapies. Subsequently, they engage in rigorous research and clinical trials to assess the efficacy and safety of these possible treatments. Despite the extensive duration of this process, it ultimately culminates in the development of new drugs and therapies that have the potential to improve patient health outcomes significantly.

In conjunction with developing novel therapeutic interventions, healthcare professionals examine healthcare delivery and practices. By scrutinizing patient outcomes data, practitioners can identify gaps in care or opportunities for enhancement. Consequently, new protocols and strategies are developed to elevate the overall quality of care, resulting in improved outcomes and heightened patient satisfaction.

Challenges and Rewards of Doctor's Multidimensional Role:

The medical profession is an intensely demanding yet gratifying occupation. Despite the challenges inherent to being a physician, the gratification associated with this profession is immeasurable.

One of healthcare professionals' most significant challenges is the arduous workload, which often requires extended hours and shifts beyond the traditional 9-to-5 schedule. Physicians, in particular, are usually needed to work nights, weekends, and holidays and must be prepared to respond to emergencies at any time. In addition to the job's physical demands, physicians must remain up-to-date with the latest research and clinical practices, which requires great dedication and effort. The emotional and psychological toll of the job can also be overwhelming, as physicians are frequently needed to confront severe illnesses and death, which can have a profound impact on their mental well-being.

Despite the profession's challenges, the rewards of being a physician are genuinely remarkable. Physicians enjoy the privilege of providing medical care and alleviating physical ailments, which brings great satisfaction and fulfillment. Notably, they also have the opportunity to participate in innovative research and technology and work alongside a team of highly motivated professionals committed to providing the best possible care to their patients.

Conclusion:

The evolving healthcare landscape necessitates that doctors adapt and take on various roles beyond their primary duty of patient care. Their responsibilities have expanded exponentially, requiring them to be educators, policymakers, leaders, researchers, and advocates for their patients. There are challenges in balancing these multi-dimensional roles, with notable demands including rigorous workloads, frequently confronting severe illnesses and death, and the need to learn and adapt to the latest in medical practice continuously. However, amidst these challenges, the benefits of being a physician are substantial. Managed correctly, these multi-faceted roles offer professional fulfillment, growth opportunities, the capacity to contribute to medical advancements, and the privilege to deliver high-quality, patient-centered care. Doctors' embracing these various roles is vital to superior healthcare provision and its continual advancement.

Suggested Readings

- Denis, J. L., & Van Gestel, N. (2016). Medical doctors in healthcare leadership: Theoretical and practical challenges. BMC Health Services Research, 16(2).
- Bartle, E., & Thistlethwaite, J. (2014). Becoming a medical educator: Motivation, socialisation and navigation. BMC Medical Education, 14(1).
- Leadership Is a Learned Skill -- Family Practice Management. (2003).
- Rahman, S., Majumder, M . A. A., Shaban, S. F., Rahman, N., Ahmed, M., Abdulrahman, K. Bin, & D'souza, U. J. A. (2011). Physician participation in clinical research and trials: Issues and approaches. In Advances in Medical Education and Practice (Vol. 2, pp. 85–93). Dove Medical Press Ltd.
- Zajac, S., Woods, A., Tannenbaum, S., Salas, E., & Holladay, C. L. (2021). Overcoming Challenges to Teamwork in Healthcare: A Team Effectiveness Framework and Evidence-Based Guidance. Frontiers in Communication, 6.

Charisma in Healthcare: An Essential Quality for Doctors

"Charisma is the fragrance of soul."

— Toba Beta

Overview:

Historically, the medical field, with its deep-rooted cultures and stringent norms, has often been associated with rigidity. This perception is distinct from the charismatic leadership styles known for their captivating charm and inspiring dynamism. In medicine, where expertise and precision are highly valued, the importance of charisma is often overlooked. However, a doctor's charm, confidence, and warmth are deeply woven into every interaction with patients, every life-changing diagnosis, and every word of support. In this article, we highlight the vital role of charisma as a quality for healthcare professionals. Beyond medical knowledge and surgical skills, a doctor's influence can provide comfort and motivation and inspire trust during moments of vulnerability. We will explore how doctors' charisma can be demonstrated, its tangible impact on patient outcomes, and its transformative power in the doctor-patient relationship.

The Concept of Charisma:

Charisma, a unique trait identified by Max Weber, a renowned sociologist, is defined as a compelling attractiveness or charm that can inspire devotion in others.

While charisma may be perceived as an innate ability or something one is born with, research proves that it can be learned and enhanced. According to leadership expert Glen Llopis, charisma is not just a personality trait but a set of behaviors that can be cultivated.

It is a quality frequently attributed to leaders; it infuses an individual with an irresistibly charming aura, an impactful presence, and an inspiring personality that can dramatically influence others around them.

Promoting charismatic qualities in medical professionals is essential for enhancing interpersonal relationships in healthcare settings and boosting the overall patient experience. This developmental process aims to equip healthcare providers with unique attributes such as profound empathy, stellar communication skills, inspirational leadership, stunning enthusiasm, compelling confidence, and a therapeutic presence. These qualities can have a transformative impact on patient care, ensuring healing extends beyond the physical to the emotional and psychological well-being of the patient. The introduction of charisma in the medical field signifies a potent blend of competence and compassion, empowering medical professionals to offer optimal healthcare with a human touch.

The Importance of Charisma in the Medical Field:

Developing charisma in medical practice is beneficial not only for patients but also for doctors. Charismatic doctors are better able to connect with their patients, find meaning in their work, and tend to experience less burnout.

Patients who perceive their physician as charismatic are more likely to comply with treatment plans and return for follow-up visits. Charismatic physicians can also establish a robust rapport with patients quickly, enabling patients to feel more comfortable sharing personal information and concerns.

Charisma is a significant factor that contributes to effective teamwork within medical staff. Physicians with magnetic charm can motivate and inspire their colleagues, creating a more productive and optimistic work environment. Furthermore, teamwork is a vital component of the medical field, and charismatic physicians can foster open communication and trust among team members, leading to improved patient outcomes.

However, it is essential to acknowledge that charisma alone is insufficient for a medical professional's success. Clinical expertise, practical communication skills, and ethical conduct are all equally vital in providing exceptional healthcare. It should be considered a complementary attribute to these core competencies.

The Role of Charisma in Patient-Doctor Relationships:

In the healthcare sector, the allure of a physician's personality dramatically contributes to creating solid connections between doctors and their patients. A doctor's captivating persona can cultivate trust, establishing a deep-seated connection that optimizes patient care. A doctor's charm enhances their capacity for meaningful engagement, showing awareness and empathy towards their patients' ailments and worries.

This commanding yet congenial attribute enables doctors to alleviate patients' anxiety, enabling them to adhere to prescribed treatment plans fully. Simply put, a doctor's charisma can thus create a reassuring and encouraging atmosphere, yielding significant therapeutic advantages. It is an echo of empathy, compassion, and understanding – a potent tonic that can facilitate the healing process – reflecting that the art of medicine is intrinsically a 'people-oriented' science.

However, experts caution against overemphasizing the role of charisma in healthcare. It may be advantageous but not a substitute for high-quality medical care. Furthermore, even doctors who may not possess a charismatic demeanor can provide excellent healthcare services. It is also essential to recognize that patients may respond differently to different types of doctors. What works well for one patient may not work as well for another.

Charismatic Leadership in Hospital Settings:

Inspirational leaders are crucial in hospital settings, as they nurture a unified setting that enhances the proficiency of healthcare service delivery. This leadership style centers on galvanizing and stirring the team with a robust and compelling zest that encourages commitment and proactive engagement in duties. Charismatic hospital leaders drive their teams with a compelling vision, promoting a patient-centric approach that values compassion and empathy. They use their strong interpersonal skills to nurture a sense of trust, respect, and confidence among the hospital staff, encouraging an atmosphere of positivity and collaboration. Such an innovative and transformative leadership style results in enhanced employee satisfaction, increased patient satisfaction, and overall improvement in the quality of healthcare services and patient outcomes. Charismatic leadership is indispensable in shaping a competent and dynamic workforce in hospital settings, contributing massively to establishing a high-performing and patient-centered healthcare system.

Overcoming Challenges to Charisma in the Medical Field:

While the benefits of charisma are undeniable, specific challenges like hierarchical nature, lack of time for personal interaction, high stress levels, and language & cultural barriers within the medical field potentially inhibit these magnetic qualities. Despite these challenges, the following techniques and strategies can be employed to enhance charismatic appeal among medical professionals:

1. **Improve Communication**: Understanding and addressing individual patient needs is critical. By showing empathy and active listening, a doctor can create a safe and comfortable environment for the patient.

2. **Managing Stress Levels**: Effective stress regulation is crucial for flourishing charismatic qualities. It allows medical professionals to maintain their enthusiasm and passion. Yoga, meditation, and regular physical exercise can help manage stress.

3. **Effective Time Management**: Medical professionals, through better time management, can create room for deeper interaction with patients, colleagues, and subordinates, allowing their charisma to shine.

4. **Cultural Sensitivity**: Healthcare professionals can overcome language and cultural barriers by acquiring knowledge about and sensitivity to various cultures.

Ethical Considerations of Charisma in Medical Practice:

Charisma in medical practice is a double-edged sword, yielding significant benefits but imposing ethical challenges that require careful navigation.

The application of charisma must be carefully balanced with the ethical principle of informed consent. Informed consent is the cornerstone of medical ethics, emphasizing the patient's right to make voluntary, well-informed decisions about their healthcare. A doctor's allure should never eclipse the clarity of information provided, nor should it unduly influence a patient's choices. Upholding patient autonomy remains paramount in all healthcare interactions.

Furthermore, the engaging doctor must guard against the unconscious bias of delivering an overly optimistic prognosis, which can distort the patient's expectations and understanding of their medical condition. Ethical practice demands accurate and honest communication, even when the news is adverse, ensuring patients are genuinely informed.

The ethical implications of charisma also extend to the realm of healthcare equity. Since it is not equally distributed among physicians, this individual variation can inadvertently result in unequal patient experiences and satisfaction levels, challenging the ideal of justice in healthcare.

Fundamentally, although charm can significantly enhance the relationship between therapist and patient, this charm must be balanced with an unwavering adherence to ethical standards like doing good, avoiding harm, and upholding fairness within medical environments. Doctors must be cautious of their natural magnetism, possibly crossing moral lines. They must work diligently to guarantee that their charisma acts as a positive contributor and not a detriment in their medical practice.

Conclusion:

Charisma in healthcare emerges not as an extra embellishment but as an indispensable asset in the noble profession of medicine. A charismatic doctor provides medical expertise, fosters trust, encourages adherence to treatment plans, and promotes a positive and harmonious work environment, ultimately leading to improved patient outcomes. Nevertheless, it cannot replace the need for clinical knowledge, practical communication skills, and ethical conduct. Moreover, while charisma may greatly enhance healthcare delivery, potential challenges like stress, time constraints, and cultural differences must be adequately addressed. Thus, cultivating a charismatic presence in healthcare professionals is essential, but it should be coupled with unwavering adherence to ethical standards to ensure patient-centered, high-quality healthcare delivery. By achieving this balance, the sacred art of healing will mend bodies and empower spirits, reaffirming that within each healing touch lies an echo of a soul's fragrance—the quintessence of charisma in medicine.

Suggested Readings

- Fond, G., Ducasse, D., Attal, J., Larue, A., MacGregor, A., Brittner, M., & Capdevielle, D. (2013). Charisme et leadership: de nouveaux défis pour la psychiatrie. Encephale, 39(6), 445–451.
- Learna.ac. (2022). Three Types of Leadership Styles in Healthcare.
- Hollin, G., & Giraud, E. (2017). Charisma and the clinic. Social Theory and Health, 15(2), 223–240.
- MLD. (2023). Advantages And Disadvantages Of Charismatic Leadership | MTD Training. Mldtraining.Com.

Professional Boundaries: A Critical Aspect in Medicine

"Boundaries are part of self-care. They are healthy, normal, and necessary."

- Doreen Virtue

Overview:

Maintaining professional boundaries within the complex healthcare framework is not merely a suggestion but an imperative. Frequently invisible but immensely significant, professional boundaries are crucial guiding principles in any medical setting. They govern the relationship between healthcare professionals and their patients, fostering respect, trust, and mutual understanding. This exploration draws attention to and facilitates meaningful conversations about these critical boundaries. It spotlights its gravity, role in forming professional patient-doctor relationships, the consequences when these boundaries are violated, and the need for clear guidelines in today's rapidly evolving healthcare environment. In today's world, where personal and professional realms frequently overlap, it is critical to grasp the importance of maintaining professional limits in the medical field. Such understanding sheds light on the intricate and sensitive manner in which healthcare workers skillfully manage their roles.

Understanding the Concept of Professional Boundaries in Medicine:

Professional boundaries in medicine refer to the limits that protect the space between a healthcare professional's power and their patient's vulnerability. These boundaries ensure that a relationship between a professional and a patient stays safe, therapeutic, and focused on the patient's needs. Understanding such boundaries is critical to maintaining trust in the patient-practitioner relationship, ensuring clear communication, and, ultimately, enhancing the quality of patient care. Misunderstanding or violating these boundaries can lead to ethical dilemmas, misunderstandings, and potential harm to the patient. Therefore, understanding and maintaining professional boundaries in medicine is essential for effective doctor-patient relationships.

Here are a few examples of professional boundaries being overstepped in the healthcare industry:

1. A doctor inappropriately discusses personal issues with a patient during his/her consultation, making the patient uncomfortable.

2. A surgeon operating without gaining the patient's informed consent, representing a blatant disregard for patient autonomy and legal standards.

3. A healthcare provider discussing a patient's private health information in public areas, breaking confidentiality agreements and compromising patient privacy.

4. A doctor accepting personal gifts from a patient could lead to a biased care provision and a potential conflict of interest.

5. A physician allows their personal beliefs to override evidence-based clinical recommendations, thus affecting the standard of care provided to the patient.

6. A pharmacist recommending unproven therapies to patients in a bid to market specific products violates the principle of honesty and integrity in professional practice.

7. A medical student performing procedures without adequate supervision or consent breaches ethical guidelines and patient trust and can risk patient safety.

8. A caregiver in a long-term care facility who accepts monetary or inheritable gifts from a patient can be seen as exploitation and a serious breach of professional conduct.

9. A nurse sharing confidential patient information with non-medical personnel breaches data protection and patient confidentiality.

10. Physical relationships between a healthcare provider and a patient intrude into professional ethics and can lead to conflicts of interest.

The Significance of Professional Boundaries for Healthcare Workers:

Establishing and maintaining professional boundaries is paramount in defining the relationship between healthcare professionals and their clients. These boundaries provide a framework for upholding ethical standards and ensuring the delivery of high-quality care. They also serve as a crucial means for clinicians to develop an appropriate emotional distance from their patients, which is essential to maintain impartiality, objectivity, and respect for patients' autonomy and privacy.

Moreover, professional boundaries protect patients from potential harm from exploitative or inappropriate behavior from healthcare providers. Simultaneously, it also safeguards healthcare providers from burnout and compassion fatigue.

Recent research has indicated that upholding professional boundaries can significantly impact patient satisfaction. Patients who perceive that their healthcare provider has maintained an appropriate distance report feeling more respected, validated, and engaged in their care. Conversely, patients who perceive a lack of professional boundaries may experience discomfort, mistrust, or a sense of violation, negatively impacting their overall satisfaction with their healthcare experience.

Neglecting professional boundaries can severely affect patient outcomes and future therapeutic engagements. Inappropriate intimacy or abusive conduct with patients can undermine public trust in the medical profession and lead to significant negative consequences for the healthcare provider and the medical institution.

Professional boundaries can have legal and ethical implications for healthcare providers. Failing to observe appropriate boundaries may result in allegations of malpractice, licensing issues, and disciplinary actions, underscoring the significance of clearly defined and ethical practices regarding professional boundaries.

Ethical Implications of Breaching Professional Boundaries:

In healthcare, it is crucial to establish and maintain healthy and ethical relationships between professionals and their patients.

One of the most significant concerns regarding violating professional boundaries is exploiting professionals' power. As individuals in positions of authority, these professionals must maintain ethical boundaries and avoid abusing their power. Breaching these boundaries can result in a power imbalance, leaving the client feeling vulnerable and powerless. For professionals to use their position of power to gain personal benefits or to maintain a relationship with a client beyond their professional responsibilities is highly unethical and can cause harm to the client. Therefore, professionals must establish clear boundaries and maintain a professional code of conduct to ensure their client's safety and well-being.

Confidentiality and privacy are crucial aspects of any professional-client relationship. Professionals are responsible for not breaching their client's trust by divulging sensitive information. The consequences of violating confidentiality can be severe and long-lasting, causing irreparable harm to the client's trust, mental well-being, and overall quality of life. In some cases, it may even lead to legal action against the professional, resulting in the loss of their license or significant financial damages.

Strategies to Maintain Professional Boundaries in Medicine:

1. **Set Clear Expectations**: Make sure everyone involved, including all staff and patients, understands the professional behavior expected in each situation.

2. **Communication Rules**: One crucial approach for upholding professional boundaries is establishing transparent patient communication. This involves healthcare providers clarifying their roles and responsibilities to patients, enabling them to understand comprehensively what they can expect from their healthcare provider. Furthermore, healthcare providers must carefully consider patients' opinions and preferences and communicate with them respectfully and attentively. Define acceptable communication methods and times. For instance, avoid personal topics during professional conversations and discourage communication outside office hours or official channels.

3. **Abstain from Dual Relationships**: Dual relationships refer to personal, financial, or social relationships that healthcare providers may have with their patients outside the healthcare setting. Such relationships can blur the lines between professional and personal boundaries and may compromise the quality of care provided to the patient.

4. **Patient Autonomy:** Always respect the wishes and decisions of patients, even if they differ from your personal beliefs. This will be crucial in avoiding attachment and bias while treating patients.

5. **Use of social media**: Limit or prevent personal social media interactions with patients. This can help avoid any professional boundary breaches.

6. **Emotional Intelligence**: Strive to be empathetic and compassionate towards patients, yet managing these emotions well is vital to avoid any relationship that breaches professional conduct.

7. **Regular Training and Education**: Regular training programs focus on professional boundaries to reinforce best practices among medical staff.

8. **Peer Support**: Encourage a culture of supporting and advising each other when faced with boundary issues. This will enable everyone to learn from others' experiences and avoid making the same errors.

9. **Review and Assess:** Regularly assess the practice's professional boundaries. Update strategies as needed to ensure they're effective and practical.

10. **Seek Professional Guidance**: If faced with a complex situation, do not hesitate to seek advice from a senior or ethical committee. It's better to discuss potential boundary issues beforehand rather than to regret an error later.

Conclusion:

Maintaining professional boundaries is a critical aspect of healthcare practice. These boundaries ensure a safe and therapeutic relationship between patients and healthcare professionals, characterized by respect, trust, and mutual understanding. Violating these boundaries can lead to ethical dilemmas, breaches of trust, and imposition of harm to patients. Therefore, healthcare providers must understand and uphold them strictly. Besides, healthcare providers must undergo regular training, adhere to clear communication rules, abstain from dual relationships, respect patient autonomy, and seek advice from seniors or ethics committees when required. Professional boundaries are not merely about maintaining an emotional distance; they fundamentally support the ethical standards of the healthcare industry, ensuring the well-being of both patients and healthcare providers. Hence, they should be suitably prioritized, communicated, and upheld in the culturally diverse and often emotionally charged healthcare environment.

Suggested Readings

- Reyes Nieva, H., Ruan, E., & Schiff, G. D. (2019). Professional-Patient Boundaries: a National Survey of Primary Care Physicians' Attitudes and Practices. Journal of General Internal Medicine, 35(2), 457–464.
- Standing, H., Patterson, R., Dalkin, S., Exley, C., & Brittain, K. (2020). A critical exploration of professional jurisdictions and role boundaries in inter-professional end-of-life care in the community. Social Science & Medicine, 266, 113300.
- Lampe, L., Hitching, R., Hammond, T. E., Park, J., & Rich, D. (2023). Being a 'good' doctor: Understanding and managing professional boundaries is challenging and can lead to stress and burnout. Australasian Psychiatry, 31(6), 764–767.
- Gaye Cunnane. (2021). Boundaries in medicine: How can we preserve our wellbeing, while still sharing our humanity? - The BMJ.

- Kaonga, N. N. (2015). Professional Boundaries and Meaningful Care. AMA Journal of Ethics, 17(5), 416–418.
- Sara Bird. (2013). RACGP - Managing professional boundaries.

Living on the Edge: Juggling Personal and Professional Life Effectively

"Never get so busy making a living that you forget to make a life."

- Dolly Parton

Overview:

In the high-stakes healthcare arena, practitioners are routinely called upon to prioritize patient care, often at the expense of their well-being and family life. Nevertheless, achieving equilibrium doesn't always mean walking on a tightrope. This discourse delves into practical strategies that allow doctors and other medical professionals to flourish in both domains of their lives. The text delves into the intricate realities of working in the fast-paced and high-pressure field of medicine. It aims to provide valuable insights and strategies on effectively balancing one's obligations and goals with the critical responsibilities of one's professional career. Whether you're a medical practitioner, a student in the field, or someone seeking an optimal work-life balance, this insightful text offers actionable guidance, fostering a roadmap for a harmonious life where the white coat complements rather than dominates one's identity.

Understanding the Doctor's Dual Role: Personal and Professional Life:

Healthcare providers must understand the boundaries between their personal and professional roles and ensure that neither role negatively affects the other. This requires them to understand ethical principles and avoid conflicts of interest.

In their personal lives, physicians should prioritize self-care, engage in stress-reducing activities, and maintain positive relationships with their friends and family. They must also always conduct themselves professionally, avoiding any unprofessional behavior.

As part of their professional duties, doctors are responsible for putting the needs and well-being of their patients first. To do so, they must remain unbiased and impartial in their treatment, avoiding personal relationships outside the healthcare setting. By upholding these standards of professionalism, doctors can guarantee the highest quality of care for their patients.

The Impact of Professional Commitments on Doctor's Personal Life:

The medical profession can put a lot of pressure on practitioners, affecting their mental and physical well-being. Long working hours, a high-pressure environment, and the need to consistently perform at a high level can all contribute to this. In addition to these challenges, physicians may struggle to maintain personal relationships, pursue leisure activities, or care for their health.

Balancing professional and personal commitments can be difficult due to work demands, making spending quality time with loved ones challenging. This can lead to missed family events, such as birthdays, anniversaries, and vacations, causing feelings of depression and frustration. These negative emotions can ultimately affect their work, making it challenging to provide the best possible care to patients.

One of the most challenging parts of the medical profession is the emotional burden it places on healthcare professionals. They often face life-or-death situations that can cause high levels of stress and anxiety. Additionally, they may have to deliver unfavorable news to patients and their loved ones. This can take a significant personal and professional toll on healthcare providers, leading to negative emotions such as anger, frustration, and sadness.

Effects of work-life Imbalance on Doctors' Health:

The adverse effects of work-life imbalance extend beyond mental and behavioral health and also manifest in physical health. This imbalance has been demonstrated to have numerous unfavorable health outcomes among physicians, including burnout, depression, anxiety, insomnia, substance abuse, and cardiovascular conditions. Exhaustion on an emotional level, a sense of detachment, and a decline in feelings of personal achievement characterize burnout, a prevalent problem among doctors. It has been linked to adverse consequences, such as decreased patient satisfaction and increased medical errors.

Strategies to Balance Work and Personal Life:

1. Establish clear boundaries:

Given their work's physically and mentally demanding nature, it can be challenging for physicians to set clear boundaries and establish specific working hours. Nonetheless, doing so is crucial to their overall well-being. They must prioritize activities that promote relaxation and rejuvenation. This approach will help them avoid burnout and lead a more fulfilling and productive career.

2. Prioritize self-reflection:

Healthcare experts are recommended to engage in regular self-reflection. This exercise offers a chance to evaluate performance, pinpoint areas that need improvement, and stay aware of one's emotional health. Setting aside time to introspect, analyze complicated cases, and acknowledge accomplishments is crucial. This approach increases self-awareness and prepares doctors to provide excellent patient care.

3. Cultivate a support network:

In medicine, it is crucial to establish strong relationships with colleagues to manage stress effectively. Being part of a supportive community can create a safe and private space for open discussions, sharing personal experiences, and seeking or providing advice. Camaraderie and teamwork can promote comfort and security, even during challenging times. A support system like this is essential for professionals to thrive and maintain their well-being while working in a high-pressure environment.

4. Practice stress management techniques:

Physicians should develop and utilize various practical techniques to manage work stress effectively. These techniques may include deep breathing exercises, mindful meditation, or physical activities such as yoga or running. By integrating these practices into their daily routine, physicians can improve their ability to cope with stress and enhance their overall well-being.

5. Make room for fun stuff:

Medical professionals must prioritize their leisure activities and hobbies outside work to maintain a balanced lifestyle. These hobbies do not necessarily have to be related to their field of practice, but they can counterbalance the demands of their job. Engaging in creative and relaxing hobbies can effectively prevent burnout and rejuvenate them. Participating in activities that bring joy, whether spending time with loved ones, pursuing a passion, or engaging in other activities, is essential. By prioritizing these endeavors, medical practitioners can maintain their health and well-being.

6. Prioritize your physical health:

Maintaining a healthy lifestyle is crucial for achieving optimal health and overall well-being. A balanced diet, regular physical activity, and sufficient restorative sleep are all essential components of a healthy lifestyle. Getting enough sleep and eating a nutritious diet contribute to overall wellness and enhance one's ability to cope with demanding work situations.

7. Don't hesitate to ask for help:

Healthcare professionals need to acknowledge that they are susceptible to stress and anxiety and that it is okay to seek assistance when needed. It can be highly beneficial for doctors to avail themselves of mental health resources, such as counseling or therapy, especially during times of uncertainty and pressure. By prioritizing their mental health, physicians can continue to provide exceptional care to their patients while caring for their personal and emotional needs.

8. Continuous learning:

Doctors can boost their confidence levels and reduce the stress associated with uncertainty by staying updated with the latest medical research and advancements. Such an approach can significantly improve the doctor's well-being, leading to better patient outcomes and overall quality of care. Therefore, it is of utmost importance for medical professionals to prioritize ongoing education and professional development to ensure they possess the latest knowledge and skills required to provide the best possible care to their patients.

9. Delegation strategy

By implementing a delegation strategy, medical professionals can optimize their productivity and reduce their workload. It is essential to identify and delegate non-expertise-related, time-consuming tasks to other members of the healthcare team. This approach allows healthcare professionals to focus on critical tasks requiring their expertise, leading to improved patient outcomes.

10. Prioritize the tasks

To achieve a healthy work-life balance, healthcare professionals must prioritize their activities based on their importance and urgency. They should also practice the art of declining unnecessary commitments and learn to say no to activities that do not align with their professional and personal goals. This approach will enable healthcare professionals to manage their time more efficiently, increasing job satisfaction and reducing burnout rates.

11. Institutional assistance.

It is essential to recognize that doctors are an integral part of the healthcare system, and their well-being is critical to the organization's success. Therefore, healthcare organizations must proactively promote work-life balance among their employees. This can be achieved by implementing flexible work arrangements, reducing workload, providing counseling and mental health support, and encouraging healthy lifestyle habits. By prioritizing the well-being of their staff, healthcare organizations can enhance the quality of patient care and improve employee health and job satisfaction.

Role of Time Management in Balancing Personal and Professional Life in Medicine:

Good time management skills are essential for healthcare professionals to balance work and personal life. They often face the challenges of managing long work hours, unexpected emergencies, and keeping up with the latest developments. If healthcare professionals don't manage their time effectively, they can experience burnout, stress, and a decline in the quality of patient care.

Healthcare professionals can improve their time management skills by adopting various strategies. For instance, they can seek guidance from a mentor, participate in time management training programs, or utilize technology-based tools to streamline their workflow. The most popular technology-based tools for managing time effectively include calendar apps, task organizers, and project management software. These tools assist healthcare professionals in planning and prioritizing tasks, setting deadlines, and monitoring progress, which leads to improved productivity and efficiency. Utilizing such tools can be particularly beneficial for healthcare professionals who must juggle multiple tasks and responsibilities simultaneously, as it can help them manage their time more effectively and reduce stress levels.

Conclusion:

The medical field can be immensely demanding, often stressing the balance between professional obligations and personal life. However, healthcare professionals can attain a healthy work-life balance by adopting practical strategies such as establishing boundaries, prioritizing self-reflection and physical health, cultivating a supportive network, practicing stress management techniques, continuing learning, deploying delegation strategies, and prioritizing tasks. Furthermore, healthcare organizations have a central role in encouraging this balance, with interventions like flexible work arrangements, mental health support, and reduced workload. Time management, aided by technology-based tools, can also be a significant asset in juggling responsibilities. The well-being of healthcare professionals is as important as the quality of patient care they provide, as their wellness indirectly enhances the effectiveness of their occupational responsibilities. Hence, achieving an equilibrium between personal life and professional duties is not only possible but essential for a successful and sustainable medical profession.

Suggested Readings

• Baum, N. (2008). Balancing Your Personal and Professional Lives. The Ochsner Journal, 8(4), 160.

• Lampe, L., Hitching, R., Hammond, T. E., Park, J., & Rich, D. (2023). Being a 'good' doctor: Understanding and managing professional boundaries is challenging and can lead to stress and burnout. Australasian Psychiatry, 31(6), 764–767.

• Hanganu, B., & Ioan, B. G. (2022). The Personal and Professional Impact of Patients' Complaints on Doctors—A Qualitative Approach. International Journal of Environmental Research and Public Health, 19(1).

• Shahvari, Z., Alipour, F., Asghari, F., Samadi, S., & Amini, H. (2020). Personal factors affecting medical professionalism: a qualitative study in Iran *

• Australia, H. (2023). Work-life balance.

• Sermo Team. (2023). Guide for Doctors: Work-Life Balance Best Practices | Sermo.

• Aymes, S. (2020). Work-life balance for physicians: The what, the why, and the how-tips-for-finding-your-work-life-balance Work-life balance for physicians: The what, the why, and the how.

Medicine's Dual Challenge: Balancing Risk and Uncertainty

"Uncertainty is the only certainty there is, and knowing how to live with insecurity is the only security."

- John Allen Paulos

Overview:

In medicine, practitioners often grapple with two simultaneously occurring phenomena - risk and uncertainty. These elements represent medicine's dual challenge – determining the ideal balance between the inherent risks associated with treatments or procedures and the pervasive uncertainty that permeates most medical decisions. The text explores the complexities of mitigating risk and managing uncertainty in the exhaustive and intricate field of medical science. It elaborates on how these two factors often act as significant deterrents in the decision-making process within healthcare. Additionally, it sheds light on the strategies to balance these challenges, thereby bringing about a profound improvement in ensuring better patient outcomes.

Understanding Risk and Uncertainty in Medical Practice:

Both risk and uncertainty are fundamental elements of medical practice and can profoundly affect the decision-making process of healthcare providers. It is essential to comprehend these concepts to ensure patients receive the best possible care while minimizing potential adverse outcomes.

Risk refers to the likelihood of harm or injury to a patient due to medical intervention.

Uncertainty is the absence of knowledge or information regarding a patient's condition or the effectiveness of treatment.

Examples of Risk and Uncertainty in Medical Practice:

1. **Risk**: There's a risk involved when performing organ transplants. The patient's body may reject the new organ, leading to serious health complications or even death.

2. **Uncertainty**: A situation of uncertainty in the medical field could be when a new vaccine or drug is launched. Despite the rigorous testing and trials, there can be uncertainty about its effectiveness and potential side effects in some patients, especially in the long term.

3. **Risk and Uncertainty**: A patient with severe heart disease may be recommended for bypass surgery. Here, the 'risk' is associated with complications during or after surgery, such as infection, bleeding, stroke, etc; the 'uncertainty' pertains to the unpredictability of the surgery's long-term success and how effectively it would improve the patient's quality of life.

The Impact of Uncertainty on Patient Care and Outcomes:

In the medical field, professionals often encounter situations wherein they are uncertain about a patient's condition or the most appropriate course of treatment. For instance:

1. A cardiothoracic surgeon had a case wherein his patient was showing symptoms of both angina and heart failure. The overlapping symptoms made it hard for him to ascertain the accurate condition, causing a delay in treatment. Such uncertainty led to a prolonged stay of the patient at the hospital, and his health condition worsened over time.

2. A neurologist misdiagnosed his patient's migraine for stress-induced headaches due to some conflicting symptoms. The patient's recurring pain accelerated since the treatment for stress headaches did not improve the condition, culminating in an urgent hospital admission.

3. Due to the overlapping symptoms of COVID-19 and seasonal flu, a family physician failed to diagnose his patient correctly. This resulted in the patient unknowingly spreading the virus to others in the community and delayed appropriate care for her condition.

Such uncertainty can deleteriously affect the quality of patient care and outcomes. When healthcare providers are uncertain, it can result in significant delays or errors in diagnosis and treatment. Consequently, patients may experience prolonged hospital stays, an increased risk of complications, and poorer health outcomes.

Uncertainty is a salient variable that can engender heightened levels of anxiety and distress among patients and their families. The challenge can be incredibly daunting when confronted with an unclear diagnosis or treatment plan, as they may feel uncertain about their care and may not fully comprehend the implications of their condition. This can hurt their ability to make informed healthcare decisions and erode their trust in healthcare providers.

Comprehensive Analysis of Medical Risk:

Medical risk assessments are critical for predicting the likelihood of adverse health outcomes such as morbidity, mortality, hospitalization, or disability. These assessments rely on various factors, including individual characteristics, medical history, environmental exposures, and lifestyle. As such, they play a critical role in preventive care, disease management, and clinical decision-making.

Several medical risk assessment methods have been developed and validated for diverse health conditions and populations, including the Framingham Risk Score, Charlson Comorbidity Index, ECOG Performance Status, and APACHE II etc.

The efficacy of medical risk assessment methods may vary depending on the context and intended use and may require customization or validation for specific populations or settings. As such, it is crucial for healthcare providers, researchers, and policymakers to carefully scrutinize the suitability and pertinence of different methods before their adoption into practice or policy-making.

Role of Evidence-Based Medicine in Reducing Risk and Uncertainty:

The application of Evidence-based Medicine (EBM) has been an invaluable tool in reducing uncertainty in healthcare decision-making processes. EBM encompasses an extensive approach that combines clinical expertise with the latest systematic research findings to make informed decisions concerning patient care. By adopting EBM, healthcare practitioners are better equipped to make sound judgments based on the best available evidence, thus providing patients with high-quality healthcare services.

The core principles of EBM are widely employed in diagnosis, where healthcare providers rely on validated diagnostic tests and screening tools that have undergone rigorous research and analysis. These tools help providers accurately identify the presence and extent of disease or injury, allowing for the development of appropriate treatment strategies.

EBM principles also inform the selection of treatment strategies that have been proven effective in clinical trials, ensuring that patients receive the most appropriate, evidence-based care possible. By adhering to EBM principles, healthcare providers can ensure that their practices are anchored in the latest scientific evidence and that patients receive the highest quality care.

EBM has gained popularity recently, yet healthcare professionals have slowly adopted its principles in daily practice. Recently, a concerted effort has been made to expand the application of EBM principles in healthcare decision-making. As a result, organizations such as the Evidence-Based Medicine Foundation have emerged as invaluable resources for healthcare providers seeking to augment their knowledge and understanding of EBM principles. Through their comprehensive educational programs and resources, these organizations play a pivotal role in promoting the widespread adoption of EBM principles in modern healthcare.

Risk Management in Medical Practice:

The ability to balance risk is a crucial skill for healthcare providers. Inpatient treatment must achieve a harmonious equilibrium between caution and action to deliver high-quality, patient-centered care and ensure optimal outcomes.

Mastering this skill allows healthcare providers to mitigate the likelihood of adverse events and complications, enhance patient satisfaction and trust, and ultimately drive superior patient health outcomes. When the risk is managed effectively, patients can be confident that they receive the highest quality care. At the same time, healthcare providers can be assured that they provide safe, effective, and compassionate care.

To ensure effective risk management in medical practice, healthcare professionals must adopt a proactive approach. This entails continuous learning, ongoing monitoring of outcomes, and staying current with the latest research and best practices. Additionally, healthcare professionals should remain open to reflecting on their decisions and learn from mistakes or unexpected outcomes. This enables them to make informed decisions that minimize patient risk, ultimately leading to enhanced patient safety and improved quality of care. By implementing a proactive approach to risk management, healthcare professionals can effectively mitigate potential hazards and safeguard the welfare of their patients while optimizing overall patient care standards.

Addressing Uncertainty in Healthcare:

The medical decision-making process is an intricate and demanding task that requires healthcare professionals to navigate with precision and confidence. However, uncertainty remains a significant challenge, with numerous unknown and unpredictable critical factors. To tackle this uncertainty effectively, healthcare professionals must possess diverse skills, including the ability to gather and interpret information accurately, think critically, and adapt promptly to changing circumstances. By honing these skills, they can deliver patients the highest quality of care and ensure favorable outcomes.

To effectively manage the inherent uncertainty in healthcare, it is crucial to establish a work environment that cultivates transparency and open communication. Medical practitioners must communicate candidly and honestly about various procedures and treatments' risks and potential outcomes. By adopting this approach, patients receive complete and accurate information that empowers them to make informed decisions about their healthcare, which can help to mitigate uncertainty and reduce the risk of unfavorable outcomes.

Strategies for Balancing Risk and Uncertainty in Healthcare:

In the healthcare industry, decision-making carries inherent risk and uncertainty, as each decision can profoundly impact a patient's life. Therefore, healthcare professionals must carefully balance these factors to provide the best possible care while minimizing potential harm. To achieve this goal, various strategies must be employed, such as gathering and analyzing data, consulting with experts, assessing patient preferences, and considering ethical and legal issues related to patient care. By adopting these approaches, healthcare providers can make informed decisions that account for the complexities of the healthcare landscape while upholding the highest standards of ethical practice.

One of the most successful approaches to achieving this is through evidence-based decision-making. However, in cases where high-quality data is not readily available or the condition being treated is rare, reliance on the clinical expertise and judgment of healthcare professionals may be necessary. In such cases, the healthcare provider's clinical experience and knowledge of best practices remain vital in making informed decisions.

Shared decision-making is a widely accepted strategy in healthcare that seeks to involve patients in the decision-making process. This approach aims to ensure that patients' preferences, values, and needs are taken into account and can lead to better patient satisfaction and outcomes. However, for shared decision-making to be effective, it requires open and effective communication and trust between patients and healthcare providers. Both parties must collaborate to make informed decisions about the most suitable treatment options for the patient.

Healthcare providers are entrusted with evaluating the advantages and disadvantages of various treatments, particularly in end-of-life care. This is where ethical considerations become crucial. To make informed decisions, healthcare providers must consider several ethical principles, such as patient autonomy, beneficence, non-maleficence, and justice. These principles guide healthcare providers, enabling them to make impartial and equitable decisions that prioritize patients' well-being while respecting their preferences.

Emerging Trends in Managing Medical Risks and Uncertainty:

To ensure the safety of patients and promote the highest standards of care, healthcare professionals must stay abreast of the latest trends in managing medical risks and uncertainty.

One emerging trend gaining momentum in the industry is using data analytics to identify potential risks and prevent them before they cause harm to patients. Electronic health records, which serve as primary patient data repositories, provide a wealth of information that can be subjected to advanced analytics to detect patterns and identify potential areas of concern. By leveraging data analytics to identify and mitigate risks proactively, healthcare professionals can enhance patient safety, improve clinical outcomes, and reduce overall healthcare costs.

The healthcare industry is witnessing a growing trend in adopting telemedicine, which involves remotely providing medical care to patients. This approach has proven effective in minimizing the risk of exposure to infectious diseases and improving access to care in remote and underserved areas. The significance of telemedicine has been further highlighted by the COVID-19 pandemic, which has served as a crucial tool in ensuring continuity of care while reducing the risk of transmission.

The healthcare sector increasingly leverages advanced technologies such as artificial intelligence and machine learning to enhance patient care and safety. These technologies enable healthcare professionals to identify potential risks and predict patient outcomes, facilitating proactive intervention before adverse events occur. Predictive analytics and decision support systems are among the applications of technology augmenting patient care and safety.

Incorporating healthcare systems and adopting interdisciplinary teams can significantly improve communication and collaboration among healthcare professionals. This, in turn, can play a pivotal role in mitigating the risk of errors and enhancing patient outcomes. The utilization of interdisciplinary teams is associated with superior decision-making skills and the provision of customized care that caters to the unique requirements of individual patients.

However, integrating artificial intelligence (AI) and machine learning (ML) in healthcare decision-making poses new challenges regarding data security, confidentiality, and ethical implications. As such, healthcare professionals must keep abreast of these emerging trends and make informed decisions on the potential risks and benefits. This is crucial in ensuring that patient care remains the top priority and that these technologies are conducted safely and ethically.

Conclusion:

The complexities of risk and uncertainty inherent in medical practice necessitate a balanced and strategic approach to healthcare decision-making. Risk, defined as the potential harm that may arise from medical interventions, along with uncertainty and the lack of surety in the efficacy of treatments, profoundly influences healthcare outcomes. Evidence-based medicine (EBM), comprehensive risk assessments, and communicative transparency have fostered more informed and secure healthcare practices. Moreover, shared decision-making, which relies heavily on patient involvement, can improve patient satisfaction and outcomes. Emerging trends such as data analytics, telemedicine, artificial intelligence, machine learning, and interdisciplinary teams are revolutionizing risk management and decision-making in healthcare. However, healthcare professionals must vigilantly navigate these progressive technologies, contemplating their potential risks, security implications, and ethical considerations to ensure beneficial, patient-centered care. Ultimately, balancing risk and uncertainty is a dynamic and continuous process, necessitating continuous learning, reflection, and adaptation.

Suggested Readings

• Makridakis, S., Kirkham, R., Wakefield, A., Papadaki, M., Kirkham, J., & Long, L. (2019). Forecasting, uncertainty and risk; perspectives on clinical decision-making in preventive and curative medicine. International Journal of Forecasting, 35(2).

• Kim, K., & Lee, Y. M. (2018). Understanding uncertainty in medicine: Concepts and implications in medical education. In Korean Journal of Medical Education (Vol. 30, Issue 3).

• Hatfield, T., & Fritz, Z. (2023). How and why do doctors communicate about diagnostic uncertainty: an experimental vignette study. Patient Education and Counseling, 109.

• Abeysinghe, S., Leppold, C., Ozaki, A., & Morita, M. (2020). Risk, uncertainty and medical practice: changes in the medical professions following disaster. Evidence and Policy, 16(2).

• Pascarella, G., Rossi, M., Montella, E., Capasso, A., De Feo, G., Snr, G. B., Nardone, A., Montuori, P., Triassi, M., D'auria, S., & Morabito, A. (2021). Risk analysis in healthcare organizations: Methodological framework and critical variables. Risk Management and Healthcare Policy, 14.

• Khan, A., Farooq, A., Ahmad, S., & Fraser, J. M. (2022). Optimizing the complexities of unforeseen risk in healthcare with innovation and technology: a proposed framework. In Journal of Hospital Management and Health Policy (Vol. 6).

• Sur, R. L., & Dahm, P. (2011). History of evidence-based medicine. Indian Journal of Urology, 27(4).

• Masic, I., Miokovic, M., & Muhamedagic, B. (2008). Evidence Based Medicine - New Approaches and Challenges. Acta Informatica Medica, 16(4).

• Sheridan, D. J., & Julian, D. G. (2016). Achievements and Limitations of Evidence-Based Medicine. In Journal of the American College of Cardiology (Vol. 68, Issue 2).

Bridging the Gap: Addressing Weaknesses in the Medical Profession

"Our greatest frailty is giving up; the surest way to succeed is always to try one more time. In medicine, failure is not an option."

- Thomas Edison

Overview:

The medical profession plays a critical role in society, ensuring the health and well-being of individuals. However, like any other field, it has its challenges. Identifying these areas of weakness is crucial to improving healthcare quality and addressing the concerns of patients and medical professionals. This segment aims to analyze the current shortcomings in medical practice and identify potential solutions to address these gaps. Throughout this discourse, we will examine the various weaknesses that affect the healthcare system and explore practical strategies and innovations that can help alleviate the weaknesses and bridge the gaps in the medical profession. The text emphasizes the importance of teamwork in problem-solving and offers success stories from reputable hospitals that prove the effectiveness of these strategies. The aim is to serve as a roadmap for medical professionals and institutions to improve their practices and ultimately benefit their patients.

Evaluating the Common Weaknesses in the Medical Profession:

Medical Errors

One area of weakness in the medical profession is the issue of medical errors. These errors can range from misdiagnosis to medication and surgical errors. Misdiagnosed medical conditions result in the death or permanent disability of around 795,000 Americans every year.

Lack of Coordination

Another area of concern is the need for coordination and fragmented care within the healthcare system. Patients often receive care from multiple healthcare providers who may not effectively communicate or coordinate their efforts. This can lead to errors, duplication of services, and gaps in care.

Lack of evidence-based practice:

Another area for improvement that warrants attention is the failure to adhere to evidence-based guidelines. This can manifest in administering outdated or ineffective treatments and unnecessary tests and procedures that harm patient health.

Poor customer service:

Medical practices must address any deficiencies in their customer service practices to provide an optimal patient experience. Such deficiencies may manifest as prolonged wait times, inattentive staff, and inadequate communication with patients, all of which can contribute to adverse patient experiences.

Neglecting patient-centered care:

In the ever-changing healthcare landscape, failing to prioritize patient-centered care is an oversight and a critical mistake with severe repercussions. Adopting a patient-centered approach enhances the quality of care and strengthens the bond between patients and caregivers. However, without this empathetic and personalized approach, patients may feel neglected, their voices unheard, and their needs unmet, leading to unsatisfactory health outcomes.

Overcoming weaknesses:

Effective communication and collaboration

One effective strategy for strengthening medical practices is to enhance communication and collaboration among healthcare team members. This can be done through regular team meetings, where doctors, nurses, and other staff members can discuss patient cases, share updates and insights, and work together to improve clinical outcomes. By fostering a collaborative environment, medical practices can enhance the quality of care provided to patients.

Shift from paper-based systems to Electronic Health Records

Investing in advanced technologies and electronic health records (EHR) systems is essential. By transitioning from paper-based systems to EHRs, medical practices can streamline administrative tasks, improve documentation accuracy, and enhance efficiency in delivering patient care. EHRs also facilitate data sharing and interoperability with other healthcare providers, ensuring continuity of care and reducing medical errors.

Patient Engagement

Medical practices should prioritize patient engagement and satisfaction. Implementing patient portals and online appointment scheduling systems can empower patients to access their medical records, request prescription refills, and communicate with their healthcare providers easily. Additionally, patient satisfaction surveys and feedback mechanisms can provide valuable insights into areas that need improvement, helping medical practices tailor their services to meet patient needs better.

Improving diagnostic skills

Improving diagnostic skills is a critical area that demands doctors' constant attention. Misdiagnoses can have severe implications for patients' health and well-being. Therefore, practitioners must focus on enhancing their ability to identify and treat illnesses. One way to achieve this goal is by pursuing continuing education and keeping abreast of the latest medical research. By doing so, doctors can stay up-to-date with the most advanced diagnostic techniques, treatments, and technologies. This, in turn, can lead to improved patient care and better health outcomes.

Developing Emotional Intelligence

Physicians must give equal attention to their emotional intelligence as they do to their medical expertise. It is critical for physicians to be compassionate and empathetic toward their patients, as patients expect doctors to provide not only medical care but also emotional support. Doctors who engage with their patients emotionally can cultivate trust and deliver better care. Therefore, developing emotional intelligence is essential to becoming an excellent physician.

Role of Continuous Learning in Strengthening Medical Practice:

Continuous learning is an essential component of the medical profession, as it provides healthcare practitioners with the necessary knowledge and skills to stay up-to-date with the latest advancements in medical treatments and technologies. This keeps them better equipped to integrate these advances into their practice, resulting in more favorable patient outcomes.

Continuous learning in the medical field can take various forms, such as attending conferences, seminars, or workshops to learn about the latest research and trends in their respective specialties. Medical professionals may also participate in online courses, webinars, or peer-to-peer learning networks to exchange knowledge and best practices with colleagues worldwide.

Collaborative Brainstorming to Improve Medical Practice:

Collaborative brainstorming has emerged as a valuable tool in improving medical practice. With the ever-advancing field of healthcare, it is crucial to continuously brainstorm and find innovative solutions to enhance medical procedures, patient outcomes, and overall healthcare quality.

Furthermore, collaborative brainstorming fosters a culture of communication, teamwork, and innovation within healthcare institutions. By involving various stakeholders, such as surgeons, nurses, administrators, and even patients, healthcare organizations can tap into a wealth of knowledge and expertise. Each individual brings unique insights and experiences to brainstorming, leading to more comprehensive and practical solutions.

In addition to the immediate benefits, collaborative brainstorming also provides long-term advantages. It encourages a continuous improvement mindset, where healthcare professionals constantly seek new and better care delivery methods. This collaborative approach also promotes a culture of learning and adaptability, allowing medical professionals to evolve alongside advancements in technology and medical knowledge.

Certain practices can be implemented to ensure the success of collaborative brainstorming sessions in healthcare. Firstly, creating a safe and non-judgmental environment is crucial, encouraging participants to express their ideas and opinions freely without fear of criticism. Additionally, effective facilitation techniques, such as structured brainstorming frameworks or the use of facilitators trained in group dynamics, can help guide discussions and ensure that all voices are heard.

Effective Strategies for Strengthening Medical Practices:

Case Studies: Successful Improvements in the Medical Field:

The medical field constantly evolves and improves, driven by numerous case studies identifying successful strategies and improvements. These case studies are valuable references for healthcare professionals and organizations looking to enhance patient care, streamline processes, and optimize outcomes. Here, we will explore two notable case studies that have resulted in significant advancements in the medical field.

1. Improving Patient Safety: The Johns Hopkins Hospital

One noteworthy case study comes from The Johns Hopkins Hospital, which successfully implemented a comprehensive patient safety program. The hospital identified the need for a systematic approach to reduce medical errors and enhance patient safety. Through the implementation of various initiatives, such as mandatory safety training, improved communication protocols, and the use of technology for medication administration, The Johns Hopkins Hospital witnessed a remarkable reduction in adverse events and medical errors. This case study demonstrates that a proactive approach to patient safety can significantly improve healthcare outcomes.

2. Enhancing Surgical Outcomes: Mayo Clinic

Mayo Clinic is widely recognized for its commitment to quality and patient-centered care. A case study conducted at the Mayo Clinic focused on enhancing surgical outcomes through a multidisciplinary approach. By involving various healthcare professionals, including surgeons, anesthesiologists, nurses, and physical therapists, in the pre-operative, operative, and post-operative phases, Mayo Clinic achieved remarkable results. Implementing standardized protocols, comprehensive patient education, and close postoperative follow-up significantly reduced the rate of surgical complications and unplanned readmissions. This case study demonstrates the value of collaboration and comprehensive care in optimizing surgical outcomes.

Conclusion:

In conclusion, despite the medical profession's critical role in society, there is a significant need to address its weaknesses. The profession struggles with medical errors, lack of coordination and evidence-based practice, poor customer service, and negligence of patient-centered care. However, effective strategies to overcome these problems include enhancing communication and collaboration, adopting advanced technologies like Electronic Health Records (EHR), improving diagnostic skills, enhancing Emotional Intelligence, and embracing continuous learning. Collaborative brainstorming also stands as a promising strategy, fostering an environment of innovation and improvement. Successful case studies from institutions like Johns Hopkins Hospital and Mayo Clinic serve as examples, illustrating that when these strategies are put into action, the result is safer, higher quality care, satisfaction among patients, and improved healthcare outcomes. Hence, the medical profession must continue addressing these weaknesses to benefit patients and the healthcare system.

Suggested Readings

• Makary, M. A., & Daniel, M. (2016). Medical error-the third leading cause of death in the US. BMJ (Online), 353.

• Rodziewicz, T. L., Houseman, B., & Hipskind, J. E. (2022). Medical Error Reduction and Prevention. StatPearls [Internet].

• Stevens, E. L., Hulme, A., & Salmon, P. M. (2021). The impact of power on health care team performance and patient safety: a review of the literature. In Ergonomics (Vol. 64, Issue 8).

• Vest, J. R., & Gamm, L. D. (2010). Health information exchange: Persistent challenges and new strategies. Journal of the American Medical Informatics Association, 17(3).

• Pronovost, P. J., Mathews, S. C., Chute, C. G., & Rosen, A. (2017). Creating a purpose-driven learning and improving health system: The Johns Hopkins Medicine quality and safety experience. Learning Health Systems, 1(1).

• Novack, D. H., Suchman, A. L., Clark, W., Epstein, R. M., Najberg, E., & Kaplan, C. (1997). Calibrating the physician: Personal awareness and effective patient care. JAMA, 278(6).

• Murphy, D. R., Singh, H., & Berlin, L. (2014). Communication breakdowns and diagnostic errors: A radiology perspective. In Diagnosis (Vol. 1, Issue 4).

• Khawar, A., Frederiks, F., Nasori, M., Mak, M., Visser, M., Van Etten-Jamaludin, F., Diemers, A., & Van Dijk, N. (2022). What are the characteristics of excellent physicians and residents in the clinical workplace? A systematic review. In BMJ Open (Vol. 12, Issue 9).

• Hatfield, T., & Fritz, Z. (2023). How and why do doctors communicate about diagnostic uncertainty: an experimental vignette study. Patient Education and Counseling, 109.

• Shibli, A. (2020). 4 Ways to Identify Your Strengths and Weaknesses to Land Your Dream Job.

• (Linda Wu, et al,. 2017 Physician know thyself). (2017).

• (Dr. Rahul Khemani et al., How to Turn Weakness into Strength? (2024).

• Real Staffing, et al., 2021 How to turn your weaknesses into strengths at work _ Real Staffing. (n.d.).

What Do Patients Expect And Value In A Doctor?

"Expectations won't hurt as long as they are realistic."

-Garima Soni

Overview:

Patient contentment and well-being are pivotal in the medical sector, profoundly affecting both the delivery and outcomes of healthcare services. This discourse offers an empathetic understanding of what patients genuinely desire and appreciate in a doctor. It will allow us to gain insight into what patients look for when choosing a doctor and what they consider essential in their interactions. This understanding can be crucial in improving patient care, fostering a better doctor-patient relationship, and improving the healthcare service. By appreciating and incorporating these expectations into the practice, doctors can ensure their patients feel valued, understood, and cared for. The aim is not only to unravel the ideal qualities of a physician from a patient's perspective but also to pose crucial insights into improving and maintaining satisfactory medical services.

Decoding Good Medical Practice: Patient Perspectives:

Effective medical practice constitutes a critical facet of providing superior healthcare services. It is a framework of guiding principles and conduct that healthcare professionals must uphold to ensure optimal care delivery to their patients.

This practice is not only indispensable for healthcare providers but is also pivotal for patients themselves.

In the healthcare industry, patients hold healthcare providers to high standards. The expectation is that healthcare providers are transparent about their knowledge and expertise, possess integrity, and maintain confidentiality. Additionally, patients expect healthcare providers to remain updated with the latest best practices in their field.

Above all, patients anticipate receiving an accurate and timely diagnosis and gaining an understanding of their condition. They are interested in the most effective treatment options, requiring a thorough evaluation, appropriate testing, and a clear and comprehensive diagnosis. Furthermore, a customized treatment plan considering each patient's unique needs is crucial.

What Patients Value in a Doctor?

Patients value physicians who demonstrate an active listening approach, giving patients a sense of being heard and understood. Moreover, patients appreciate doctors who adopt a personalized approach to their care, catering to their unique needs and circumstances.

Patients value physicians who demonstrate transparency and openness about their treatment options and actively engage them in decision-making. This openness empowers patients to feel more in control of their healthcare, resulting in higher satisfaction. Conversely, a physician's lack of communication and transparency can lead to patient mistrust and frustration.

Empathy fosters a positive and constructive relationship between physicians and patients. Physicians' empathy helps patients feel more comfortable and at ease, creating an environment allowing them to share their concerns and experiences freely. As a result, patients are more likely to adhere to treatments and recommended lifestyle changes, leading to better health outcomes.

Exploring Doctor-Patient Relationship Dynamics:

Given its importance, it is vital to recognize that the doctor-patient relationship is a complex dynamic involving various social, psychological, and ethical considerations. By acknowledging and addressing these factors, healthcare providers can build trust and rapport with their patients, ultimately leading to better outcomes and higher patient satisfaction.

Many factors, including communication, trust, and shared decision-making, can influence the dynamics of the doctor-patient relationship.

Effective communication is fundamental in establishing trust and developing a therapeutic alliance between healthcare providers and their patients. Patients who feel comfortable and perceive their healthcare provider as genuinely interested in their concerns are more inclined to adhere to treatment recommendations, resulting in higher satisfaction with their care.

Shared decision-making is increasingly gaining recognition as a crucial component of patient-centered care. It involves a collaborative effort between healthcare providers and patients to make healthcare decisions consistent with the patient's unique values, preferences, and requirements. By empowering patients to take an active role in their healthcare decisions, better health outcomes, improved patient satisfaction, and enhanced quality of care can be achieved.

Studies have revealed that certain factors, including gender, age, race, and cultural background, can significantly affect the dynamics of the doctor-patient relationship. As a result, healthcare providers must remain aware of these potential barriers and take proactive measures to address them, ensuring that their patients receive equitable care tailored to their needs. Healthcare providers can cultivate trust, enhance engagement, and promote superior health outcomes by providing care sensitive to each patient's unique characteristics.

Cultural and Personal Factors Affecting Patient Expectations:

A patient's cultural background can significantly affect how they view their health and illness and their trust in healthcare professionals. This can lead to differences in their expectations and treatment plan outcomes. Therefore, healthcare professionals must recognize and understand these cultural differences to provide adequate care and build trust with their patients.

Additionally, a patient's personal experiences and beliefs can play a significant role in their expectations. Patients may have preconceived notions about specific treatments or medications based on their own experiences or those of their family and friends.

It is worth noting that older adults tend to prioritize care coordination and communication with their healthcare providers, while younger patients may prioritize convenience and access to technology.

Furthermore, anxiety and fear can significantly impact a patient's expectations, particularly regarding pain management or surgical outcomes.

It is essential to consider these factors when creating a comprehensive treatment plan that considers each patient's unique circumstances and preferences.

The Journey Towards Being a Patient-Centered Doctor:

Developing a patient-centered approach in healthcare necessitates a significant shift in physicians' mindsets. This transformation involves moving away from a narrow focus on treating medical conditions to adopting a comprehensive understanding of individual patient's needs and concerns. Although this shift poses a considerable challenge, the benefits of a patient-centered approach are substantial for both physicians and their patients. Embracing this approach fosters a deeper understanding of patient needs, facilitates better communication, and promotes shared decision-making and adherence to treatment plans, leading to improved health outcomes and patient satisfaction. Therefore, healthcare providers must prioritize the patient-centered approach for better patient outcomes.

The adoption of a patient-centered approach requires the incorporation of feedback obtained from patients into clinical practice. Feedback forms, surveys, and similar tools can offer valuable insights into patients' experiences and perspectives. By analyzing this feedback, clinicians can tailor their approach to meet the requirements of their patients more effectively. Incorporating patient feedback into clinical practice can lead to improved patient outcomes, increased patient satisfaction, and better quality of care. Therefore, healthcare providers must emphasize the importance of obtaining patient feedback and incorporating it into their clinical decision-making processes.

Conclusion:

Patients' expectations and values are pivotal in shaping their experiences and outcomes in the healthcare sector. Essential doctor qualities from a patient's perspective include transparency, integrity, up-to-date knowledge, effective communication, empathy, and a personalized approach to treatment. The dynamics of the doctor-patient relationship are complex and influenced by social, psychological, and ethical considerations and factors such as gender, age, race, and cultural background. A patient-centered approach is vital, considering individual cultural and personal differences in expectations and needs. This approach dictates shared decision-making, tailored communication, active listening and empathy, and the utilization of patient feedback in clinical practice improvements. Fostering such an environment can significantly improve outcomes and patient satisfaction and elevate the overall quality of healthcare services.

Suggested Readings

- Philpot, L. M., Khokhar, B. A., DeZutter, M. A., Loftus, C. G., Stehr, H. I., Ramar, P., Madson, L. P., & Ebbert, J. O. (2019). Creation of a Patient-Centered Journey Map to Improve the Patient Experience: A Mixed Methods Approach. Mayo Clinic Proceedings: Innovations, Quality & Outcomes, 3(4), 466–475.
- Bidmon, S., Elshiewy, O., Terlutter, R., & Boztug, Y. (2020). What patients value in physicians: Analyzing drivers of patient satisfaction using physician-rating website data. Journal of Medical Internet Research, 22(2).

- Dormohammadi, T., Asghari, F., & Rashidian, A. (2010). What Do Patients Expect from Their Physicians? In Iranian J Publ Health (Vol. 39, Issue 1).
- Banerjee, A., & Sanyal, D. (2012). Dynamics of doctor-patient relationship: A cross-sectional study on concordance, trust, and patient enablement. Journal of Family and Community Medicine, 19(1), 12–19.
- Lisa Rapaport. (2023). Castle Connolly Survey Asks What Patients Want Most From Their Doctors.
- GMC. (2023). Exploring patient and public views to inform the Good medical practice review - GMC.
- Ridd, M., Shaw, A., Lewis, G., & Salisbury, C. (2009). The patient-doctor relationship: A synthesis of the qualitative literature on patients' perspectives. British Journal of General Practice, 59(561), 268–275.
- Nápoles-Springer, A. M., Santoyo, J., Ma, K. H., Pérez-Stable, E. J., & Stewart, A. L. (2005). Patients' perceptions of cultural factors affecting the quality of their medical encounters. In Health Expectations (Vol. 8).

Enhancing Patient Trust: Strategies for Healthcare Professionals

"To be trusted is a greater compliment than being loved."

- George MacDonald

Overview:

Earning and preserving patient trust is paramount in healthcare's dynamic and crucial world. From dealing with life-defining diagnoses to navigating complex treatment options, it is pivotal that patients wholeheartedly trust their healthcare providers. This article delves into the nuances of interpersonal relationships within medical environments, focusing on enhancing trust. The manuscript is a valuable tool highlighting the moral standards and guiding principles involved in patient-caregiver relationships while shedding light on practical methods healthcare providers can employ to build and fortify trust within their professional conduct. Whether you are a seasoned healthcare provider or a novice, this guide is invaluable for building fruitful and enduring patient relationships.

Strategies to Enhance Trust with Patients:

Several key elements contribute to the development of trust in healthcare relationships. These include:

1. **Respect** —Demonstrating a high degree of respect toward patients is an essential responsibility of all healthcare

providers. This responsibility includes upholding patients' privacy, an inherent right that must not be compromised. In addition, healthcare providers must recognize and honor patients' values and beliefs, as these factors can significantly influence their overall well-being and healthcare outcomes. Adherence to these principles fosters a culture of professionalism in healthcare settings and ensures patients receive the best possible care with the utmost dignity and respect.

2. **Competence** - Patients expect their providers to have extensive knowledge, proficiency, and expertise in their healthcare field and be fully equipped to deliver the necessary care and treatment. To maintain such trust and confidence, healthcare providers must strive to meet these expectations by continually advancing their skills and knowledge and providing compassionate and effective patient care.

3. **Empathy**—Providing adequate healthcare services depends on healthcare providers displaying empathy toward their patients. By demonstrating empathy, healthcare providers can establish a robust rapport with their patients, earn their trust, and furnish them with the best possible care and treatment.

4. **Honesty and Transparency**—Patients rely on their healthcare providers for accurate and dependable information regarding their health status, diagnosis, and potential treatment options. As such, healthcare providers must prioritize honesty and transparency in their communication with patients to foster a robust and trustworthy relationship. This trust makes patients feel confident and well-informed as they navigate their health and medical decisions. Patients who perceive their

healthcare provider as honest and open are likelier to trust their physician and display confidence in their treatment. This trust and confidence can result in better patient outcomes and heightened satisfaction with the healthcare experience.

5. **Communication** - Effective communication is crucial in cultivating trust between healthcare providers and their patients. To achieve this, it is essential to engage in open and empathetic communication, which enables healthcare professionals to furnish information clearly and concisely while also responding to patient inquiries and concerns with sensitivity. Active listening on the part of healthcare providers is equally important, as it demonstrates respect and empathy and can lead to better patient outcomes. By prioritizing transparent and compassionate communication, healthcare providers can create a positive and supportive environment that fosters trust, confidence, and improved healthcare experiences.

Case Studies: Successful Trust-Building Practices in Healthcare:

Several healthcare organizations have implemented effective trust-building practices to achieve this objective and successfully establish positive and productive patient-provider relationships.

Kaiser Permanente is an organization that has taken significant strides to improve the communication skills of its physicians through a specialized training program. The program is designed to help physicians enhance their listening and empathizing abilities, leading to higher patient satisfaction.

The Cleveland Clinic has introduced the "Patients First: Empathy and Innovation Summit" program to encourage caregivers to think creatively and solve problems to provide personalized patient care. These initiatives demonstrate a commitment to enhancing patient care by prioritizing effective communication and innovative thinking in the healthcare industry.

The Mayo Clinic, a distinguished medical institution, has implemented a distinctive initiative called the **"Sharing Mayo Clinic" program.** The program's primary objective is to encourage patients and employees to share their experiences, opinions, and stories about the clinic with the general public. This initiative has proven to be highly successful in enhancing overall patient satisfaction rates and establishing trust between patients and healthcare providers. Employing this program, the Mayo Clinic has established a platform allowing patients and employees to communicate and share their first-hand experiences with others, promoting transparency and strengthening the bond between the clinic and its community.

Challenges and Solutions in Maintaining Patient Trust:

One of the primary obstacles that healthcare providers face in maintaining patient trust is communication barriers. Medical jargon and complex terminologies can confuse and intimidate patients, making it difficult to comprehend their diagnosis, treatment options, and potential risks. Consequently, patients may hesitate to ask questions or express their concerns, leading to a breakdown in communication that can negatively impact the patient-provider relationship.

Healthcare providers can overcome these barriers by utilizing clear and straightforward language, encouraging patients to ask questions, and offering educational resources in various formats, such as videos or brochures, to make the information more accessible. By communicating clearly and concisely, healthcare providers can help establish a rapport with their patients and ensure mutual understanding and trust.

Medical errors and malpractice are significant challenges that can seriously impact patients and undermine their trust in the healthcare system. To address this, healthcare providers must prioritize transparency when errors occur, taking responsibility for their mistakes and implementing measures to prevent similar errors. This can help reassure patients that their well-being is a top priority and help restore their confidence in the healthcare system.

In the healthcare industry, cultural differences can pose a significant barrier to building and maintaining patient trust. Healthcare providers must remain vigilant of their patients' cultural norms and practices to ensure their actions and recommendations align with their cultural backgrounds. As such, healthcare providers should make a concerted effort to identify and address any biases they may have that could negatively impact the care they provide. This can help build stronger relationships with patients and improve their care quality.

Conclusion:

Establishing and nurturing patient trust is a crucial aspect of the healthcare sector. Critical strategies for building such trust include demonstrating competence, empathy, honesty, and respect; practicing open and effective communication;

promoting transparency; and establishing friendly patient relations. Several healthcare organizations, including Kaiser Permanente, the Cleveland Clinic, and the Mayo Clinic, have successfully implemented innovative programs to enhance trust-building practices. However, challenges persist, such as communication barriers, medical errors, and patient cultural differences. Overcoming these obstacles requires clear and straightforward communication, transparency in the face of mistakes, consideration of cultural backgrounds, and eliminating biases. By adopting these strategies, healthcare providers can create a positive and supportive environment to enhance patient trust, optimize care, and ultimately lead to better health outcomes.

Suggested Readings

• Ambula. (2023). Challenges of Patient Engagement - Ambula Healthcare.

• Ambula-Health. (2023). Grow your practice & build trust with patients using these healthcare marketing.

• Dana Sparks. (2018). Sharing Mayo Clinic: Making the workforce welcoming to all - Mayo Clinic News Network.

• Garrubba M & Yap G. (2019). Trust in Health Professionals Executive Summary Background.

• Performance Heath. (2023). Patient Engagement Strategies: Creating a Safer Future in Healthcare.

• Philomath. (2023). Building Trust in Healthcare: Leveraging Market Research to Enhance Patient Engagement | by Philomath Research | Medium.

• Yuan, C. T., Dy, S. M., Yuanhong Lai, A., Oberlander, T., Hannum, S. M., Lasser, E. C., Heughan, J. A., Dukhanin, V., Kharrazi, H., Kim, J. M., Gurses, A. P., Bittle, M., Scholle, S. H., & Marsteller, J. A. (2022). Challenges and Strategies for Patient Safety in Primary Care: A Qualitative Study. American Journal of Medical Quality, 37(5), 379–387.

Healing Together: Family-oriented Medical Practice

"Family is the most important thing in the world."

- Princess Diana

Overview:

The family unit is an indispensable and irreplaceable aspect of human life, comprising individuals who share biological, marital, or adoptive bonds. "Healing Together" offers a deep dive into the interwoven fabric of healthcare and family dynamics. This compelling narrative vividly depicts the undeniable connection between family support and patient well-being. It explores diverse aspects of family-oriented practices within the medical field, delving into the psychological, social, and emotional factors accompanying any health ordeal. Embrace a transformative perspective on medicine—one where the family is not merely present but profoundly integrated into the path toward wellness.

Understanding the Concept of Family in Medical Practice:

The involvement of family members in healthcare plays an integral role in ensuring comprehensive care. It encompasses various aspects, including emotional support, effective communication, decision-making, and caregiving. The invaluable insights provided by family members into their loved one's medical history, symptoms, and treatment preferences can significantly aid healthcare providers in developing personalized treatment plans.

Emotional support is essential for patients' well-being in addition to medical treatment. Family members can play a pivotal role in providing this support, which can significantly impact the patient's mental health. Moreover, they can act as advocates, ensuring that their loved one's medical needs and preferences are considered while making treatment decisions. The involvement of family members can also foster a collaborative and trustful relationship between healthcare providers, patients, and their families, leading to better health outcomes.

However, the extent of family members' involvement must be customized based on the patient's needs and preferences. While some patients may prefer greater autonomy and control over their treatment decisions, others may necessitate more support and guidance from their families. As a result, healthcare professionals must consider each patient's unique needs and collaborate with families to achieve optimal treatment outcomes.

Requirement for a family-oriented approach:

The successful adoption of family-oriented care necessitates a significant shift in mindset of healthcare professionals and institutions. It requires the recognition of the family as an indispensable member of the care team and the involvement of family members in all aspects of the care process. This may entail providing education and support for family caregivers, facilitating communication between family members and healthcare providers, and empowering them to participate in decision-making. In essence, family-oriented care has the potential to yield significant benefits for both patients and healthcare providers and, therefore, should be considered an essential component of contemporary healthcare practices.

The Importance of Treating the Whole Family, Not Just Parts:

In healthcare, medical practitioners have historically focused solely on treating a patient's symptoms, often disregarding the potential influence of the patient's family on their overall well-being. However, recent research has emphasized the advantages of treating the entire family unit instead of individual members. Such an approach not only addresses the patient's medical concerns but also helps to enhance the overall quality of life for the entire family.

Treating families as a composite entity can significantly improve communication and rapport between family members. Additionally, this approach has the potential to uncover and address any underlying factors contributing to the patient's condition, such as familial disagreements, financial strains, or unhealthy lifestyle practices.

Incorporating Family Dynamics into Medical Treatment Plans:

In developing medical care plans, it is crucial to account for a patient's medical history and present condition and the impact of family dynamics on the treatment trajectory. The family environment is essential in determining a patient's physical and mental health outcomes. Hence, healthcare professionals must consider family dynamics when devising patient treatment pathways. This approach will ensure that patient care is comprehensive and tailored to their needs.

Examples:

1. A 45-year-old male with a history of diabetes and currently showing signs of kidney problems may need a specialized care plan. Suppose this patient lives with his

elderly parents, who may be unable to provide the necessary care. In that case, healthcare professionals may need to consider home nursing services or regular check-ups.

2. A young female diagnosed with an eating disorder whose family has a history of ignoring or belittling her problem. In formulating a treatment plan, healthcare professionals must pay particular attention to this family dynamic and possibly incorporate psychological counseling for the whole family in the care plan.

3. A child with acute leukemia currently undergoing chemotherapy. Suppose the child is from a large family, with many siblings competing for the parent's attention and love. In that case, healthcare professionals must consider that the child may need additional emotional support during treatment. In this case, treatment pathways may involve social services or mental health professionals.

4. An elderly patient diagnosed with Alzheimer's disease will require a different approach if she lives alone compared to if she lives with her family. If she is on her own, professionals might need to consider assisted living facilities; if her family is there to support her, treatment could focus more on home care with specific instructions given to family members.

When designing treatment plans, it is crucial to consider family dynamics and their potential influence on a patient's health. Unresolved family conflicts or dysfunctional relationships can contribute to stress and anxiety, which can worsen a patient's condition. Healthcare professionals can offer better support for their patient's overall health and well-being by identifying and addressing these issues. This approach enables them to provide personalized care considering the complex interplay between a patient's physical and emotional well-being. By doing so, healthcare professionals can improve patient outcomes, decrease healthcare costs, and promote a healthier society.

The Impact of Family-oriented Approach on Patient Outcomes:

The recovery rates of patients are a critical indicator of the quality of healthcare provided. Various factors, including family involvement, have positively influenced patient recovery rates.

Several studies have highlighted that patients whose families were involved in their care exhibited higher rates of successful recovery than patients whose families were absent. Family involvement was also positively associated with patient satisfaction and overall healthcare experience.

The Future of Family Involvement in Medical Practice:

Over the past few decades, family involvement has emerged as a crucial component of medical practice, facilitating the delivery of high-quality care to patients. However, with the advent of cutting-edge technologies and rapidly evolving healthcare policies, the future of family involvement in medical practice remains to be determined.

Modern healthcare policies and privacy regulations pose a significant challenge to family involvement in healthcare decision-making, primarily for patients aged 18 years or older who can make decisions.

The advent of telemedicine has introduced new complexities in family members' involvement in medical practice. Virtual consultations, while convenient, may provide a different level of family participation than in-person visits. This may impact the effectiveness and quality of care provided, as family members often serve as crucial sources of emotional and logistical support for patients.

As such, healthcare providers and policymakers must consider innovative solutions to help bridge this gap and ensure patients receive the highest care possible, regardless of the consultation mode.

Conclusion:

Integrating family-oriented perspectives in medical practice significantly affects recovery and overall patient health outcomes. The involvement of family members in healthcare is more than just essential support; it's a unique resource vital for comprehensive care. It facilitates effective communication, decision-making, and caregiving and provides critical emotional support to patients. A personalized approach acknowledging the family's role within the healthcare process can ultimately lead to improved patient outcomes and satisfaction while lowering healthcare costs. However, the future of family involvement in healthcare demands further evaluation, given the changing dynamics in healthcare technology, such as telemedicine and evolving healthcare policies. To uphold the advantages of family-oriented medical practice, medical practitioners and policymakers must navigate these challenges and create innovative solutions that continue to incorporate family members effectively into patient care.

Suggested Readings

• Bohart, S., Møller, A. M., Andreasen, A. S., Waldau, T., Lamprecht, C., & Thomsen, T. (2022). Effect of Patient and Family Centred Care interventions for adult intensive care unit patients and their families: A systematic review and meta-analysis. Intensive and Critical Care Nursing, 69, 103156.

• Fakhry, M., & Mohammed, W. E. (2022). Impact of family presence on healthcare outcomes and patients' wards design. Alexandria Engineering Journal, 61(12), 10713–10726.

• Scherr, S., Reifegerste, D., Arendt, F., van Weert, J. C. M., & Alden, D. L. (2022). Family involvement in medical decision making in Europe and the United States: A replication and extension in five Countries. Social Science & Medicine, 301, 114932.

• Newman, M. C., Lawless, J. J., & Gelo, F. (2007). Family-Oriented Patient Care.

• Kuo, D. Z., Houtrow, A. J., Arango, P., Kuhlthau, K. A., Simmons, J. M., & Neff, J. M. (2012). Family-centered care: Current applications and future directions in pediatric health care. In Maternal and Child Health Journal (Vol. 16, Issue 2, pp. 297–305).

Emotional Intelligence: The Unseen Power in Medicine

"When awareness is brought to an emotion, power is brought to your life."

- Tara Meyer Robson

Overview:

Healthcare professionals often experience high levels of stress and emotionally demanding situations in their daily work. They may have to deal with critical emergencies, communicate complex diagnoses with patients and their families, or work in challenging environments. To effectively manage these challenges, healthcare professionals must develop emotional intelligence. This discourse delves deep into the heart of our emotions, uncovering their powerful impact on medicine. The text highlights emotional intelligence (EI) and its invaluable role as a secret weapon in enhancing the quality and success of patient care. It is a thought-provoking guide designed to explore emotions' profound influence on health, patient care, and medical outcomes and initiate a conversation on how healthcare professionals can harness and hone this critical skill to usher in a new era of empathy-based, patient-centric medicine. If you are involved in healthcare, studying medicine, or fascinated by the interplay between emotions and healthcare, you must explore this compelling exploration. It reveals the often-overlooked strength of emotions, transforming it into a practical tool in the medical field.

Understanding the concept of Emotional intelligence:

Emotional intelligence is a valuable skill that encompasses recognizing, comprehending, and managing one's emotions and those of others. It significantly impacts an individual's ability to navigate challenging situations effectively, communicate with others meaningfully, and cultivate positive relationships.

The skill comprises several elements: self-awareness, empathy, communication, and emotional regulation. By nurturing emotional intelligence, individuals can enhance their personal and professional lives and positively influence those around them.

It is crucial to acknowledge that emotional intelligence should not be considered a substitute for clinical knowledge and expertise but should complement medical skills and knowledge. Medical practitioners must balance their emotional intelligence and scientific understanding to provide the best possible care to their patients. Medical professionals who possess both emotional intelligence and clinical expertise are better equipped to handle the challenges of their profession, sustain their well-being, and offer optimal patient care.

The Role of Emotional Intelligence in Successful Medical Practice:

Emotional intelligence has emerged as a crucial factor in enhancing communication and empathy in the medical profession. Healthcare practitioners with high levels of emotional intelligence can comprehend and respond appropriately to the emotions and requirements of patients, their families, and their colleagues. They can actively listen, empathize, and offer emotional support that conveys understanding and care, fostering trust and reinforcing the doctor-patient relationship. Ultimately, this leads to better patient outcomes.

The incorporation of emotional intelligence into the medical profession has the potential to significantly aid medical professionals in managing conflicts and working collaboratively in multidisciplinary teams. Comprehending and navigating different perspectives and emotions is critical in high-pressure medical environments where teamwork is essential. By cultivating a positive and supportive environment, professionals can enhance collaboration, reduce conflicts, and promote a culture of mutual respect and understanding.

Influence of Emotional Intelligence on Patient-Doctor Interaction:

Establishing a solid patient-physician relationship is critical in achieving favorable health outcomes in medical practice. Emotional intelligence (EI) has emerged as a crucial skill healthcare providers must possess to enhance patient outcomes.

Numerous studies have demonstrated that healthcare professionals with high levels of EI demonstrate superior communication skills, empathy, and a more profound comprehension of patients' emotions. These qualities are known to improve patient satisfaction and compliance with treatment and ultimately lead to better health outcomes. As such, high EI levels among healthcare professionals are a valuable asset for institutions seeking to enhance the quality of patient care and satisfaction.

These findings highlight the importance of emotional intelligence in the medical field and suggest that incorporating emotional intelligence training into medical education could significantly benefit patients and healthcare providers.

The Integration of Emotional Intelligence into Clinical Decision-Making Practices:

The clinical decision-making process in medical settings is intricate and involves considering medical factors and patients' emotional well-being. Emotional intelligence plays a pivotal role in this process, as empirical evidence suggests that healthcare providers who exhibit elevated levels of emotional intelligence are better equipped to recognize their patients' emotional needs and adjust their communication styles accordingly. This skill is linked to increased patient engagement in the decision-making process, which, in turn, leads to elevated levels of satisfaction among patients.

Cultivating Emotional Intelligence: Strategies for Medical Professionals

In medicine, cultivating emotional intelligence (EI) is a crucial attribute that can significantly impact the quality of patient care. Regrettably, numerous healthcare professionals disregard the significance of developing EI. Medical professionals can employ various tactics to enhance their EI.

One effective method for achieving this goal is to practice mindfulness. Mindfulness involves being fully present and aware of one's thoughts and emotions without judgment. By regularly practicing mindfulness, medical professionals can develop a heightened sense of self-awareness, which can help them better understand their emotional states and those of their patients. This understanding can lead to more effective communication and improved patient outcomes. Here are a few examples of mindfulness practice:

1. A physician has a busy schedule with back-to-back consultations. In between sessions, he practices mindfulness by focusing on his breath and the sensation of his feet touching the ground, anchoring him in the present moment. This quick mindfulness exercise improves his self-awareness of any stress and anxiety, which allows him to handle his emotions better. He is, therefore, more attuned to his patients' needs, improving their overall healthcare experience.

2. During a counseling session, a psychiatrist encounters a challenging patient unresponsive to traditional therapy techniques. Instead of becoming frustrated, the psychiatrist practices mindfulness, acknowledging his feelings of frustration without judgment. This self-awareness allows him to assess the situation objectively and explore alternative ways of communication, resulting in a productive session for both him and the patient.

3. A surgeon about to perform a high-risk procedure takes a few moments to practice mindfulness before starting the operation. He centers himself by focusing on his breathing and acknowledging the weight of the situation without judgment. This practice reduces his stress, thus increasing his focus and precision during the surgery, leading to successful patient outcomes.

Incorporating feedback is a valuable approach that can aid medical professionals in enhancing their communication skills and emotional intelligence. To achieve this end, medical practitioners can solicit feedback from their patients and colleagues, which can provide insightful feedback regarding areas that require improvement. This continuous feedback loop facilitates ongoing development, enabling medical professionals to broaden their expertise and augment their capabilities.

Empathy, the ability to recognize and share the feelings of others, is crucial for developing emotional intelligence. Medical professionals who practice empathy can create a more positive and supportive environment for their patients, leading to increased trust and improved patient outcomes.

Emotional Intelligence: The Future of Medical Practice

The medical profession has historically emphasized physicians' technical skills and knowledge. However, a growing consensus is that EI is vital to patient care and medical practice. As a result, medical schools and residency programs increasingly incorporate EI training into their curricula. This emphasis on EI is expected to foster more empathetic and patient-centered care, improving patient health outcomes.

It should be noted, however, that certain external factors, such as time constraints, administrative duties, and inadequate resources, may impede the development of EI. Consequently, healthcare institutions and organizations should make concerted efforts to integrate EI training and support systems into medical education and professional development. By doing so, they can ensure that healthcare professionals possess the necessary skills to provide compassionate and effective care to patients.

Conclusion:

Emotional intelligence (EI) is integral in the medical field, significantly impacting patient care, communication, decision-making processes, and overall patient outcomes. While it does not replace clinical expertise, it enhances and complements medical skills, empowering healthcare professionals to navigate challenging situations and foster stronger patient relationships. Therefore, incorporating EI training in medical education and professional development should be prioritized to cultivate a more empathetic and patient-centered healthcare environment. In doing so, the medical community can successfully transition towards an approach that addresses physical ailments and considers patients' emotional well-being, optimizing the quality of care and boosting patient satisfaction. However, medical institutions and organizations must also address external constraints that may hinder the development of this critical skill.

Suggested Readings

- Arora, S., Ashrafian, H., Davis, R., Athanasiou, T., Darzi, A., & Sevdalis, N. (2010). Emotional intelligence in medicine: A systematic review through the context of the ACGME competencies. In Medical Education (Vol. 44, Issue 8, pp. 749–764).
- Dott, C., Mamarelis, G., Karam, E., Bhan, K., & Akhtar, K. (2022). Emotional Intelligence and Good Medical Practice: Is There a Relationship? Cureus.
- AscendHealth. (2017). Ascend Health | The Importance of understanding and developing Emotional Intelligence in Healthcare.

- ESS Global. (2024). Cultivating Emotional Intelligence for Healthcare Leadership - Soft Skills for Healthcare.
- Kendra Cherry, Mse. (2024). Emotional Intelligence: How We Perceive and Express Emotions.
- Weng, H. C. (2008). Does the physician's emotional intelligence matter? Impacts of the physician's emotional intelligence on the trust, patient-physician relationship, and satisfaction. Health Care Management Review, 33(4), 280–288.
- Cherry, M. G., Fletcher, I., O'Sullivan, H., & Dornan, T. (2014). Emotional intelligence in medical education: A critical review. Medical Education, 48(5), 468–478.
- Kozlowski, D., Hutchinson, M., Hurley, J., Rowley, J., & Sutherland, J. (2017). The role of emotion in clinical decision making: An integrative literature review. BMC Medical Education, 17(1).

A Triad for Effective Healthcare: Empathy, Understanding, and Communication

Empathy has no script. There is no right way or wrong way to do it. It is simply listening, holding space, withholding judgment, emotionally connecting, and communicating that incredibly healing message:

"You are not alone."

- Brene Brown

Overview:

Thriving in healthcare is not just about knowledge or skill but also about connecting with your patients. It is about getting to the heart of their concerns, sharing in their journey, and ensuring their treatment is ideally in tune with what they hope for. We often race against the clock and rely on machines and protocols, but taking a moment to listen and relate can positively impact us. This enlightening read unravels the three cornerstones of successful healthcare - empathy, understanding, and communication. This unique blend of elements has the potential to redefine the healthcare experience for both practitioners and patients alike. By embracing these three critical components, healthcare professionals can elevate the standard of care, ensuring optimal patient satisfaction and overall wellness. Transform your health-providing approach and make a meaningful difference in the lives of your patients with "Triad for Effective Healthcare."

Empathy in Medical Practice:

Exploration and rigorous training in healthcare require comprehensive knowledge of medicine paired with an acute awareness of cognitive, emotional, and psychological dimensions. At the heart of this discipline lies empathy: It enables healthcare practitioners to step into their patients' shoes, comprehend their fears, concerns, and emotions, and provide them with personalized care.

However, building empathy can be challenging for healthcare providers, necessitating establishing personal connections with their patients. Therefore, healthcare providers must proactively foster empathy towards their patients.

The acquisition of empathy within the healthcare profession is contingent upon the active practice of listening, nonverbal communication, and the validation of patients' emotions. Healthcare providers must endeavor to eradicate personal biases and assumptions and approach each patient with an open mind and a willingness to comprehend their unique perspective. As such, healthcare professionals must strive to develop and maintain empathetic skills, which can, in turn, improve the quality of care and lead to better health outcomes.

The Impact of Empathy on Patient Care:

One of the most notable impacts of empathy on patient care is the enhancement of patient satisfaction. Healthcare providers who actively listen to their patients, validate their concerns, and demonstrate genuine care and understanding establish a positive rapport with their patients. This fosters a sense of being valued and heard, increasing patient satisfaction with their healthcare experience.

Such empathetic care is especially crucial in healthcare settings, where patients often feel vulnerable and anxious. Empathy, therefore, serves as a cornerstone of compassionate patient care, promoting positive outcomes and enhancing the overall delivery of healthcare services.

In addition to improving patient satisfaction, empathy significantly impacts patient adherence to treatment plans. By taking the time to understand their patients' perspectives, fears, and challenges, healthcare providers can better customize treatment plans to meet each patient's unique needs. This personalized approach, founded on empathy, drives patient engagement and motivation to follow prescribed treatments and recommendations.

The Intersection of Empathy and Self-Care in Medicine:

In the fast-paced and demanding field of medicine, the intersection of empathy and self-care plays a vital role in providing quality care to patients.

Empathy and self-care allow healthcare professionals to better connect with their patients and provide compassionate care tailored to their needs. By prioritizing their physical, mental, and emotional well-being, healthcare professionals can prevent burnout and better cope with the challenges they face in their profession. Self-care encompasses regular exercise, healthy eating habits, adequate sleep, engaging in hobbies, and seeking support from colleagues, friends, or therapists.

Self-care plays a significant role in promoting empathy among healthcare professionals. By enabling caregivers to regulate their emotions, manage stressors, and maintain a positive outlook, self-care equips them to establish meaningful connections with patients, express genuine empathy, and provide compassionate care. In turn, this contributes to better patient outcomes and overall satisfaction.

The Role of Professional Boundaries in Empathy and Self-Care:

In healthcare, it is essential to maintain professional boundaries to benefit patient's and healthcare professionals' well-being. Individuals working in healthcare often face emotionally challenging situations that can expose them to suffering and trauma. The following are a few examples of healthcare providers working without clear boundaries and becoming overwhelmed by their emotional responses, leading to burnout.

1. A psychologist overwhelmed by his patients' distressing circumstances starts to lose sleep and feels constantly fatigued. He must realize the need for professional boundaries and allocate specific hours to empathize and discuss his client's future treatment. This helps him maintain his emotional stability and continue to provide the necessary care to his patients without feeling exhausted.

2. A pediatrician has a soft spot for young patients and often crosses the line between empathy and getting emotionally involved with the plight of the children and their families. She must realize that this could impair her professional judgment. So, she should strictly adhere to boundaries by

focusing on treatment plans and remaining empathetic without becoming overly invested.

3. A doctor who spends prolonged hours working with a challenging case may feel an overwhelming responsibility to do more than his professional obligation requires. Regardless of the emotional toll, he must maintain his role as a healthcare provider without becoming personally involved with the patient's situation.

The establishment of professional boundaries is a crucial aspect of healthcare practice. One of the critical elements of this is setting clear limits and expectations, which encompasses defining boundaries around the extent of care that can be provided, the nature of the therapeutic relationship, and appropriate behavior. These boundaries prevent healthcare providers from overstepping their role and creating unhealthy dependencies with their patients. By defining expectations, healthcare professionals can ensure that their empathy remains within the confines of professional boundaries and does not become overly intrusive or inappropriate. This approach upholds ethical and legal standards and fosters a respectful and trustworthy relationship between healthcare providers and their patients.

The Central Role of Understanding in Patient Care:

A skilled doctor must be able to put himself in his patients' position, comprehend their situation, and provide compassionate care that respects the patient's dignity and autonomy. Understanding the patient's apprehensions, values, and preferences is essential in delivering patient-centered care.

One critical factor in developing personalized care plans is understanding the socio-economic and cultural aspects that can influence a patient's health. This comprehension also aids in mitigating medical errors that can have dire consequences.

The Significance of Effective Communication:

Effective communication is pivotal in the medical sector, as it significantly impacts patient outcomes, satisfaction, and safety. It requires healthcare providers to actively listen to patients' concerns, provide unambiguous and concise information to patients and their families, utilize appropriate language and medical terminology when discussing medical conditions and treatments, and ensure that all parties comprehend the conveyed medical information. It is crucial to note that communication is an interactive process, meaning that healthcare providers must facilitate patients' questions, clarify information, and encourage the expression of concerns to ensure optimal care.

Accurate and clear communication of medical information by professionals is crucial in ensuring optimal patient care and preventing medical errors. The timely and precise transmission of patient data is essential in facilitating accurate diagnoses, appropriate treatment, and comprehensive patient care.

In contrast, poor communication can result in medical errors, increased healthcare expenses, and significant risks to patient safety. Patients who feel heard and understood by their healthcare providers are more likely to report better health outcomes and higher satisfaction levels than those who do not.

Numerous studies have demonstrated that communication between healthcare providers and patients is vital to patient satisfaction. Patients are more prone to be content with their treatment and overall experience when they perceive that their healthcare provider is actively attending to their concerns, considering their viewpoints, and providing Clear and easily understood—explanations of their diagnosis and treatment alternatives.

In contrast, suboptimal communication can have serious consequences, such as patient dissatisfaction and adverse health outcomes. When patients do not receive clear information about their diagnosis or treatment options, they may become confused, leading to anxiety, mistrust, and dissatisfaction. Additionally, a lack of clear communication can result in diagnostic or treatment errors, severely affecting patient health and safety.

Factors Affecting: Triad for Effective Healthcare" in Doctor-Patient Relationships:

Healthcare providers face various challenges that can hinder their ability to empathize and connect with their patients. These challenges may include time constraints, burnout, cultural disparities, and personal biases, among other factors.

Nevertheless, healthcare providers can overcome these barriers by adopting strategies to enhance their empathy and understanding skills. Such methods include active listening, validation, and non-judgmental communication tactics. By implementing these strategies, healthcare providers can improve their ability to connect with their patients and provide more effective care.

It is imperative to acknowledge that empathy and comprehension are not universal concepts, and patients exhibit different preferences regarding how their healthcare providers should approach and treat them. While some patients prefer a highly empathetic approach, others prefer a more practical and technical communication style. Therefore, healthcare providers must remain mindful of these individual differences and exhibit flexibility in their approach to providing care.

Future vision:

In recent years, medical schools and residency programs have begun acknowledging the critical importance of empathy, understanding, and communication in healthcare delivery. As a result, they have taken steps to integrate courses and training programs that focus on these aspects into their curricula. These efforts aim to assist aspiring doctors in acquiring the skills necessary to provide patient-centered care.

An area worthy of investigation is using technology to advance empathy and self-care in medicine. Virtual reality (VR) simulations, for instance, have the potential to enable healthcare providers to understand their patients' emotions better by experiencing different viewpoints. By immersing themselves in virtual scenarios, healthcare professionals can refine their empathy abilities and learn to respond more effectively to a range of patient needs and concerns.

Practicing doctors can benefit from continued education and training opportunities to enhance their communication and patient-centered care skills. These initiatives help ensure that healthcare providers are equipped with the skills needed to provide high-quality care that is respectful, compassionate, and responsive to their patients' needs.

Conclusion:

Empathy, understanding, and communication are the essence of effective healthcare delivery. Empathy allows healthcare providers to grasp and share in their patients' emotional and physical experiences, while understanding involves grasping their socio-economic, cultural, and individual contexts. Communication is crucial, serving as the bridge that facilitates clear, accurate, and patient-centric information exchange. However, executing this triad can pose challenges for healthcare providers due to time constraints, professional burnout, cultural disparities, and personal biases. Nourishing these pillars requires personal and professional growth, supported by continuous education, self-care, and professional boundaries. Incorporating these skills into healthcare curricula and providing ongoing training opportunities for current practitioners will help ensure their application in real-life patient interactions. Furthermore, innovative solutions like Virtual reality simulations could be instrumental in advancing the cultivation of these skills. With these core principles at the forefront of healthcare, practitioners can genuinely transform their approach, adding depth, authenticity, and human compassion to their roles - creating a healthcare experience that is profoundly enriching for both patients and providers.

Suggested Readings

- Derksen, F., Bensing, J., & Lagro-Janssen, A. (2013). Effectiveness of empathy in general practice: A systematic review. In British Journal of General Practice (Vol. 63, Issue 606).

- Moudatsou, M., Stavropoulou, A., Philalithis, A., & Koukouli, S. (2020). The role of empathy in health and social care professionals. In Healthcare (Switzerland) (Vol. 8, Issue 1). MDPI AG.
- Jeffrey, D. (2016). Empathy, sympathy and compassion in healthcare: Is there a problem? Is there a difference? Does it matter? Journal of the Royal Society of Medicine, 109(12), 446–452.
- ESS Global. (2024). The Impact of Empathy on Patient Outcomes.
- Oben, P. (2020). Understanding the Patient Experience: A Conceptual Framework. Journal of Patient Experience, 7(6), 906–910.
- Poole, A. D., & Sanson-Fisher, R. W. (1979). Understanding the patient: A neglected aspect of medical education. Social Science & Medicine. Part A: Medical Psychology & Medical Sociology, 13(C), 37–43.
- King, A., & Hoppe, R. B. (2013). "Best Practice" for Patient-Centered Communication: A Narrative Review. Journal of Graduate Medical Education, 5(3), 385–393.
- Yue, Z., Qin, Y., Li, Y., Wang, J., Nicholas, S., Maitland, E., & Liu, C. (2022). Empathy and burnout in medical staff: mediating role of job satisfaction and job commitment. BMC Public Health, 22(1).
- Wilkinson, H., Whittington, R., Perry, L., & Eames, C. (2017). Examining the relationship between burnout and empathy in healthcare professionals: A systematic review. In Burnout Research (Vol. 6, pp. 18–29). Elsevier GmbH.
- Härkänen, M., Pineda, A. L., Tella, S., Mahat, S., Panella, M., Ratti, M., Vanhaecht, K., Strametz, R.,

Carrillo, I., Rafferty, A. M., Wu, A. W., Anttila, V. J., & Mira, J. J. (2023). The impact of emotional support on healthcare workers and students coping with COVID-19, and other SARS-CoV pandemics – a mixed-methods systematic review. BMC Health Services Research, 23(1).

From Turmoil to Tranquility: Achieving Proficiency in Handling Difficult Patients

"Patients demand our attention and understanding. They may be difficult, but they are just calling for help in their way."

- Florence Nightingale.

Overview:

Healthcare professionals often face the challenging task of managing difficult patients. Studies consistently indicate that healthcare professionals find approximately 15% of patient interactions challenging. Identifying such patients can be difficult for healthcare providers, as certain traits and characteristics complicate effective care delivery. This chapter aims to provide a comprehensive guide to assist the caregiver in dealing with uncooperative or aggressive individuals in a more manageable and less stressful way. The guide delves deep into the roots of complex behaviors, exposing the psychological and environmental triggers that may cause patients to act out. It presents techniques and communication strategies that are immediately empathetic and firm, ensuring respect and understanding prevail even in tumultuous circumstances. By fostering greater awareness of patients' diverse needs and concerns and adopting a solution-oriented mindset, healthcare providers can create a more serene and therapeutic environment for all. From the examination room to the long-term care facility, mastering the art of handling difficult patients is an invaluable skill that promises to enhance the therapeutic alliance and the overall quality of care.

The profiles of Difficult Patients: key Traits and Characteristics:

Demanding and entitled: These patients often display demanding and entitled behavior, with a sense of superiority and an expectation of immediate attention and accommodation to their needs. They may have a solid inclination to scrutinize medical professionals, hold unattainable standards, and desire greater recognition for efforts to safeguard their health.

Non-Compliant: These patients are primarily non-compliant with treatment plans or medical advice. The underlying causes of non-compliance may stem from fear, denial, or a lack of understanding regarding the importance of adhering to prescribed interventions. Non-compliant patients may disregard medical advice, skip appointments, or fail to comply with medication regimens, further complicating their care needs.

Aggressive or hostile: These patients often display aggressive or hostile behavior towards healthcare providers. They may use offensive language, become quickly angered, or even engage in physical confrontations. Such behavior can be influenced by mental health issues, past negative experiences within the healthcare system, or feelings of frustration and helplessness.

Nervous or frightened: In addition, difficult patients may experience high levels of anxiety or fear surrounding medical procedures or diagnoses. They may display excessive worry, panic, or reluctance to undergo necessary tests or treatments. Anxiety can arise due to a lack of understanding, past traumatic experiences, or an underlying fear of the unknown.

It is important to note that the term "difficult patient" should not be used as a label to stigmatize or belittle individuals seeking healthcare. Instead, it should be viewed as an opportunity for healthcare providers to recognize and address each patient's needs and concerns individually. By understanding difficult patients' unique traits and characteristics, healthcare professionals can implement strategies to enhance patient-provider communication, promote adherence to treatment plans, and ultimately improve patient outcomes.

Practical Techniques for Managing Difficult Patients:

Building Trust and Rapport: Active listening, empathy, and communication skills build trust and rapport with these individuals. By demonstrating a genuine interest in their concerns and validating their feelings, healthcare providers can help alleviate tensions and foster a more collaborative relationship.

Empowering patients: Patient education and involving patients in shared decision-making empower them to actively participate in their care, leading to increased compliance and improved health outcomes. Additionally, providing clear and concise explanations about medical procedures, diagnoses, and treatment options can mitigate patient anxiety and enhance their understanding.

Behavioral changes: Recognizing that challenging behavior may manifest in complex emotional or psychological issues enables healthcare providers to respond with compassion and empathy. Additionally, healthcare professionals should be mindful of their reactions and emotions when dealing with difficult patients. Personal biases or frustrations may inadvertently impact the quality of care provided. Regular self-reflection and emotional well-being support can assist healthcare professionals in maintaining compassion and professionalism when faced with challenging situations.

Establish Clear Limits: Establishing boundaries and setting realistic expectations is crucial in managing such patients. Healthcare providers should communicate the limitations of their practice, respond assertively to inappropriate behavior, and adopt conflict resolution strategies when necessary.

Effective De-escalation Techniques: In some cases, de-escalation techniques may be necessary to manage agitated or aggressive patients. Healthcare professionals should receive appropriate training on responding to challenging situations, ensuring the safety of everyone involved. These techniques may include remaining calm, using non-confrontational language, and employing active listening to diffuse tensions.

Effective Communication Methods with Challenging Patients:

Effective communication strategies are vital in navigating these situations, whether it's a disgruntled patient or uncooperative. Here are some strategies that can help healthcare professionals handle such patients:

1. **Active Listening**: One of the most essential skills in handling difficult patients is active listening. Patients feeling heard and understood can mitigate tensions and allow for effective communication. Healthcare professionals should listen attentively, maintain eye contact, and use verbal and

non-verbal cues to show interest and empathy toward the patient's concerns.

2. **Empathy and Understanding**: Empathy and understanding can go a long way in creating a positive rapport with aggressive patients. Acknowledge their feelings, frustrations, or fears and validate their concerns. By showing empathy, healthcare professionals can create a safe and nonjudgmental environment where patients feel comfortable expressing themselves.

3. **Maintain Calmness**: Healthcare professionals must remain calm and composed when dealing with difficult patients. This can help prevent conflicts from escalating and ensure that communication stays productive. Take deep breaths, use a calm and reassuring tone, and avoid reacting defensively to the patient's challenging behavior.

4. **Use Open-Ended Questions**: Instead of asking closed-ended questions that can result in a simple "yes" or "no" response, utilize open-ended questions to encourage the patient to express themselves more fully. This can help you gather relevant information, address their concerns more effectively, and uncover any underlying issues contributing to their problematic behavior.

5. **Validate and Redirect**: When faced with patients who are being confrontational or aggressive, it can be helpful to validate their emotions and redirect the conversation toward finding a solution. For example, if a patient expresses frustration with long wait times, acknowledge their feelings and propose alternatives or reassurances to help alleviate their concerns.

6. **Set Clear Boundaries**: Establishing clear boundaries with challenging patients is essential to maintaining a

professional environment. Communicate what behavior is acceptable and what is not, ensuring you enforce any necessary consequences respectfully.

7. **Collaborative Problem-Solving**: Collaborating with difficult patients can help find mutually agreeable solutions. Involve the patient in decision-making, discuss available options, and explore compromises if necessary. This can empower patients and make them feel actively involved in their healthcare decisions.

8. **Seek Support if Needed**: Despite employing all these strategies, some patients may need to be more complicated. In such cases, seeking support from supervisors, colleagues, or other healthcare professionals is crucial. Their perspective, guidance, or intervention may be valuable in resolving challenging situations while ensuring patient safety.

Remember, effective communication takes time to develop and hone. By implementing these strategies and approaching difficult patients with patience, empathy, and professionalism, healthcare professionals can navigate such situations more effectively, maintain quality care, and foster positive patient relationships.

Resolving non-compliance in healthcare:

Non-compliance is a pervasive issue in the healthcare industry that poses a significant challenge for patients and healthcare providers. It refers to patients' failure to adhere to the prescribed medical treatments, including following medication regimens, attending follow-up appointments, or making necessary lifestyle changes. This lack of adherence can severely affect patients' health outcomes, leading to increased healthcare costs and reduced quality of life.

One of the primary reasons behind non-compliance is the complexity of medical treatments and the associated instructions. Patients often need help understanding and implementing the information given to them by healthcare professionals. This could be due to a lack of health literacy, language barriers, or simply the overwhelming nature of dealing with illness. As a result, patients may unintentionally miss doses, misunderstand instructions, or forget essential steps in their medical care.

Another contributing factor is the patient's circumstances and beliefs. Some patients may have financial constraints that prevent them from obtaining the necessary medications or accessing required healthcare services. Others may have cultural or religious beliefs that conflict with specific treatment methods. Additionally, patients may have fears or misconceptions about their condition or the prescribed treatments, leading them to resist complying with medical advice.

Addressing non-compliance requires a multi-faceted approach involving healthcare providers, patients, and the healthcare system. Healthcare professionals must enhance their communication skills to ensure patients understand their instructions clearly. This consists of utilizing plain language, visual aids, and culturally sensitive approaches, mainly when dealing with diverse patient populations.

Furthermore, healthcare providers should actively involve patients in the decision-making process regarding their treatment plans. By engaging patients in shared decision-making, healthcare professionals can establish trust, address concerns or reservations, and increase patients' commitment to following the prescribed treatments.

The healthcare system also plays a crucial role in addressing non-compliance. It should prioritize patient education and provide necessary resources to support patients in managing their healthcare. This may involve developing user-friendly educational materials, implementing reminders and notifications for medication adherence, or providing financial assistance programs for patients in need.

Moreover, technology can significantly help address non-compliance challenges. Mobile applications, reminder systems, and telehealth platforms can help patients stay on track with their treatment plans and receive timely support from healthcare professionals, regardless of their geographical location.

Ethics in Dealing with Difficult Patients:

Ethics is crucial in healthcare interactions, mainly when dealing with difficult patients. Healthcare professionals are called upon to navigate challenging situations while upholding their ethical obligations, such as respecting patient autonomy, maintaining confidentiality, and providing the best possible care.

One ethical principle that guides the handling of difficult patients is goodwill, which emphasizes the responsibility to promote their well-being. It is essential to remember that even the most challenging individuals may be experiencing fear, pain, or frustration, which can manifest in challenging behaviors. By acknowledging these emotions, healthcare providers can adopt a compassionate approach to addressing their needs and concerns.

Respecting patient autonomy is another essential ethical principle in dealing with such patients. Even in challenging situations, it is crucial to involve patients in decision-making processes, providing them with the necessary information and support to make informed choices about their care. In cases where a patient's autonomy is compromised due to mental illness or cognitive impairment, healthcare professionals should work collaboratively with the patient's family or legal guardian to determine the best course of action while considering the patient's best interests.

Confidentiality is another ethical obligation that healthcare providers must uphold. Regardless of the patient's behavior or challenges, healthcare professionals must protect their personal health information, sharing it only with those involved in the patient's care. This commitment to confidentiality fosters trust, which is vital in building effective doctor-patient relationships, especially with challenging patients.

Sometimes, healthcare providers may face ethical dilemmas when dealing with difficult patients. For example, patients may refuse necessary treatment, risking their health. In such cases, healthcare professionals should balance respecting the patient's autonomy and acting in their best interest. A collaborative approach involving open communication, education, and negotiation can help find a resolution that aligns with the patient's values and the healthcare provider's duty not to harm.

Ethics also call for healthcare professionals to practice self-care while dealing with difficult patients. The demanding nature of these interactions can impact providers' emotional well-being. Taking the time to process challenging encounters, seeking colleague support, and engaging in self-reflection are essential elements in maintaining ethical behavior and avoiding burnout.

Conclusion:

Managing difficult patients can be a challenging task for healthcare providers. Such patients may exhibit traits such as demanding or entitled behavior, non-compliance, aggressiveness, or high levels of anxiety. However, understanding these traits and developing effective management strategies can significantly enhance healthcare delivery. This involves active listening, empathy, setting clear boundaries, educating patients, and making them active participants in their healthcare journey. Maintaining effective communication and implementing de-escalation techniques is crucial for handling challenging situations. Non-compliance, often due to misunderstanding, fear, or obstacles, can be addressed through improved communication, shared decision-making, and leveraging technology. Adherence to ethical principles, such as goodwill, respect for autonomy, and maintaining confidentiality, is critical in managing difficult patients. At the same time, self-care is essential for healthcare providers to support their emotional well-being. With patience, empathy, and professionalism, healthcare professionals can navigate the challenges of interacting with difficult patients, ultimately improving patient outcomes and fostering positive patient relationships.

Suggested Readings

• Hinchey, S. A., & Jackson, J. L. (2011). A cohort study assessing difficult patient encounters in a walk-in primary care clinic, predictors and outcomes. Journal of General Internal Medicine, 26(6), 588–594.

• Varkey, B. (2021). Principles of Clinical Ethics and Their Application to Practice. In Medical Principles and Practice (Vol. 30, Issue 1, pp. 17–28). S. Karger AG.

• Nicolaus, S., Crelier, B., Donzé, J. D., & Aubert, C. E. (2022). Definition of patient complexity in adults: A narrative review. Journal of Multimorbidity and Comorbidity, 12, 263355652210812.

• Raina, R. S., & Thawani, V. (2016). The zest for patient empowerment. In Journal of Clinical and Diagnostic Research (Vol. 10, Issue 6, pp. FE01–FE03). Journal of Clinical and Diagnostic Research.

How to Deal with Death and Dying: A Forgotten Skill

"Honest listening is one of the best medicines we can offer the dying and the bereaved."

- Jean Cameron.

Overview:

The inevitability of death is a reality that permeates all aspects of human life, particularly in the medical profession. This segment delves into the profound yet uncomfortable discussion surrounding death and dying—a subject often sidelined in the field of medicine. Constant developments in healthcare and an obsessive focus on the preservation of life sometimes overshadow the importance of understanding the process of dying and dealing with death. This text echoes the critical need to master the Art of dealing with Death and Dying, a forgotten skill for many in the medical profession. Throughout the discourse, the theme centers around the necessity for healthcare professionals to not only focus on saving lives but also to be equipped to handle the death of their patients, facing the inevitable with sensitivity and empathy. It seeks to promote conversations about death to enhance the quality of end-of-life care and stresses revitalizing this overlooked aspect in medical education and practice. The need to assimilate the complexities of death, in all its finality and certainty, is highlighted as a vital attribute to be nurtured within the medical community.

Understanding the Concept of Death and Dying:

One prevalent perspective on death and dying in the medical field is the biomedical model. This model characterizes death as a biological event when vital functions cease, including the cessation of the heart's beating, respiration, and brain activity. In this model, healthcare practitioners focus primarily on the physical aspects of death and dying and often employ medical interventions and life-sustaining treatments to prolong life.

The psychosocial model stands in stark contrast to the biomedical model by emphasizing the emotional and psychological aspects of death and dying. The model recognizes that individuals who are facing death, as well as their families, experience a range of emotions such as fear, grief, and loss. As such, the psychosocial model seeks to provide holistic care that addresses patients' medical and emotional needs. Healthcare professionals who embrace the psychosocial model engage in therapeutic communication and supportive counseling and facilitate arrangements for end-of-life care to provide comprehensive care to patients and their families.

The cultural perspective bears a significant impact on the development of attitudes and customs surrounding the subject of death and dying. Distinct cultural beliefs, practices, and traditions about death exist across different societies. Healthcare practitioners must demonstrate recognition and respect for these cultural differences to offer culturally sensitive care and support to patients and their families. For instance, in many Asian cultures, especially Chinese, discussing death is prohibited and is feared to cause bad luck. Healthcare workers should sensitively address the topic with these populations, using indirect communication and involving relatives. Culture shapes the perception and handling of death in healthcare delivery.

Acquiring a comprehensive understanding of the concept of death and dying is imperative for healthcare professionals to provide compassionate and patient-centered care. By possessing knowledge regarding diverse perspectives on death and dying, healthcare professionals can effectively address the physical, emotional, and cultural aspects of this experience. Such a holistic approach can significantly enhance patient satisfaction, improve end-of-life care, and support grieving families. It is indispensable for healthcare professionals to possess expertise in this area to ensure optimal patient outcomes and provide quality care.

The Lost Skill: Dealing with Death in the Medical Field

Historically, the healthcare industry adopted a more comprehensive approach to death and dying. In addition to the technical aspects of their profession, healthcare practitioners were also trained to provide emotional support and guidance to patients and their families. They possessed the knowledge and empathy to navigate these challenging conversations with compassion and sensitivity. They were aware of the significance of honest and open discussions about death.

However, this skill has been deprioritized in favor of efficiency and productivity in the current fast-paced medical environment. Healthcare professionals are often overwhelmed and overworked, leaving little time for the emotional aspects of patient care. As a result, there has been a decline in the ability to deal with death and its associated emotional consequences, leading to a loss of touch with this critical skill.

The ramifications of the lost skill in question are profound and far-reaching. Patients and their families are left feeling disconnected and unsupported during one of the most challenging periods of their lives. They may have unanswered inquiries, concealed fears, and unsettled emotions, resulting in increased grief, guilt, and regret. Healthcare professionals also experience the consequences of losing this skill. They may become exhausted and emotionally detached from their work, hurting their well-being.

Studies have demonstrated that healthcare professionals who receive training in addressing death and dying are better equipped to provide adequate support to their patients and families. Additionally, they reported higher levels of satisfaction with their ability to meet the emotional needs of patients and their families. This indicates that training programs that include end-of-life care can be instrumental in improving the quality of care provided by healthcare professionals.

By providing a well-organized and continuous training program, we can help healthcare professionals acquire the essential skills to navigate this tricky landscape. Developing these skills is crucial for providing effective and compassionate care to patients and their families.

The Emotional Impact of Death on Medical Professionals:

The experience of witnessing death and being involved in end-of-life care can cause immense distress for medical professionals. These professionals often form strong bonds with their patients and invest significant time and effort into providing optimal care. The loss of a patient can evoke feelings of profound sadness, grief, and self-doubt. Additionally, witnessing the suffering and deterioration of a patient's health can be emotionally draining, mainly when medical interventions are unable to alter the outcome. The emotional impact of these experiences can extend beyond the workplace, affecting medical professionals' personal lives and mental well-being.

Communicating tragic news to families is an arduous task for medical professionals. Physicians and nurses frequently find themselves in the heart-wrenching position of informing loved ones of a patient's demise. This responsibility demands high empathy, tact, and practical communication skills. However, it also places an enormous emotional burden on healthcare professionals as they confront raw emotions and mourning from distressed family members. The weight of delivering such news may engender guilt and enduring apprehension of causing emotional distress to others.

In addition to the challenges of providing adequate healthcare, medical professionals must also confront the loss of patients. Despite their expertise and dedication, healthcare providers inevitably experience the loss of patients for various reasons. Coping with these losses can be particularly taxing, as medical professionals often hold themselves to high standards and are committed to saving lives. Combining personal investment and professional responsibility can lead to feelings of failure, helplessness, and unresolved grief. As such, healthcare providers need access to resources and support to manage the emotional toll of patient loss.

Importance of Grief Management Skills in Medicine:

Studies from Harvard University indicate that annually, more than 700,000 individuals lose their lives within medical facilities throughout the United States. Medical professionals, including doctors, nurses, and aides, provide the primary source of comfort for families who have lost loved ones.

To provide appropriate care to patients experiencing grief, healthcare professionals must thoroughly understand the different phases and manifestations of grief. By recognizing the various signs and symptoms of grief, medical practitioners can provide apt support and interventions that can prevent the development of complications such as prolonged grief disorder and complicated grief.

Professionals in healthcare must possess practical grief management skills to establish constructive communication with patients and their families. The loss of a loved one or an encounter with a significant loss can be overwhelming and emotionally charged. Physicians who demonstrate empathy and provide compassionate care during these difficult times can establish a trusting relationship with the patient and their family members. This has the potential to result in improved patient satisfaction and overall well-being.

Cultivating grief management skills is indispensable for preventing physician burnout and promoting the mental health of healthcare professionals. The consistent exposure to loss and grief can impose a toll on physicians, leading to emotional exhaustion and compassion fatigue. By employing grief management techniques such as self-care, debriefing, and seeking support, healthcare providers can safeguard their well-being and ensure quality patient care.

Strategies for Coping with Death in Healthcare:

Self-care has emerged as a promising approach for healthcare professionals who frequently encounter death. Maintaining physical, emotional, and mental well-being through regular exercise, sufficient sleep, and engaging in relaxing and joyful activities can help reduce stress levels. Seeking support from peers, family, or friends can also create a safe space for healthcare professionals to share their emotions, which can help them process feelings of grief and loss.

In the context of healthcare, mindfulness and meditation have emerged as valuable strategies for coping with grief associated with death. Mindfulness involves being fully present in the moment and acknowledging one's thoughts and emotions without judgment. Through mindfulness exercises and meditation, healthcare professionals can develop emotional strength and resilience, enabling them to cope more effectively with the emotional challenges of their work.

Education and training are critical in preparing healthcare professionals to handle end-of-life situations. By delivering comprehensive education on grief and bereavement, healthcare organizations can equip their workforce with the knowledge and skills necessary to navigate the complexities of loss. Training programs can focus on understanding the stages of grief, developing practical communication skills while delivering bad news, and fostering empathy and compassion. Such initiatives can help healthcare professionals to better manage the emotional and psychological impact of end-of-life care, ultimately leading to better patient outcomes.

Creating a supportive work environment is of utmost importance in aiding healthcare professionals in coping with death. Facilitating open communication channels and providing debriefing opportunities can enable healthcare providers to share experiences, process emotions, and obtain peer support. Moreover, implementing organizational policies that foster a work-life balance and address the emotional needs of healthcare professionals can contribute to their overall well-being.

Medical institutions should consider implementing policies prioritizing work-life integration and flexibility. This can be achieved by providing sufficient time off, ensuring fair workload distribution, and fostering a supportive work environment that acknowledges the importance of personal time and family commitments.

Routine mental health assessments and unfettered access to mental health resources are of paramount importance. Healthcare workers should have access to private psychological evaluations to identify indicators of stress or exhaustion promptly. Furthermore, they should have easy access to counseling services or support from mental health practitioners. By removing the stigma associated with mental health challenges, medical institutions can promote early intervention and support.

Future Vision

Incorporating grief management skills within medical instruction and training programs is necessary for future healthcare professionals. By providing medical students with the knowledge and tools required to address grief, they can be better equipped to support their patients throughout the grieving process. This, in turn, can contribute to better patient outcomes and a more comprehensive approach to healthcare.

Conclusion:

Dealing with death and dying is a vital aspect of healthcare that needs to be given priority. A comprehensive understanding of death's biomedical, psychosocial, and cultural aspects is crucial for healthcare professionals to provide compassionate and whole-person care. Such skills must be taught and emphasized in medical education to equip healthcare workers with the necessary tools and reinstate the importance of this aspect lost in the fast-paced healthcare field. In addition, healthcare professionals are bound to experience emotional impact due to professional involvement and personal investment in patient care. Coping strategies such as self-care, mindfulness, education and training, supportive work environment, work-life integration, and access to mental health resources should be incorporated to cater to healthcare professionals' emotional and psychological needs. By rejuvenating the lost skill of dealing with death and dying, we can enhance end-of-life care, support grieving families, and ensure optimal patient outcomes in the healthcare field.

Suggested Readings

- Kathleen Franco, M. D. (2021). How to Cope With Death as a Future Doctor.
- PCC. (2015). Tips for Dealing with Loss and Grief in the Healthcare Field.

- A Guide to Understanding Death & Dying.
- Take-Home Message the Four Concepts and Why They're Important,
- Ibrahim, H., & Harhara, T. (2022). How Internal Medicine Residents Deal with Death and Dying: a Qualitative Study of Transformational Learning and Growth. Journal of General Internal Medicine, 37(13), 3404–3410.
- Heiner, J. D., & Trabulsy, M. E. (2011). Coping With the Death of a Patient in the Emergency Department. Annals of Emergency Medicine, 58(3), 295–298.
- Batley, N. J., Bakhti, R., Chami, A., Jabbour, E., Bachir, R., El Khuri, C., & Mufarrij, A. J. (2017). The effect of patient death on medical students in the emergency department. BMC Medical Education, 17(1).
- HSC. (2022). Coping with death and grief as a healthcare worker - HSE.ie.

Mastering The Art Of Learning From Mistakes: Thriving Through Failures

"Your mistakes do not define you; they educate, empower, and enable you to reach your true potential."

- John C. Maxwell

Overview:

In every field, mistakes serve as an opportunity for growth and improvement. However, the learning curve becomes more crucial in medicine, directly impacting human lives. Recent research on healthcare mistakes suggests that such errors could be responsible for up to 251,000 deaths every year in the United States, ranking as the third most common reason for mortality in the country. The FDA receives more than 100,000 reports of medication errors annually in the U.S. This article delves into how professionals can turn failures into stepping-stones for advancement and perfection. The upcoming text discusses the significance of developing a learning attitude towards mistakes in the medical field. It emphasizes the importance of creating a culture where errors are acknowledged without fear of retribution, with the mutual aim of enhancing patient safety and care quality. This fosters an environment of support and learning, instilling a better work ethic and motivating constant improvement. In essence, the narrative aims to guide medical professionals on harnessing lessons from their mistakes and driving transformative change in healthcare.

Embracing Failure: Fostering a Culture of Learning in Medicine:

Medicine is characterized by the utmost importance of precision, where even the slightest mistake can lead to dire consequences. Consequently, medical professionals often feel overwhelmed by the prospect of failure. However, the culture of perfectionism and fear can hinder the industry's learning and growth. Therefore, medical professionals must recognize failure as an opportunity for improvement and professional development. By embracing failure as a chance to learn and better themselves, medical professionals can work towards providing superior and safer care for their patients.

Below is a set of imagined situations that exhibit typical errors in the medical field, intended as instructional content for medical personnel.

1. An experienced surgeon accidentally made a minor surgical error due to his team's lack of clear communication. Instead of ignoring the slip-up, he took it as an opportunity to analyze the issue and identify its root cause. He found that the communication channels within his team were not as efficient as they should be, which led to the error. As a result, he devised an effective team communication strategy to minimize future mistakes, drastically improving teamwork and patient outcomes.

2. A seasoned pharmacist unintentionally gave the wrong medication to a patient. By thoroughly analyzing the error, he discovered it occurred due to confusing labeling and packaging of the medicines. He used this incident as a learning experience and initiated a new policy of double-checking a medication's name, dosage, and instructions

before dispensing it. This strategy helped reduce the frequency of similar errors, enhanced her performance, and improved patient satisfaction.

3. At a tertiary care hospital, the management encouraged an environment where every medical error was seen as a learning opportunity. When a nurse injected the wrong vaccination due to a misinterpretation of the vaccine schedule, the healthcare center investigated and identified the underlying issue. They realized that the vaccine schedule was poorly explained, leading to mistakes. This realization helped the center improve the schedule's clarity and train its staff to interpret it better, reducing such errors in the future.

4. The maternity ward faced a crisis when an infant was handed over to the wrong parents due to similar names and incorrect labeling. Upon analyzing the error, they discovered a flaw in their newborn identification system and immediately rectified it. Training was provided to all staff members to ensure proper implementation of the updated system. This incident improved the ward's system and highlighted the importance of learning from errors to prevent future mistakes.

5. The nurse administered a larger medication dosage to a patient because she misread the doctor's prescription. This error served as a wake-up call, and she took it upon herself to sit with the prescribing doctor whenever she had doubts about a medication. Her proactive approach to learning from her error minimized her chances of making the same mistake, enhancing patient care and the hospital's safety measures.

6. A diligent lab technician once mislabeled a patient's blood sample, causing a delay in the test results. He acknowledged

his error and created a checklist to verify the patient's details before labeling the samples. This approach significantly reduced the risk of such errors, increased the lab's efficiency, and improved overall patient care.

The Psychological Impact of Mistakes in the Medical Profession:

The healthcare industry is paramount in safeguarding the population's welfare, with medical professionals playing a crucial part. The decisions made by healthcare providers can alter the course of their patients' lives, and any inadvertent mistake could be catastrophic for the patient's health.

Consequently, the apprehension of committing errors can have a profound psychological impact on healthcare professionals, leading to stress and anxiety, which, in turn, could exacerbate burnout and other mental health issues. Moreover, this apprehension may cause healthcare providers to become excessively cautious, resulting in delayed treatment and adversely affecting the quality of patient care.

Numerous research studies have indicated that medical errors can trigger a range of adverse emotions like guilt, shame, and self-doubt among healthcare providers. These emotions can significantly impact the mental well-being of the affected providers and may hinder their ability to deliver optimal care. In specific scenarios, the fear of committing errors can cause healthcare professionals to distance themselves from their colleagues and patients, thereby further aggravating their feelings of anxiety and stress.

Importance of Learning from Mistakes in Medicine:

In medicine, the practice of learning from mistakes can bring forth a host of benefits. One of the most notable advantages is that it can foster a culture of progress, innovation, and continual improvement. When healthcare professionals can openly discuss their mistakes without fear of disciplinary action, they are more likely to engage in constructive dialogue and collaborate to find solutions. This leads to better patient outcomes and promotes a sense of trust and cooperation among healthcare professionals. Ultimately, this type of culture propels advancements in medicine and enhances the overall quality of healthcare delivery.

However, a culture of transparency, accountability, and open communication is essential for this process to be genuinely productive. This involves moving away from a blame-centric approach and fostering an ongoing education and improvement environment. In such an environment, errors are perceived as opportunities for growth and improvement, and healthcare professionals are motivated to openly deliberate and tackle errors to prevent their recurrence in the future.

The Role of Mentors in Teaching How to Learn from Errors:

Learning from mistakes is critical to growth, yet young learners often need help to grasp these lessons. Mentors are vital in helping them see failures as chances for improvement by offering guidance, support, and positive feedback. They instill a resilient and optimistic growth mindset, encouraging continuous learning. Mentors use techniques like thought-provoking questions to help learners analyze their errors and avoid repeating them. Through feedback, they reinforce the view of mistakes as natural learning steps, building learners' confidence to tackle future challenges.

How Learning from Mistakes Can Influence Medical Policies:

Medical policies are a fundamental aspect of healthcare systems, as they provide a framework for medical professionals to adhere to while delivering care. However, despite their significance, these policies are not immune to errors, which can arise from gaps, inconsistencies, or ambiguous language. Such errors can yield serious repercussions, ranging from patient injuries to escalated healthcare expenses. Consequently, it is crucial to analyze these mistakes and modify policies to prevent the recurrence of similar errors in the future.

Mistakes in medical policies can act as a catalyst for identifying gaps or inconsistencies in the existing policies. By scrutinizing the root causes of errors, healthcare organizations can revise their policies to address these issues and prevent similar mistakes from occurring in the future.

Furthermore, mistakes can reveal areas where policies could be clearer or more clear, leading to misinterpretations by healthcare providers. In such scenarios, policy revisions can include clarifications that ensure healthcare providers correctly understand the guidelines. These revisions can go a long way in preventing errors and ensuring the delivery of quality healthcare services.

Methods for Effectively Learning from Medical Mistakes:

A practical approach for improving patient safety is using root cause analysis (RCA). RCA is a structured method that comprehensively examines an incident to uncover its underlying causes. This is achieved by gathering data, analyzing the incident, identifying contributing factors, and developing precise recommendations for improvement. By recognizing the fundamental causes of the incident, RCA can help healthcare providers and organizations prevent similar mistakes from occurring in the future, thereby enhancing patient safety. RCA is a valuable tool for improving patient outcomes and reducing the likelihood of medical errors.

Regular audits and evaluations of clinical processes are recommended to learn from medical errors. These evaluations allow healthcare institutions to identify weaknesses and pinpoint improvement opportunities to enhance patient safety. Furthermore, it is essential to encourage the reporting of near-miss incidents and safety issues to identify areas of concern.

Promoting transparency and collaborative discussions in the medical field is essential to cultivate a work environment that endorses trial and error. Following a patient's case or procedure, healthcare professionals can convene to engage in a productive exchange about the positive aspects and areas that need improvement for future cases. Such debriefing sessions enhance communication and foster a more interconnected and efficient team dynamic, resulting in better patient outcomes and augmented job satisfaction among team members.

Implementing protocols and strategies prioritizing safety and minimizing the likelihood of errors is one of the most fundamental ways to enhance patient safety. Electronic medical records are a prime example of such measures, contributing to reducing medication errors in healthcare facilities.

Simulation training is a highly effective approach that can foster a culture of continuous learning within the medical profession. It lets them practice challenging tasks safely without risk to patients. It has many benefits. It keeps patients safer, allows learning from mistakes, and improves skills and confidence. It also helps find areas for improvement and creates new ideas for patient care.

Additionally, leaders should extend their unwavering support to employees who commit errors so that they can learn from their experiences and hone their skills. This approach can engender a constructive and productive work environment where employees feel motivated to take calculated risks and innovate.

Conclusion:

Learning from mistakes in the medical industry is complex and challenging, yet it is vital for improving patient care outcomes. A culture that embraces error analysis without fear of compensation fosters a constructive and collaborative environment, which, in turn, can encourage continual learning and improvement. Various techniques, such as root cause analysis, clinical process audits, and simulation training, can be adopted to enhance the quality of healthcare delivery. Additionally, mentors are crucial in teaching emerging professionals to gain insights from their errors and utilize them as stepping stones toward progress.

Furthermore, learning from past mistakes can significantly inform the revision and development of medical policies, leading to more effective and efficient practices. Therefore, it is imperative for the healthcare industry to continually encourage an environment where errors are seen as valuable opportunities for growth, progression, and the enhancement of patient care.

Suggested Readings

- Anderson, J. G., & Abrahamson, K. (2017). Your health care may kill you: Medical errors. Studies in Health Technology and Informatics, 234, 13–17.
- Thomas L. Rodziewicz; Benjamin Houseman; John E. Hipskind. (2023). Medical Error Reduction and Prevention - StatPearls - NCBI Bookshelf.
- Fischer, M. A., Mazor, K. M., Baril, J., Alper, E., DeMarco, D., & Pugnaire, M. (2006). Learning from mistakes: Factors that influence how students and residents learn from medical errors. Journal of General Internal Medicine, 21(5), 419–423.
- Steven Zauderer. (2023). 29 Medication Errors Statistics & Facts (2023).
- Parecki, G., & Student, M. (2021). Why Making Mistakes Should Be an Assignment in Medical School.
- Robertson, J. J., & Long, B. (2018). Suffering in Silence: Medical Error and its Impact on Health Care Providers. Journal of Emergency Medicine, 54(4), 402–409.
- Bari, A., Khan, R. A., & Rathore, A. W. (2016). Medical errors; causes, consequences, emotional

response and resulting behavioral change. Pakistan Journal of Medical Sciences, 32(3), 523–528.

- Gemmete, J. J. (2024). Learning from medical errors. In CVIR Endovascular (Vol. 7, Issue 1). Springer Science and Business Media Deutschland GmbH.
- EMPOWER YOUR PRACTICE Journal for Practice Managers Improving Patient Safety: The Role of Learning from Medical Errors. (n.d.).

Turning Criticism into Positive Change: Building a Better Self

"The only man who never makes a mistake is the man who never does anything."

- Theodore Roosevelt

Overview:

Criticism is an inevitable part of any profession, including medicine. Handling criticism is an indispensable skill that medical professionals must cultivate to effectively navigate their profession's demanding and high-pressure environment. Criticism may emanate from various sources, including patients, colleagues, supervisors, or the general public. Our focus in this text provides an insightful perspective on transforming criticism into positive change, specifically in medicine. This thought-provoking text explores the potential benefits of adopting a participative approach toward criticism within medical professions. It sheds light on using criticism as a stepping stone for improvement and development. As medical practitioners strive to improve their professional selves, criticism can be a constructive tool rather than a demotivating factor. Let's explore how this paradigm shift can revolutionize individual and institutional growth within the medical domain.

Managing a reflexive response to criticism:

In any profession, handling criticism with composure and poise is essential. When faced with questioning one's competence or judgment, it is natural to feel defensive or angry. However, responding emotionally can only exacerbate the situation and potentially damage professional relationships. Instead, taking a step back, maintaining a sense of calmness, and responding thoughtfully is recommended. This approach will showcase one's professionalism and enhance their reputation in the field.

In medicine, professionals should remain receptive to constructive criticism and perceive it as an opportunity for growth and advancement. Acknowledging and learning from such criticism indicates professionalism, demonstrating a commitment to enhancing patient care. Here are a few examples of constructive criticism,

1. "While your knowledge of medical terminologies is commendable, it would benefit you and the patient if you could explain the diagnosis in simpler terms. Not everyone is familiar with complex medical jargon."

2. "Your attention to detail in diagnosing the disorders is exemplary. However, ensuring friendly conduct towards the patients would further improve their comfort levels during consultations."

3. "Your surgical skills are top-notch, yet it would work better if you spent more time explaining the procedure and possible complications to the patient before surgery. This can alleviate their fear and boost their confidence in the procedure."

4. "While your availability for patients is highly appreciated, regular breaks will help you refocus and avoid burnout over time."

5. "You have an incredible ability to handle emergencies effectively. However, communication with your team during

critical situations can be improved, leading to better overall results and efficient patient care."

Regarding critical evaluations in the medical profession, cautiousness is necessary to prevent undermining healthcare professionals' morale and confidence. To achieve this balance, fostering an environment that encourages feedback while maintaining a respectful and constructive approach is crucial. In this context, constructive criticism entails identifying areas that require improvement and suggesting ways to address them without resorting to harmful or personal attacks.

Role of a Great Doctor in Embracing Constructive Criticism:

A competent physician recognizes that constructive criticism is not a personal insult but a chance for self-improvement. They remain open to feedback from peers, patients, and the broader medical community, as they understand that no individual is immune to mistakes and that there is always room for growth. Physicians exhibit humility, open-mindedness, and a deep commitment to continuous learning by actively seeking and considering constructive feedback.

Furthermore, physicians' solicitation and appreciation of constructive criticism engender a culture of cooperation and perpetual enhancement within the medical community. This culture facilitates exchanging ideas, disseminating best practices, and establishing a supportive environment wherein physicians can learn from each other. Ultimately, this joint effort contributes to advancing medical knowledge and formulating innovative approaches to patient care.

How Criticism Influences Change in Healthcare:

Criticism is an essential element in maintaining accountability among healthcare professionals and systems. Patient feedback, regulatory inspections, and quality assurance assessments are crucial checks and balances ensuring healthcare providers comply with established standards. Criticism can prompt implementing corrective measures, staff training, or policy changes if deficiencies are identified, improving patient safety and overall quality of care.

For instance, if a hospital receives feedback regarding extended waiting times in the emergency department, it can conduct a root cause analysis and devise suitable strategies to reduce wait times, such as optimizing triage processes or increasing staffing levels. By addressing such issues, hospitals can enhance patient experiences and ensure prompt access to care.

Criticism in healthcare can have a negative impact, but it can also prompt healthcare providers to adopt evidence-based approaches. When healthcare professionals receive constructive criticism backed by studies and research, they are more likely to adjust their protocols accordingly. This shift towards evidence-based practice can lead to better patient outcomes and increased patient safety, ultimately improving the quality of care.

Constructive feedback and criticism can lead to meaningful conversations among healthcare professionals and institutions, fostering an environment of cooperation and knowledge exchange. This collaboration can help medical practitioners learn from one another and collectively drive change, thereby enhancing the quality of patient care.

Embracing Modifications in Healthcare Via Constructive Criticism:

The rapid evolution of medical devices and technologies offers the potential for improved diagnostic accuracy and treatment outcomes. However, integrating new technologies can be challenging and may pose risks if not thoroughly validated. Constructive criticism can help identify potential flaws in new technologies, ensuring their safety and efficacy before widespread implementation. By evaluating new medical technologies critically, the medical community can make informed decisions and maximize the benefits of technological advancements in healthcare.

In today's age of widespread medical information availability, it is imperative to rigorously scrutinize research studies and clinical trials to determine their validity and reliability. By promoting constructive criticism among healthcare professionals, the field can foster a culture of evidence-based practice, where treatments and interventions are supported by robust scientific evidence.

In healthcare settings, embracing constructive criticism can create an environment conducive to collaboration and multidisciplinary teamwork. Critiquing and questioning protocols, treatment plans, and clinical decisions fosters open and transparent communication among healthcare professionals, ultimately improving patient outcomes. By valuing the opinions and expertise of others, healthcare professionals are better equipped to work together to overcome challenges and provide the best possible care for their patients.

Implications of mishandling Criticism for Medical Professionals:

Given the nature of their work, medical professionals are often exposed to challenging and emotionally charged situations. Criticism, if not managed appropriately, can significantly impact their mental health and lead to burnout, poor teamwork, and decreased job satisfaction, but it can also negatively impact patient care. Therefore, a failure to handle criticism effectively may limit professional growth and the potential for improved patient outcomes. Moreover, it may foster an unhealthy work environment that could lead to medical errors. Hence, it's of utmost importance for medical professionals to understand the art of handling criticism constructively and professionally to ensure optimal function within the healthcare system.

Effective Ways to Handle Criticism in Healthcare Settings:

Remember that dealing with criticism in healthcare is an ongoing process, and it takes time to develop the skills to handle feedback effectively. By implementing these practical techniques, healthcare professionals can create a supportive culture that fosters growth and patient-centered care.

1. **Maintain a Professional Attitude**: It is essential to approach criticism with a professional mindset. Instead of taking it personally, consider it valuable feedback that can benefit you and your practice. Maintaining emotions and responding professionally sets the tone for a constructive resolution.

2. **Listen and Understand**: Actively listen to the criticism and try to understand the raised concerns. Take a step back

and put yourself in the shoes of the person giving the feedback. Consider their perspective and the underlying reasons for their criticism. This approach can help you gain insight and find common ground for resolution.

3. **Respond with Empathy**: Medical professionals should approach criticism with empathy and professionalism, acknowledging the critique and expressing concern for the individual. Conflicts can be diffused, trust can be established, and strong relationships can be fostered by validating their concerns and demonstrating a willingness to address the issue.

4. **Seek Feedback Regularly**: Encourage regular feedback from patients, colleagues, and supervisors. By proactively seeking feedback, you demonstrate your commitment to improvement and open the door for constructive criticism. This approach also helps identify potential issues early on, enabling you to address them before they become significant problems.

5. **Separate Valid Criticism from Personal Attacks**: It is essential to distinguish between valid criticism and personal attacks. Valid criticism focuses on specific areas for improvement and offers constructive suggestions. On the other hand, personal attacks are often fueled by emotions and lack a constructive purpose. Knowing the difference allows you to filter out the noise and focus on the feedback that can help you grow.

6. **Reflect and Take Action**: After receiving criticism, take some time to reflect on the feedback. Consider its validity and potential impact on patient care or your professional development. Use the criticism as a catalyst for self-

improvement and develop an action plan to address the concerns raised.

7. **Continuous Learning**: Embrace a mindset of continuous learning and improvement. Keep updated with the latest research, attend relevant workshops or conferences, participate in peer consultations, and engage in professional development activities. Enhancing your skills and knowledge can mitigate potential criticisms and improve patient care.

Conclusion:

Criticism is an inevitable and crucial aspect of the medical profession, motivating positive change and further professional development. Constructive criticism propels the advancement of medical knowledge and improvement of services and fosters collaboration among healthcare professionals. It also allows for the safe implementation of new medical technologies and contributes to validating research studies. However, the process of handling criticism warrants careful navigation. Falling short in effectively managing criticism can lead to severe implications such as burnout, decreased job satisfaction, and even jeopardized patient care. To counter these potential issues, medical professionals can employ several strategies, ranging from managing emotional responses and differentiating between valid criticism and personal attacks to actively seeking feedback for personal growth. With a continuous learning and improvement mindset, healthcare professionals can turn criticism into a valuable tool for improving the medical practice and ensuring the best possible patient care.

Suggested Readings

- Mukherjee, S. (2020). EMPLOYEE FEEDBACK 7 Real-Life Examples of Constructive Criticism.
- Babatunde, F., & Cardiology, •. (2019). Negative Feedback Changed the Way I Practice Medicine.
- Harris, J. (2021.). How to Handle Constructive Criticism in a Healthy Way.
- Devin (2023)What Doctors Are Doing About Bad Reviews Online_ How to Leverage Negative Feedback for Positive Change.
- Kuang, S. Y., Kamel-ElSayed, S., & Pitts, D. (2019). How to Receive Criticism: Theory and Practice from Cognitive and Cultural Approaches. Medical Science Educator, 29(4), 1109–1115.
- Hardavella, G., Aamli-Gaagnat, A., Saad, N., Rousalova, I., & Sreter, K. B. (2017). How to give and receive feedback effectively. Breathe, 13(4), 327–333.
- Understanding constructive criticism_ definition, examples, and effective application _ Samelane. (2023).
- My Hub 2020 Strategies For Handling Destructive Criticism In The Workplace

Feedback and Clinical Audit: Optimizing Quality

"True intuitive expertise is learned from prolonged experience with good feedback on mistakes."

- Daniel Kahneman

Overview:

The healthcare industry constantly strives to improve patient outcomes, affordability, and quality of service. Continuous monitoring, evaluation, and upgrading practices are essential to ensure the best possible patient care. A pivotally significant approach to realize this aim is through the efficient utilization of feedback and clinical audits in medical practice, which is the focus of our discussion in this article. It explores the impact of constructive feedback and effective clinical audit implementation on enhancing the quality of care rendered in medical settings. It explains their role in systematically examining patient care quality and safety, identifying areas that require attention, making improvements, tracking progress, and driving the commitment toward delivering excellent patient care.

The Importance of Feedback in Healthcare:

Effective feedback enables healthcare professionals to identify areas for growth and development, which, in turn, facilitates the delivery of more personalized and efficient care to their patients.

The importance of feedback in healthcare is primarily attributable to its impact on patient outcomes. When healthcare providers receive feedback from their patients, they gain valuable insights into the effectiveness of their treatment plans and interventions. Such insights allow healthcare providers to make necessary adjustments to enhance patient outcomes and satisfaction.

Providing constructive feedback from colleagues and supervisors is equally significant in Promoting professional advancements and promoting competence among healthcare professionals. This feedback facilitates the identification of areas in which colleagues can enhance their skills and knowledge, resulting in continuous development of clinical expertise and improvement in decision-making concerning patient care.

To ensure effective feedback, it is crucial to establish a supportive and non-judgmental environment that facilitates open communication channels. Such a culture cultivates trust and collaboration among healthcare providers, allowing them to share their experiences and learn from one another freely. Building a feedback culture also helps to break down hierarchies, allowing feedback to flow in all directions, from junior staff to senior leaders. By promoting a culture of feedback, healthcare organizations can nurture professional development, improve patient outcomes, and enhance overall organizational performance.

Patient Feedback as a Tool for Improvement:

Collecting and analyzing patient feedback provides several benefits to the healthcare system.

By examining feedback, healthcare providers can uncover recurring issues or areas where patients have reported dissatisfaction. For instance, if several patients complain about long waiting times or difficulty scheduling appointments, it indicates an opportunity for healthcare organizations to streamline their processes and improve patient experience.

Additionally, patient feedback enables a more patient-centric approach to healthcare delivery. By actively seeking outpatient feedback, healthcare providers can better understand individual needs, preferences, and expectations. This information is essential in tailoring healthcare services to meet patients' needs. It promotes a sense of patient empowerment and ensures their voice is heard in decision-making.

Furthermore, patient feedback plays a significant role in enhancing patient satisfaction. When patients feel that their opinions are valued and their concerns are addressed, their overall satisfaction with the healthcare experience increases. Satisfied patients are more likely to adhere to treatment plans, have better health outcomes, and even recommend the healthcare organization to others.

The Significance of Clinical Audit in Medicine:

Clinical audits are integral to modern healthcare practice, measuring medical practices against established guidelines and standards. By comparing current practices to existing benchmarks, healthcare professionals can identify variations and discrepancies, enabling them to standardize medical care, enhance patient safety, and optimize treatment outcomes.

Clinical audits also play a critical role in monitoring the effectiveness of interventions and treatment plans. By collecting data on clinical outcomes, healthcare professionals can determine the impact of specific interventions and identify areas where modifications are necessary. This allows for adjustments to treatment plans based on evidence-based practices and real-world results, ultimately leading to better patient care.

Furthermore, clinical audits foster a culture of continuous improvement in healthcare settings. By regularly reviewing and evaluating medical practices, healthcare professionals are encouraged to reflect on their performance, identify areas for improvement, and implement changes accordingly. This leads to a continuous cycle of learning, growth, and enhanced patient care.

Apart from self-assessment, clinical audits facilitate peer review and external scrutiny. By sharing audit findings with colleagues, healthcare professionals can learn from each other's experiences and identify the best practices. Moreover, external review by regulatory bodies or audit committees ensures accountability and helps to maintain high standards of care.

The clinical audit also serves as a valuable tool for research and education within the medical community. The data collected through audits can contribute to research studies, providing evidence for clinical practice guidelines and decision-making. By incorporating audit findings into medical education curricula, future healthcare professionals can learn from past experiences and deliver improved care.

Long-term Impact of Clinical Audits on Patient Care:

Clinical audits have a significant long-term impact on patient care, specifically in reducing medical errors. By conducting regular reviews of clinical practices and processes, audits enable the identification of errors or deviations from established protocols. This presents an opportunity to address these issues promptly, preventing potential patient harm and enhancing overall safety.

Furthermore, clinical audits have proven effective in reducing hospital readmission rates. By monitoring the quality of care provided to patients during their hospital stay and post-discharge, audits can identify areas that require improvement. For instance, audits may reveal gaps in communication and coordination among different healthcare providers, leading to readmissions or complications. Hospitals can enhance care coordination and provide effective interventions by implementing changes based on audit findings, thereby reducing readmissions.

Clinical audits have the potential to support healthcare equity by evaluating care delivery across different patient populations and identifying disparities in access to healthcare services and quality of care. Such audits may reveal treatment outcome variations based on age, gender, ethnicity, or socioeconomic status. By highlighting these disparities, clinical audits can promote targeted interventions and policy changes to ensure equitable healthcare provision.

Barriers to Effective Clinical Audits:

Resistance to change within healthcare organizations is a significant obstacle to implementing changes based on the findings of clinical audits. Such changes often necessitate modifying existing processes and systems, which may be met with reluctance from healthcare providers. A fear of the unknown, concerns about increased workload, or a lack of confidence in the benefits of proposed changes may all contribute to such resistance. Overcoming this resistance demands effective communication and collaboration between audit teams and healthcare professionals, focusing on highlighting the potential positive impact on patient outcomes.

The limited availability of resources is a significant barrier to the successful implementation of clinical audits. To conduct such audits, substantial time, staff, and financial resources are required. These constraints can pose a challenge in resource-limited settings, affecting the ability to conduct regular audits and act upon the findings. Healthcare organizations must allocate adequate resources to support clinical audit programs and ensure sustainability.

The lack of standardized audit processes and tools can hinder the efficacy of clinical audits. The absence of a uniform approach can pose a challenge in comparing and benchmarking audit results, thus impeding the identification of best practices and areas for improvement. Developing and implementing standardized audit protocols, data collection tools, and reporting formats can overcome this barrier, facilitating consistent and meaningful audits. Implementing such measures can help ensure that clinical audits are effective and can contribute to improving healthcare quality and patient outcomes.

In addition to the intrinsic value of audits in healthcare, the efficacy of clinical audits can be impeded by a lack of motivation among healthcare professionals. This could be attributed to the perception that audits add to the already substantial workload of healthcare providers. To overcome this, creating a culture that recognizes and appreciates the significance of audits and promotes an environment of continuous quality improvement is imperative. This can be achieved by incentivizing and rewarding healthcare professionals for their contributions to audits, providing them with learning opportunities, and involving them in the audit process to instill a sense of ownership and engagement.

Another significant challenge lies in integrating technological advancements into clinical audit processes. As healthcare becomes increasingly digital, it is essential to leverage electronic health records and data analytics to streamline and automate the audit process. This can enhance data collection, analysis, and reporting, leading to more efficient audits and timely implementation of improvements.

Strategies to implement and Improve Clinical audit:

Successful implementation of clinical audits requires a robust strategy encompassing an understanding of the audit's objectives, stakeholder engagement, developing actionable and measurable indicators, training and education for staff, effective communication, precise data collection, analysis, and reporting.

Promoting a culture that supports and values audit and improvement is crucial. Improvements can be made by ensuring continuing professional education, incorporating audits into decision-making processes, holding regular feedback sessions, and institutionalizing audits as part of everyday routine.

Moreover, utilizing technology like computerized audit tools and software can optimize the process further. Ultimately, the goal is to translate audit findings into concrete improvements in the quality and efficiency of healthcare services.

Collaboration among healthcare professionals, policymakers, and researchers is essential to overcome the challenges and maximize the prospects for clinical audit.

International organizations such as the World Health Organization should support and guide standardization efforts to ensure global consistency and comparability.

Conclusion:

Regular feedback and clinical audits are crucial in optimizing quality in medical practice. Feedback is a vital tool for professionals to identify areas for growth, enhance professional competence, and ensure more personalized patient care. Furthermore, patient feedback significantly influences patient-centric healthcare delivery, promoting patient empowerment and satisfaction. Clinical audits are integral to modern healthcare, functioning as a measure against established standards to improve patient safety and optimize outcomes. They play a critical role in evaluating and reviewing medical practices, fostering a culture of continuous improvement and learning. Despite some barriers like resistance to change and limited resources, effective clinical audits can be implemented with standardized processes, incentivization, and utilization of technological advancements. Both feedback and clinical audits contribute significantly to healthcare quality, patient satisfaction, and treatment efficacy, emphasizing the importance of a culture of accountability, professionalism, and continuous improvement within healthcare organizations. International organizations and stakeholders must collaborate to integrate these practices widely, drive standardization, and invest in necessary training for healthcare professionals.

Suggested Readings

• Jamtvedt, G., Flottorp, S., & Ivers, N. (2019). Observatory on Health Systems and Policies. In Health Policy Series (Issue 53).

• Foy, R., Skrypak, M., Alderson, S., Ivers, N. M., McInerney, B., Stoddart, J., Ingham, J., & Keenan, D. (2020). Revitalising audit and feedback to improve patient care. The BMJ, 368.

• Hardavella, G., Aamli-Gaagnat, A., Saad, N., Rousalova, I., & Sreter, K. B. (2017). How to give and receive feedback effectively. Breathe, 13(4), 327–333.

• Burgess, A., van Diggele, C., Roberts, C., & Mellis, C. (2020). Feedback in the clinical setting. In BMC Medical Education (Vol. 20). BioMed Central Ltd.

• (Importance of Patient Feedback & Reviews in Healthcare, 2022)

• Improving Care by Using Patient Feedback. (2019).

• Esposito, P. (2014). Clinical audit, a valuable tool to improve quality of care: General methodology and applications in nephrology. World Journal of Nephrology, 3(4), 249.

• Johnston, G., Crombie, I. K., Davies, T. O., Alder, E. M., & Millard, A. (2000.). Reviewing audit: barriers and facilitating factors for eVective clinical audit.

Selfish and Greedy Doctors: A Moral Failure in The Health Sector

"To give honest service, you must add something which cannot be bought or measured with money: sincerity and integrity."

- Donal A Adams

Overview:

Healthcare delivery should always prioritize the health and needs of the patient. Medical professionals worldwide vow to adhere to ethical standards, including dedication to human welfare, respect for patient confidentiality, and harm prevention, as they swear in by the Hippocratic Oath. However, recent concerns have highlighted a worrying trend where some doctors are accused of engaging in unethical behavior driven by personal gain. A survey conducted by the National Partnership for Healthcare and Hospice Innovation (NPHI) indicates that 82% of Americans perceive that the US healthcare system prioritizes financial gain over patient care. Furthermore, 72% of the population feels that healthcare organizations fail to provide adequate care to the aging population. This article sheds light on such alarming patterns and their effects on the medical community. While recognizing the majority's commitment, it also points out the harm done by those prioritizing financial incentives over the profession's prestige. We aim to explore the causes and consequences of doctors' selfish motives and excessive desire for wealth, revealing their impact on patient care and the erosion of public trust in healthcare. Through this narrative, we will uncover the different forms of these ethical transgressions, from blatant abuse to subtle manipulations of medical practice, and seek solutions that enforce accountability and restore the trust integral to the physician-patient relationship.

Unmasking the "Selfish and Greedy Doctors" Stereotype:

The "selfish and greedy doctors" stereotype has long been debated and controversial. An unfortunate generalization fails to acknowledge that most doctors are selflessly dedicated to caring for patients. Labeling them as greedy is unfair based on a few unethical cases. They're compassionate and committed, making sacrifices to heal others, and deserve appreciation for their work.

First, it is crucial to recognize that doctors undergo years of rigorous education, training, and experience to attain their qualifications. They invest their time, effort, and resources to acquire the necessary knowledge and skills to save lives and improve the well-being of others. This commitment alone speaks volumes about the selflessness and compassion that drives many doctors.

Furthermore, doctors often face long and demanding working hours, including being on-call during nights and weekends. They sacrifice their personal time and leisure activities to prioritize the needs of their patients. Their relentless dedication is a testament to their genuine concern for the health and welfare of those under their care.

Moreover, the financial aspect of being a doctor is often misunderstood. While it is true that doctors earn a respectable income, it is crucial to understand the reasons behind it. Medical education and training come at a considerable cost, and doctors often face significant student loan debt before starting their careers. Additionally, they are responsible for maintaining licenses and insurance and constantly updating their knowledge through continuing education. All these financial obligations can heavily impact their income.

It is also essential to recognize the countless acts of kindness that doctors regularly exhibit. Many physicians volunteer their time and expertise in underserved communities or engage in medical missions to provide care to those without access. These selfless acts showcase their commitment to serving humanity and highlight the stark contrast to the selfish and greedy stereotype.

However, it is vital to differentiate between greed and the necessity to survive and make ends meet. While undoubtedly, a few bad apples attracting media attention contribute to this stereotype, it would be wildly unfair to paint the entirety of the medical profession with such a broad stroke. Many doctors still embrace their Hippocratic Oath closely and prioritize patients' well-being, even before their financial gain.

Moreover, we need to remember the complex dynamics within the healthcare industry. Physicians often have little control over patients' high treatment and service prices. Extensive costs are usually a result of pharmaceutical companies, medical device makers, hospital executives, private practices, or insurance companies. Physicians can sometimes be mere mediums in this extensive money-driven environment, making them appear more as collateral victims than perpetrators.

Emphasizing profits over patient care is undoubtedly an unwelcome paradigm shift in healthcare. However, the 'selfish and greedy' image of physicians is largely misguided. More often than not, it is created by a few outliers prioritizing profits over patients in an increasingly commercialized healthcare industry.

Medical Industry: Profit Over Patients?

The medical industry, which plays a pivotal role in people's well-being, has long faced criticism regarding its prioritization of profit over patients. While medical professionals take an oath to prioritize the health and welfare of their patients, numerous instances suggest that profit-driven motives often overshadow patient care.

The most prevalent examples of greed in the healthcare industry are unnecessary medical procedures and overprescribing diagnostic blood and imaging tests, which align with selfish pursuits instead of medical ethics.

Pharmaceutical companies invest substantial amounts of money into influencing doctors to prescribe their medications, even if more cost-effective or safer alternatives are available. This practice drives up healthcare costs and exposes patients to unnecessary risks. Furthermore, the persistently rising prices of essential medications raise concerns about the industry's profit-oriented approach.

In addition to pharmaceuticals, the healthcare system has been accused of prioritizing profit over patients. Insurance companies frequently deny coverage or restrict access to necessary treatments to maximize profits. This often leaves individuals with limited options for affordable healthcare, especially those with pre-existing conditions.

While some argue that profit is necessary to stimulate innovation and research, balancing profit and patient care is crucial. Ethical considerations should always be at the forefront of the medical industry, ensuring that patient's needs and well-being are not compromised for financial gain.

Analysis of Medical Overcharging Practices:

Medical overcharging is a serious issue that continues to plague the healthcare industry. It refers to the unjustifiably high prices medical providers charge for various services and treatments. Such practices burden patients financially and undermine the accessibility and affordability of quality healthcare. The FBI has determined that deceitful invoicing contributes between 3% and 10% to the overall expenditure on health, which leads to unnecessary spending, inflated medical expenses, and squandering of resources. According to the National Health Care Anti-Fraud Association (NHCAA), the annual monetary damage caused by fraud in the healthcare sector is projected to be in the multi-billion-dollar range.

One of the primary factors contributing to medical overcharging is the lack of transparency in healthcare pricing. This lack of transparency allows some healthcare providers to exploit their positions and set exorbitant prices. For example, a simple procedure that may cost a certain amount at one medical facility can cost significantly more at another without any valid justification for the difference in pricing.

Furthermore, the influence of profit-driven motives cannot be ignored. Some medical providers prioritize financial gains over the well-being of their patients, leading them to engage in overcharging practices. This commercialization of healthcare goes against the ethical principles of providing quality medical care to those in need. The excessive focus on generating revenue often results in unnecessary tests, treatments, or procedures to inflate medical bills.

Consequences and Impact of Medical Greed:

The consequences of medical greed are far-reaching and affect individual patients and the healthcare system.

Medical overcharging has severe implications for patients, particularly those who lack adequate health insurance coverage or are financially vulnerable. The exorbitant costs can lead to medical debt, bankruptcy, and even the avoidance of necessary medical care. This creates a detrimental cycle where individuals forgo essential treatments or delay seeking medical attention, ultimately compromising their health outcomes.

Moreover, incidents of medical greed undermine trust in the healthcare profession, eroding the patient-doctor relationship and diminishing public confidence in the system.

From a systemic perspective, medical greed contributes to the rising cost of healthcare. Manipulated medicine prices and unnecessary medical procedures drive up healthcare expenditures, burdening patients, insurance providers, and governments.

Balancing Act: Compensation versus Compassion in Healthcare:

The modern healthcare system has an ongoing debate between compensation and compassion. On one hand, healthcare professionals deserve fair compensation for their skills, expertise, and dedication to their work. On the other hand, the essence of healthcare lies in the compassionate care provided to patients, which may sometimes be compromised in the pursuit of financial gains.

Compensation is crucial in attracting talented individuals to the healthcare industry. Medical professionals undergo rigorous training and education, accumulating substantial debt. Therefore, it is only fair that they are adequately compensated for their hard work and expertise. Competitive salaries and benefits provide financial stability to healthcare professionals and attract and retain top talent.

Moreover, fair compensation is essential in addressing the growing healthcare provider shortage. Potential medical professionals may seek alternative careers without adequate financial incentives, worsening the shortage and limiting patients' access to quality care. It is well-documented that monetary incentives significantly shape career choices, particularly in high-demand fields like healthcare.

However, the pursuit of compensation can sometimes overshadow the essence of healthcare: compassion. Compassion involves understanding and empathizing with patients' suffering, providing comfort, and ensuring patient-centered care. This aspect of healthcare should never be compromised in the quest for financial gains.

Finding the right balance between compensation and compassion is crucial. Healthcare organizations should prioritize creating a work environment that supports and fosters fair compensation and compassionate care. This can be achieved by implementing measures such as reducing administrative burdens, improving staffing levels, providing emotional support to healthcare professionals, and implementing patient-centered care models. Additionally, healthcare professionals should undergo ongoing education and training to enhance their understanding and practice of compassion in patient care.

Strategies to address the issue of medical overcharging:

There needs to be a push for greater transparency in healthcare pricing. Implementing standardized and easily understandable billing procedures would empower patients to make informed decisions about their healthcare choices. Price transparency initiatives, such as publishing the average costs of medical procedures, can help patients compare prices and choose more affordable options.

Regulatory bodies should enforce stricter oversight of medical pricing. This includes investigating and penalizing healthcare providers who engage in unjustifiably high pricing practices.

Additionally, implementing price controls or caps on specific medical procedures and treatments can help control excessive charges and promote fair pricing.

Furthermore, healthcare systems should prioritize value-based care. Instead of incentivizing medical providers solely based on the number of tests or procedures performed, reimbursement should be tied to patient outcomes and overall quality of care. This shifts the focus towards patient-centered care and discourages unnecessary medical interventions solely for financial gain.

Conclusion:

Upon a thorough review of ethical lapses in the medical field, an apparent conflict emerges between the imperative to secure financial profitability and maintaining the foundational principles centered on patient care. Most doctors selflessly give their time and resources to promote the health and welfare of those under their care, often managing considerable personal sacrifices and financial pressures. Nevertheless, a worrying trend has been highlighted wherein some doctors prioritize profit over patients, a breach that severely impacts individual patients and the healthcare system. Such behavior erodes public trust, compromises the physician-patient relationship, and contributes to escalating healthcare costs. However, it is essential to understand that the complexities of the healthcare system often render doctors victims rather than perpetrators in a profit-driven environment. The commercialization of the healthcare industry and unregulated medical pricing are significant contributors to this ethical breakdown. There's a crucial need for healthcare pricing transparency, stricter regulatory oversight, and a transition to value-based care to curtail these distressing patterns. Balancing fair compensation for medical professionals with compassionate care at the heart of healthcare is an ongoing challenge and vital to addressing these ethical violations.

Suggested Readings

• Staff MHE et al., 2022 Many Feels US Health Care Puts Profit Over Patients Choose Specialty. (2022). \

• Clements, J. (2024). Fraud Prevention and Detection in Medical Billing | Medical Billing.

• Chattopadhyay, S. (2013). Corruption in healthcare and medicine: why should physicians and bioethicists care and what should they do? Indian Journal of Medical Ethics, 10(3).

• McDonough, J. E. (2017). Our greedy health care system. In American Journal of Public Health (Vol. 107, Issue 11).

• Andre, C., & Velasquez, M. (n.d.). A Healthy Bottom Line: Profits or People?

• Angood, P. B. (2016). Caring and Compassion Vs. Compensation. Physician Leadership Journal.

• Baguley, S. I., Dev, V., Fernando, A. T., & Consedine, N. S. (2020). How Do Health Professionals Maintain Compassion Over Time? Insights From a Study of Compassion in Health. Frontiers in Psychology, 11.

• Harrison, C., Gordon, J., Henderson, J., Miller, G., & Britt, H. (2023). Under or over? General practitioner charging of Medicare. Australian Journal of General Practice, 52(4).

• Advocate et al., 2023 How to Fight Medical Bill Overcharges-PatientRightsAdvocate.org

Arrogance & Superiority Complex: The Untold Crisis Among Doctors

"An arrogant person considers himself perfect. This is the chief harm of arrogance. It interferes with a person's main task in life - becoming a better person."

- Leo Tolstoy

Overview:

This section highlights a crucial issue plaguing the medical community - the prevalence of arrogance and superiority complex among doctors. The main objective is to explore the far-reaching implications of these attitudes, not only on the doctor-patient relationship but also on the overall functioning of the healthcare system. Furthermore, it examines the significance of self-esteem for medical professionals and how it can quickly transform into detrimental arrogance if left unchecked. The text also uncovers the various factors that contribute to this behavior, sparking a vital conversation about the need for reform and transformation in the medical field. The ultimate objective is to promote a healthcare environment where humility and empathy are paramount, leading to better patient care and stronger relationships between healthcare providers and their patients.

The Significance of Self-Esteem in Medical Profession:

Self-esteem plays a crucial role in the medical profession. As healthcare professionals, individuals in this field constantly face high-stress situations, deal with life-and-death decisions, and shoulder the responsibility of improving patients' health and well-being. A healthy level of self-esteem is essential for medical practitioners to perform their duties effectively and confidently.

Self-esteem allows medical professionals to trust their abilities, make sound decisions, and take risks when necessary. Confidence in one's abilities helps reduce stress and anxiety levels, enabling physicians to focus on the task rather than second-guess themselves. This, in turn, can enhance their performance in critical situations and lead to better patient outcomes.

When the delicate balance of self-esteem is disturbed, it may develop into arrogance & superiority complex.

Arrogance is a personality trait characterized by a sense of superiority expressed through overbearing behavior, presumptuous claims, or assumptions. It involves having an inflated sense of one's worth or importance, often at the expense of others, and thinking extremely highly of oneself.

The superiority complex is a defense mechanism people use to compensate for their inferiority complex. This complex often leads to behaviors of exaggerated self-importance and a sense of superiority over others. Such people believe they are better than everyone else and usually demand special treatment or privileges.

Factors Contributing to Arrogance and Superiority Complex Among Doctors:

The competitive nature of the medical profession is a primary factor that can inadvertently lead to a sense of entitlement and superiority. Doctors constantly strive to excel in their field, leading to constant comparison and evaluation of their skills and abilities. This competitiveness can often result in a superiority complex among doctors, especially when their achievements or performance are compared to those of their colleagues. This competitive atmosphere and a lack of emphasis on humility and empathy can nurture a belief in one's superiority over others in healthcare delivery.

The hierarchical structure within the medical field may contribute to the development of arrogance and superiority complexes. The traditional hierarchy places doctors at the top, where their decisions and opinions are often regarded as unquestionable. This power dynamic can reinforce a belief that doctors are inherently superior to other healthcare professionals, weakening teamwork and collaboration.

The doctor-patient power dynamic plays a significant role in fostering the doctor complex. Patients are often in vulnerable positions, seeking guidance and treatment from doctors who can make decisions about their health. This power dynamic can lead some doctors to utilize their position to assert dominance and reinforce their superiority, further fueling the complex.

The pressure to maintain a perfect image and the fear of making mistakes can also contribute to arrogance. Doctors often face immense pressure to make accurate diagnoses and treatment decisions, as errors can have severe consequences for patients. This pressure, coupled with the expectation of knowing everything, can create an environment where admitting uncertainty or seeking input from others is perceived as a sign of weakness, further feeding into arrogance.

Another underlying cause of arrogance among doctors is the lack of adequate feedback mechanisms. In traditional medical education and practice, feedback is often limited to occasional performance evaluations or peer assessments, focusing mainly on technical skills. This lack of comprehensive feedback on communication, empathy, and interpersonal skills can reinforce doctors' belief in their infallibility and contribute to arrogance.

Furthermore, societal expectations and glorifying the medical profession can also contribute to the development of arrogance among doctors. Being admired and respected by society may lead some doctors to develop an inflated sense of self-worth, which can manifest as arrogance in their interactions with patients, colleagues, and other healthcare professionals.

Signs of Arrogance and Superiority Complex in Medical Professionals:

While confidence and expertise are valued traits in healthcare workers, it is essential to recognize when these characteristics cross over into arrogance and superiority complex, as they can significantly impact patient care and professional relationships.

One common sign of arrogance and a superiority complex in medical professionals is a disregard or dismissive attitude toward the opinions and concerns of others. Professionals with a superiority complex tend to believe that their expertise is superior to anyone else's, leading them to devalue input from colleagues, nurses, and patients. This can create a toxic work environment, hinder collaboration, and ultimately compromise patient care.

Another noticeable sign is an excessive need for control and dominance. Medical professionals with a superiority complex may exhibit a strong desire to be in charge of every decision and aspect of patient care, disregarding the input and expertise of their peers. This need for control may stem from an inflated belief that they are always right and others cannot make sound judgments. This behavior can undermine teamwork and lead to poor patient outcomes.

In addition, medical professionals with arrogance and a superiority complex often struggle with empathy and bedside manners. Their inflated sense of self-importance may hinder their ability to connect with patients on an emotional level, leading to a lack of compassion and understanding.

Furthermore, it can manifest as an unwillingness to seek advice or admit to mistakes. Medical professionals with this mindset find it challenging to acknowledge their limitations or when they have made errors. Instead, they may deny any wrongdoing and deflect blame onto others or external factors, resulting in a lack of personal growth and potentially endangering patient safety.

Implications of Arrogance and Superiority Complex:

Arrogance can lead to a lack of empathy and understanding toward patients. Arrogant healthcare professionals may dismiss or downplay patients' concerns and experiences, diminishing their ability to provide individualized care. This lack of empathy can make patients feel unheard, misunderstood, and ultimately dissatisfied with their healthcare experience.

An arrogant healthcare professional may exhibit poor communication skills. They might fail to effectively convey important medical information to patients, causing confusion and misunderstandings. When arrogance interferes with communication, patient safety can be compromised.

Arrogance and a superiority complex can impede teamwork and collaboration among healthcare professionals. Healthcare professionals with an arrogant attitude may disregard input from others, refuse to seek advice, or hesitate to ask for help when needed. This creates an environment where vital information may be overlooked, leading to medical errors and compromised patient outcomes.

Moreover, doctors who display arrogance often fail to acknowledge the value of other healthcare professionals' skills and knowledge. In today's complex healthcare landscape, patient care requires a multidisciplinary approach. Each healthcare team member brings unique expertise that, when combined, can lead to more holistic and comprehensive care. However, when doctors discount the input and recommendations of other professionals, they hinder the optimal utilization of available resources, potentially compromising patient safety and outcomes.

Furthermore, an arrogant healthcare professional may resist feedback, learning, and self-improvement. This can prevent them from staying updated with new medical knowledge and technology advancements.

Strategies for Addressing Arrogance and Superiority Complex in Healthcare Settings:

Medical schools and residency programs should emphasize the importance of empathy, listening skills, and effective communication within the curriculum. Promoting teamwork and interdisciplinary collaboration from the early stages of medical training can also help break down hierarchical barriers and foster a more inclusive and patient-centered healthcare environment.

Professional development programs allow doctors to reflect on their attitudes and behaviors, encouraging self-reflection and self-improvement. These programs can include workshops, seminars, and continuing education courses focusing on teamwork, effective communication, and empathy.

Fostering an open and non-judgmental environment is crucial. Encouraging team members to provide constructive feedback, share their experiences, and learn from one another's perspectives can help diminish the barriers created by arrogance and superiority. A culture of continuous learning and improvement will enable healthcare professionals to recognize their limitations and appreciate the expertise of others.

Implementing a mentorship or peer support program can be highly beneficial. Pairing experienced professionals with those who may exhibit arrogance or a superior attitude can help the latter better understand their impact on the team and patient care. The mentor or peer can provide guidance and support in developing humility, empathy, and practical communication skills.

Healthcare leadership also plays a significant role in addressing arrogance and superiority complex in healthcare settings. Leaders should promote a culture of accountability, where everyone is encouraged to take responsibility for their actions and behaviors. They can lead by example by demonstrating humility, active listening, and a willingness to collaborate. By emphasizing the importance of a patient-centered approach, leaders can redirect the focus from personal egos to providing high-quality care.

The Way Forward: Promoting Humility and Empathy in Healthcare:

Healthcare is constantly evolving, and one area that requires special attention is promoting humility and empathy among healthcare professionals. Humility and empathy build a stronger patient-provider relationship and improve healthcare outcomes.

Humility in healthcare refers to recognizing and acknowledging one's limitations and fallibility as a healthcare provider. It involves accepting that one does not have all the answers and being open to learning from others, including patients and colleagues.

Empathy, on the other hand, involves the ability to understand and share the feelings and perspectives of others, particularly patients in the healthcare setting. Empathetic healthcare providers show compassion, actively listen to patients, and consider their emotional and psychological needs alongside medical treatments.

However, it is essential to acknowledge that humility and empathy can sometimes decline as healthcare providers progress in their careers.

Conclusion:

Arrogance and a superiority complex among healthcare professionals are significant issues affecting the quality of patient care and intra and interprofessional relationships within the healthcare industry. Factors contributing to these traits include the competitive nature of the profession, societal expectations, a dominant hierarchical structure, and the lack of adequate feedback mechanisms. The impact of such attitudes is concerning as they inhibit empathy, collaborative teamwork, and personalized care that directly influences patient outcomes. Strategies to navigate these issues include introducing medical curriculums that highlight empathy, effective communication and teamwork, continuous professional development, mentorship, and accountable leadership. A patient-centered approach promoting humility, compassion, and teamwork is needed for improved healthcare provision. Ongoing efforts are necessary to understand and mitigate these problems, given their lasting implications for healthcare quality and organizational culture in medical settings.

Suggested Readings

• (Michael Marmot et al.,. 2003) Self Esteem and Health. (n.d.).

• Proctor, V. M. (n.d.). There is a profound lack of self-esteem in the medical profession.

• Hambley, C. (2018). Physicians Practice: Addressing overconfidence when practicing medicine.

• Egelmeer, K. (2014). What is arrogance in healthcare and how does it affect healthcare?

• Torrey, T. et al,). How to Deal with an Arrogant Doctor.

• (Tools Mind et al., 2024.) Managing Arrogant People - Developing Team Players. (n.d.).

• Burkhard, S. et al., (2022). The Relationship of Medical Provider Humility, Empathy, and Competency on Patient Satisfaction Competency on Patient Satisfaction.

• Killam Kasley, et al., 2014 Building Empathy in Healthcare _ Greater Good. (n.d.).

TRUTH UNVEILED: Doctors Are Not Always Right

"No matter what measures are taken, doctors will sometimes falter, and it isn't reasonable to ask that we achieve perfection. It is reasonable to ask that we never cease to aim for it."

- Atul Gawande

Overview:

Human error is an inherent character trait that everyone possesses, including those in the medical profession. This writing offers a frank evaluation, questioning the longstanding societal belief that medical practitioners are beyond error. This is not meant to belittle or throw suspicion upon the integrity of healthcare professionals; instead, it's an honest scrutiny of the flawed human elements behind the clinical exterior. Recent research into medical mistakes suggests that such errors could be responsible for up to 251,000 deaths each year in the U.S., rendering them the third-most common reason for mortality in the country. By scrutinizing the genuine experiences of those in the medical field, an opportunity for conversation arises about the need to understand healthcare's complexity critically. This dialogue does not undermine the skill of medical experts but promotes well-informed cooperation between patients and their healthcare providers. Recognizing that physicians do not possess complete knowledge, the article encourages individuals to take an active and informed role in their healthcare, maintaining respect for physicians' competence while engaging in critical thought. Furthermore, the article proposes methods for increasing the trustworthiness of healthcare practices to decrease the likelihood of errors and maximize patient well-being.

Causes of Doctors' fallibility:

One of the main reasons doctors are fallible is the sheer complexity of medicine and healthcare. Medicine is constantly evolving, with new research and treatments being developed daily. No single doctor can stay current with all the latest advancements and research, which means there may be gaps in their knowledge or outdated practices they are unaware of.

Lack of communication and information sharing among healthcare professionals is another factor. In a complex healthcare system where multiple specialists often treat patients, accurate and up-to-date medical records must be accessible to all relevant parties.

Another reason for doctor fallibility is the reliance on diagnostic tools and tests. While these tools are invaluable in helping doctors make accurate diagnoses, they are not foolproof. False negatives or false positives can occur, leading to incorrect treatment plans or missed diagnoses. In addition, many diagnostic tests have limitations and may not detect all conditions or diseases.

Furthermore, doctors are not immune to biases and cognitive errors. These biases, such as premature closure (the tendency to settle on a diagnosis without considering all possibilities) or confirmation bias (the tendency to seek evidence that confirms one's initial hypothesis), can lead to tunnel vision and prevent healthcare professionals from considering alternative diagnoses.

Exploring the Impact of Overconfidence in Medicine:

Overconfidence, often defined as an excessive belief in one's abilities or judgments, can profoundly impact the field of medicine. While confidence in one's skills is crucial for success, overconfidence can lead to detrimental outcomes for patients and healthcare professionals.

One critical area where overconfidence can manifest is in medical decision-making. Doctors who are overly confident may disregard alternative treatment options or fail to seek second opinions, leading to suboptimal patient care. This behavior is hazardous in complex cases where a misdiagnosis or inappropriate treatment can have severe consequences.

Another aspect of medicine where overconfidence can be problematic is in surgical procedures. Surgeons with an inflated sense of their abilities may exhibit risky behavior or take on complex cases beyond their expertise. This can result in surgical errors, complications, and even patient mortality.

Not only does overconfidence affect individual healthcare professionals, but it can also have broader implications for the healthcare system as a whole. Doctors who are overly confident may be less inclined to engage in continuous learning and professional development. This stagnation can hinder progress and impede the adoption of new, evidence-based practices and technologies.

Promoting a culture of humility and self-reflection is essential to mitigate the negative impact of overconfidence in medicine. Healthcare institutions should encourage professionals to acknowledge and address their biases while fostering an environment that values collaboration and encourages seeking input from others.

Challenging the Authority of Doctors: A Necessary Debate:

In recent years, there has been a growing debate surrounding the authority of doctors and the need for a more collaborative approach to healthcare decision-making. While doctors are highly trained professionals with a wealth of knowledge and expertise, challenging their authority is not about undermining their skills but recognizing the importance of patient autonomy, shared decision-making, and the potential for medical errors.

Patient autonomy, the fundamental principle that individuals have the right to make decisions about their health, is central to this debate. As healthcare becomes more patient-centered, involving patients in decision-making becomes increasingly crucial. Patients are more inclined to adhere to treatment plans and experience better outcomes when participating in their care. However, this shift towards patient autonomy should not be seen as a threat to doctors' authority but rather as an opportunity for a more balanced and collaborative approach.

Another important aspect of challenging doctors' authority is recognizing that medical errors can occur, even among the most experienced professionals. By questioning doctors' decisions and seeking second opinions, patients and their families can play an active role in ensuring their safety and reducing the risk of unnecessary harm.

Numerous organizations and initiatives have emerged to support the need for a debate on challenging doctors' authority further. The Patient Empowerment Foundation, for example, advocates for patients' rights to access education, information, and support to actively participate in their healthcare decisions. The Choosing Wisely campaign, led by the American Board of Internal Medicine Foundation, also encourages conversations between patients and doctors to ensure that care is evidence-based and necessary and avoids unnecessary interventions.

However, striking the right balance between challenging doctors' authority and respecting their expertise is crucial. It is essential to acknowledge that doctors undergo years of rigorous training and possess extensive medical knowledge that should not be dismissed lightly. Doctors play a vital role in diagnosing and treating illnesses; their expertise should be valued. Emphasizing collaboration and shared decision-making can foster a more effective doctor-patient relationship, where doctors provide guidance based on their knowledge and patients actively participate in the decision-making process based on their values and preferences.

Patient Advocacy: The Importance of a Second Opinion

Patient advocacy has become increasingly important in today's rapidly evolving healthcare landscape. Patients often face complex medical decisions and treatments that significantly impact their lives. One crucial aspect of patient advocacy is encouraging and facilitating the seeking of a second opinion.

A second opinion involves consulting with another healthcare professional to obtain an alternative perspective on a diagnosis or treatment plan. Prominent studies conducted by the Mayo Clinic have highlighted the critical role of seeking second opinions in healthcare. Their researchers found that approximately 88% of individuals who sought a second opinion from the Mayo Clinic had an altered or enhanced diagnosis, leading to significant modifications in their treatment strategies. It was further noted that merely 12% of the subjects in the investigation had their original diagnosis confirmed.

One reason why a second opinion matters is the potential for misdiagnosis. Medical errors, including misdiagnosis, affect millions of patients worldwide each year. Seeking a second opinion can help identify potential diagnostic errors and ensure a correct and accurate diagnosis.

Moreover, a second opinion can provide patients with alternative treatment options. Different healthcare providers may have varying expertise, experiences, and treatment approaches. Patients can make informed decisions regarding their treatment plans by considering multiple perspectives. For instance, a second opinion may reveal less invasive or more effective treatment options that were not previously discussed, ultimately leading to better health outcomes.

Furthermore, seeking a second opinion can foster a sense of trust and confidence in the patient-practitioner relationship. It demonstrates that patients value their health and are actively engaged in their care. Healthcare providers who support their patients in seeking second opinions acknowledge the complexity of medicine and the importance of collaboration in delivering the best possible care.

Strategies to Enhance Medical Practitioners' Reliability:

First and foremost, the power of continuous learning cannot be underestimated. To stay up-to-date with the dynamic nature of the medical world, doctors need to engage in lifelong learning. The advent of new diseases, therapies, and technologies necessitates continuous professional development. Attending relevant seminars, reading research publications, and participating in professional forums could help doctors to update their knowledge.

Another crucial way to improve doctors' fallibility is to encourage a culture of double-checking. A system that mandates doctors review their diagnosis or treatment plans should be in place. This move can help catch any inaccuracies before they progress to severe complications. At the same time, incorporating a hierarchical check where senior doctors scrutinize the works of their young counterparts can enhance this culture of a second opinion.

Doctors' mental and physical well-being is a significant but often overlooked factor in reducing fallibility. Long working hours, high levels of stress, and insufficient rest can seriously impede a doctor's ability to make accurate decisions. Therefore, health facilities should implement measures to ensure doctors maintain a healthy work-life balance. Regular recreational activities, adequate vacation time, and professional counseling can help enhance doctors' mental health.

In the digital era, leveraging technology is undoubtedly another effective strategy. Electronic health records (EHRs) can drastically reduce the chances of errors. These systems can alert doctors about hazards such as medication interactions, allergies, or dosage errors. Telemedicine platforms also offer consultations or referrals when doctors are unsure about specific diagnoses.

Interdisciplinary collaboration is equally important. Working closely with nurses, pharmacists, and other healthcare providers provides a comprehensive approach to patient care. This joint problem-solving approach reduces the chances of overlooking certain aspects of patient management.

Open communication with patients is also critical in reducing doctor's fallibility. When doctors take their time to listen to patients, they are likely to gather helpful information that can aid in accurate diagnosis and treatment. It also allows patients to express their concerns and ask questions that might help them understand their condition better.

Lastly, implementing a robust system for reporting and analyzing medical errors can help minimize fallibility. Healthcare organizations can learn from their mistakes and work on targeted interventions through such a system. Transparency is essential as it fosters a learning culture rather than blaming.

Conclusion:

While the role of doctors is undeniably pertinent in healthcare, the possibility of human error makes it crucial to view their authority with a healthy degree of scrutiny. Fostering a culture of continuous learning, valuing collaborative care, leveraging modern technologies, advocating for patients' active involvement in their health, and embracing the importance of second opinions and interdisciplinary collaboration can help mitigate instances of medical errors. Moreover, recognizing that doctors can be fallible encourages an atmosphere of humility and a commitment to improving healthcare practices, ultimately enhancing patient well-being. Trust and respect for medical professionals' expertise must remain intact while acknowledging that perfection may not always be achievable. The onus is on healthcare organizations to create an environment that allows for these nuanced conversations, improving patient outcomes, satisfaction, and the overall integrity of healthcare services.

Suggested Readings

• Jaklevic Mary Chris, et al., 2023 Medical errors are the third leading cause of death' and other statistics you should question _ Association of Health Care Journalists. (n.d.).

• Anderson, J. G., & Abrahamson, K. (2017). Your health care may kill you: Medical errors. Studies in Health Technology and Informatics, 234.

• Berner, E. S., & Graber, M. L. (2008). Overconfidence as a Cause of Diagnostic Error in Medicine. American Journal of Medicine, 121(5 SUPPL.).

• Croskerry, P. (2003). The importance of cognitive errors in diagnosis and strategies to minimize them. In Academic Medicine (Vol. 78, Issue 8).

• Cassam, Q. (2017). Diagnostic error, overconfidence and self-knowledge. Palgrave Communications, 3(1).

• Hambley, C. (2018). Choose a Specialty Addressing overconfidence when practicing medicine.

• M. Luciano Margaret et al., 2019) 4 Ways to Make Evidence-Based Practice the Norm in Health Care. (n.d.).

• Medfin, et al., 2023 What is a Second Opinion in Medical _ When you should Take. (n.d.).

• Rogers, S. (2022) (n.d.). Why Patient Advocacy Is Important.

The Dark Side of Medicine: Stress, Burnout, and Suicide among Doctors

"Burnout, like any difficult experience, is a great teacher. My question is: What is it trying to tell you?"

- Dr. Rebecca Ray

Overview:

In the highly demanding world of medicine, doctors are often perceived as paragons of resilience and poise. Yet beneath the surface of this esteemed profession lies a concerning reality – a triple threat of stress, burnout, and suicide that undermines the well-being of these vital healthcare providers. This segment intends to peel back the layers of the white coat, examining the critical mental health issues that so frequently escape public consciousness. Through a comprehensive exploration, we will delve into the roots of these pervasive challenges, casting light on how stress and burnout can escalate into a mental health crisis, potentially leading to the utmost tragedy of suicide among doctors. The impacts of such crises are profound, affecting not only the individuals and their families but also the quality of patient care and the healthcare system at large. Our discussion will outline the grim statistics, consider the contributing factors, and evaluate initiatives to alleviate these troubling conditions. Understanding and action are imperative to protecting our healthcare providers and, by extension, the very fabric of our healthcare system.

Difference between Stress and Burnout:

It is essential to distinguish between stress and burnout. Stress is a natural response to demanding or challenging situations, whereas burnout is a more chronic condition resulting from prolonged exposure to stress. Stress can motivate healthcare professionals to perform at their best but can lead to burnout when it becomes overwhelming and unmanaged. The World Health Organization (WHO) has recognized burnout as an occupational phenomenon characterized by emotional exhaustion, depersonalization, and reduced personal accomplishment.

Prevalence of Burnout among Doctors:

The latest Medscape National Burnout and Depression Report in the United States indicates an increase in the burnout rate among physicians, climbing from 42% in the preceding year to 47% in 2022.

A study of 4,000 Canadian physicians and trainees conducted by the Canadian Medical Association in November 2021 revealed that over half, or 53%, were experiencing high levels of burnout, a significant jump from 30% just four years earlier.

According to a 2019 survey by the British Medical Association, a staggering 80% of doctors were either at high or very high risk of burnout, with junior doctors facing the highest risk, closely followed by GP partners.

DXY, the largest online community of Chinese physicians in China, noted that over two-thirds faced burnout in 2018, as cited by The Lancet.

Furthermore, a meta-analysis involving more than 22,000 medical residents across ten countries showed a combined burnout rate of 51%.

Studies from British Columbia revealed that 80% of medical doctors experienced moderate to intense emotional burnout, 61% endured mild to extreme levels of detachment, and 44% reported experiencing reduced to moderate levels of personal achievement.

In the United Kingdom, approximately one-third of the physicians had burnout features, comparable to studies from Arab countries like Yemen, Qatar, and Saudi Arabia.

Approximately 40% of medical professionals surveyed by the Physicians Foundation admitted to experiencing fear or were aware of colleagues who hesitated to pursue mental health services because of concerns regarding the implications for medical licensing, professional credentials, and insurance paperwork.

Recognizing Burnout among Medical Professionals:

Burnout is characterized by a deep sense of emotional exhaustion, depersonalization, and diminished personal accomplishment. Medical professionals experiencing burnout often feel emotionally drained and detached and experience a loss of motivation or a sense of incompetence and inadequacy.

They often experience physical and mental fatigue, making it difficult to perform their duties effectively. Additionally, a decline in their productivity and quality of work may also be evident.

Another sign is detachment or cynicism towards patients or colleagues. They may begin to develop negative attitudes or show signs of depersonalization due to chronic stress. This detachment can hinder the development of meaningful relationships and compromise the quality of patient care.

Root Causes of mental health issues among doctors:

One significant root cause of anxiety and depression among doctors is the demanding nature of their work. The medical profession is known for long and irregular working hours, high patient loads, and the constant pressure to deliver optimal care. Physicians often face overwhelming workloads, leaving little time for self-care, personal relationships, and leisure activities. The continuous exposure to high-stress situations, coupled with the responsibility of making critical decisions, can lead to chronic stress, burnout, and the development of anxiety and depression.

In addition to the physical demands, healthcare professionals regularly face emotional challenges. They are routinely exposed to human suffering, trauma, and loss, which can take a toll on their mental well-being. The profession's emotional aspect, coupled with the need to remain empathetic and compassionate, can be emotionally draining and contribute to burnout.

The fear of medical errors or adverse outcomes can further exacerbate anxiety and depression among doctors, as they may constantly worry about the consequences of their decisions.

The prevailing culture of perfectionism, self-sufficiency, and the expectation that doctors should always be strong and emotionally stable can create barriers to seeking appropriate support. The reluctance to seek help can worsen mental health problems and hinder access to necessary treatment, continuing the pattern of deterioration.

Furthermore, healthcare professionals often have limited control over their work conditions. They may face restrictions due to bureaucratic procedures, insurance regulations, or hospital policies that hinder their ability to provide optimal patient care. This lack of autonomy can increase their stress levels and lead to dissatisfaction within their profession.

The Silent Epidemic: Suicidal Tendencies Among Doctors:

Suicide is often regarded as a silent epidemic in the medical field. The rigorous demands and high levels of stress associated with practicing medicine make medical professionals more vulnerable to mental health issues, including suicidal tendencies. This increasing trend raises serious concerns about the well-being of those entrusted with the care of others.

Globally, suicide among physicians is two to five times higher compared to the average population, with heightened risk seen in female and junior doctors. Recent statistics from the Office of National Statistics show that, in 2020, within the UK, there were 72 suicides of healthcare professionals, encompassing doctors, nurses, therapy staff, dentists, and midwives – equating to more than one such incident each week.

The stigma associated with mental health issues among medical professionals further worsens the situation. Doctors and nurses are often expected to be resilient and infallible, making it difficult for them to seek help or openly discuss their struggles. The fear of judgment, professional consequences, and concerns about confidentiality often prevent healthcare professionals from seeking the support they desperately need.

Impacts on Patient Care:

The consequences of poor mental health in the medical profession are significant. It not only affects the well-being and quality of life of healthcare professionals but also impacts patient care. Research has shown that physicians with untreated mental health conditions are more likely to make medical errors, have reduced empathy, and have lower job satisfaction. Mental health issues can impair a doctor's ability to make sound clinical decisions, affecting treatment outcomes and patient safety.

Moreover, the economic implications of burnout are significant. This includes costs related to hiring and training replacement physicians, decreased productivity, and the increased utilization of healthcare services by burned-out doctors.

Impacts on Doctor's Professional Life:

The effects of stress and burnout on doctors are substantial and can have detrimental consequences for various aspects of their lives. At the individual level, prolonged stress and burnout can lead to emotional exhaustion, reduced job satisfaction, and decreased productivity. Doctors experiencing burnout may also be at a higher risk of making medical errors, which can compromise patient safety and outcomes. Moreover, burnout has been associated with increased rates of depression, anxiety, substance abuse, and even suicidal ideation among healthcare professionals.

Moving beyond individual effects, stress and burnout can also impact the healthcare system. Burned-out doctors may be more likely to leave their profession or become less engaged, resulting in a shortage of experienced physicians. This, in turn, can lead to increased healthcare costs and reduced access to quality care. Additionally, the quality of doctor-patient relationships may suffer, as burnout can contribute to depersonalization and a lack of empathy.

One of the main consequences of mental health issues among doctors is a decline in their professional performance. Research shows that psychiatric disorders, including depression and anxiety, can impair cognitive function, decision-making abilities, and overall productivity. These conditions may lead to decreased attention, memory problems, reduced focus, and slower reaction times, harming patient care and safety.

Furthermore, mental health issues may affect doctors' willingness to seek help or disclose their conditions due to fears of professional repercussions and stigmatization within the medical community.

Potential Solutions for Mental Health Support in the Health Sector:

One potential solution is to improve mental health resources and support services for medical students, residents, and healthcare professionals. This can be achieved by establishing dedicated mental health clinics or programs within medical institutions, providing counseling services, and promoting mental wellness through various initiatives.

These resources should be easily accessible, confidential, and stigma-free, enabling healthcare professionals to seek help without fear of repercussions.

Furthermore, increasing awareness about mental health issues and providing education and training on mental health support can be instrumental in promoting a supportive culture within the medical community. Medical schools and healthcare organizations should incorporate mental health topics into the curriculum, equipping future healthcare professionals with the necessary knowledge and skills to identify and address mental health challenges among themselves and their colleagues.

Another important aspect is to address systemic issues that contribute to the mental health burden in medicine. Long working hours, high job demands, and a culture of perfectionism are some of the factors that can negatively impact the mental well-being of healthcare professionals. Implementing policies to mitigate these issues, such as setting limits on work hours, promoting work-life balance, and fostering a supportive work environment, can significantly reduce stress and burnout rates among healthcare professionals.

Furthermore, destigmatizing mental health challenges within the medical profession is crucial. This can be accomplished by sharing personal stories of healthcare professionals who have experienced mental health issues, creating platforms for open conversations, and actively challenging the prevailing culture of silence and shame around mental health.

Medical institutions, professional organizations, and policymakers must collaborate to implement these potential solutions and policy changes. By working together, these stakeholders can develop and enforce policies prioritizing mental health support, allocating resources to mental health programs, and creating a supportive ecosystem for healthcare professionals.

Maintaining Professionalism in Stressful Situations:

To provide the best possible care, healthcare professionals should practice active listening and empathy when interacting with patients. This means fully understanding and addressing patients' concerns and needs, which can help prevent misunderstandings and conflicts. Effective communication can also reduce anxiety and foster a collaborative approach to care, leading to better patient outcomes. Therefore, healthcare professionals should prioritize the development of practical communication skills to engage with patients in a compassionate and empathetic manner.

Efficient teamwork is crucial to maintaining a professional and stress-free environment in the medical industry. When healthcare professionals collaborate and cooperate, it leads to improved patient outcomes and higher levels of job satisfaction. By promoting interdisciplinary communication and shared responsibility, healthcare providers can create a feeling of unity that reduces individual stress levels. Leveraging each team member's unique insights and expertise allows healthcare professionals to come together to tackle challenging situations and deliver high-quality care. This way, healthcare providers can work towards achieving their shared goals and objectives while ensuring they provide their patients with the best possible care.

Resilience and Coping Strategies for Doctors:

Doctors must develop resilience and coping strategies to effectively handle these challenges and ensure their long-term health and well-being.

One coping strategy for doctors is seeking support from their colleagues and healthcare professionals. Sharing experiences and discussing challenges with others who understand the unique demands of the profession can provide a sense of validation and relief. This support network can offer guidance, advice, and encouragement, helping doctors navigate difficult situations and build resilience.

Another vital coping strategy is self-care. Doctors often prioritize their patients' care over their well-being, neglecting their physical and mental health in the process. Doctors must prioritize regular exercise, adequate sleep, a nutritious diet, and engaging in joy and relaxation activities. Taking time off and maintaining work-life balance can significantly contribute to their resilience and well-being.

Furthermore, doctors can benefit from adopting mindfulness and stress-reducing techniques into their daily routines. Mindfulness practices, such as meditation or deep breathing exercises, can help doctors manage stress and improve their ability to focus and make sound decisions. These techniques can be practiced during breaks or incorporated into the workplace to create a more calming and harmonious environment.

Additionally, ongoing education and professional development can significantly enhance doctors' resilience. Keeping up with the latest medical advancements, attending conferences, and participating in workshops can boost doctors' confidence and competence, increasing their ability to cope with challenging situations.

Conclusion:

The medical profession is undoubtedly stressful and challenging, and it is becoming increasingly clear that doctors are at risk of severe mental health issues due to continuous exposure to high-stress situations, long working hours, and the pressure to deliver optimal care constantly. This "triple threat" of stress, burnout, and suicide among doctors not only affects the physicians themselves but also has profound impacts on the healthcare system and the delivery of patient care. There is a pressing need for the implementation of mental health support in the health sector, including improving mental health resources and support services, increasing mental health education and awareness, tackling systemic issues contributing to the mental health burden, and breaking down the stigma surrounding mental health issues among medical professionals. By fostering a supportive and empathetic professional environment, promoting self-care and resilience strategies, and prioritizing mental health, it is possible to safeguard the well-being of doctors and ensure the continued provision of high-quality patient care. The cost, however, is high, and the responsibility falls on medical institutions, professional organizations, and policymakers alike to address this urgent issue. Through cooperation and setting priorities, we can preserve our healthcare professionals' essential physical and psychological health.

Suggested Readings

• Dr Leonid Eidelman et al., 2022, The global physician burnout pandemic-Physicians Anonymous

• Kumar, S. (2016). Burnout and doctors: Prevalence, prevention and intervention. In Healthcare (Switzerland) (Vol. 4, Issue 3).

• Landman Keren et al., 2023 The physician mental health crisis, explained - Vox. (n.d.).

• Rotenstein, L. S., Torre, M., Ramos, M. A., Rosales, R. C., Guille, C., Sen, S., & Mata, D. A. (2018). Prevalence of burnout among physicians a systematic review. In JAMA - Journal of the American Medical Association (Vol. 320, Issue 11).

• Yang Jenny, et al., 2023 Share of physicians suffering from burnout in the United States from 2011 to 2021. (2024).

• Bhatia, G., Sharma, P., Pal, A., & Parmar, A. (2023). The silent epidemic: Death by suicide among physicians. In Asia-Pacific Psychiatry (Vol. 15, Issue 1).

• Rátiva Hernández, N. K., Carrero-Barragán, T. Y., Ardila, A. F., Rodríguez-Salazar, J. D., Lozada-Martinez, I. D., Velez-Jaramillo, E., Ortega Delgado, D. A., Fiorillo Moreno, O., & Navarro Quiroz, E. (2023). Factors associated with suicide in physicians: a silent stigma and public health problem that has not been studied in depth. In Frontiers in Psychiatry (Vol. 14).

• (B Andrew Louise et al., 2022) Physician Suicide. (n.d.).

• O'Dowd, E., O'Connor, P., Lydon, S., Mongan, O., Connolly, F., Diskin, C., McLoughlin, A., Rabbitt, L.,

McVicker, L., Reid-McDermott, B., & Byrne, D. (2018). Stress, coping, and psychological resilience among physicians. BMC Health Services Research, 18(1).

From Healing to Quitting Medicine: A Doctor's Tragedy

"So, I told them the truth: the hours are terrible, the pay is terrible, the conditions are terrible; you're underappreciated, unsupported, disrespected, and frequently physically endangered. but there's no better job than a doctor in the world."

- Adam Kay

Overview:

This article delves into the hidden struggles that doctors face. It talks about the difficult decisions that doctors may face, forcing them to leave the profession they love. Meanwhile, newly released data from the AMA indicate that nearly 33% of clinicians are contemplating decreasing their professional working hours within the coming year. A 2019 Survey published in the Physician Leadership Journal indicated that over 20% of medical doctors plan to change their career paths within the next twelve months. Moreover, within two years of beginning their practice, as many as 70% of physicians across diverse healthcare disciplines are projected to pursue job prospects in alternative practice environments.

The text follows the journey of a dedicated doctor, from their hopeful beginnings to the many obstacles they encounter in the healthcare industry. The narrative exposes the inner conflict and external pressures that challenge the doctor's commitment to healing. Through this passage, we understand the emotional journey that leads to a doctor leaving their life's work. It is not only a personal tragedy but also indicative of a system that fails to support its healers.

Motives behind joining the medical profession:

The following are the key motives for individuals to join the prestigious medical profession.

1. **A Desire to Help People**: A general inclination towards helping people and improving their health conditions is a fundamental motive for many who join the medical profession.

2. **A Passion for Science**: A love for science and a keen interest in understanding human anatomy, diseases, and their cures can motivate individuals to pursue a career in the medical field.

3. **Desire to make a Difference**: The medical profession provides opportunities to make a significant impact on individuals, families, and communities, which can be a motivating factor.

4. **Job Security**: The demand for healthcare professionals is always high, which provides excellent job security. This could be a compelling motive for many individuals.

5. **Prestige and Respect**: Being a medical professional often comes with a certain level of prestige and respect, which can be a motivating factor for some.

6. **High Earning Potential**: The medical profession is often associated with a high earning potential, which can attract individuals interested in a lucrative career.

7. **Personal Experience**: People who have had personal experiences with illness or have had close family members or friends affected by health conditions may be motivated to join the medical profession to prevent or treat such conditions.

8. **Interest in Research**: Those with a keen interest in medical research and the development of new treatment methods can be drawn to the medical profession.

9. **Continuous Learning**: The constant advancements in medical science mean that doctors never stop learning, which can be a strong pull for lifelong learners.

10. **The Opportunity to Work Anywhere**: The ability to find work anywhere, in other cities and countries, is a potent motive for some to join the medical profession.

However, as time progresses, some doctors may question their original motivations and decide to leave the medical profession altogether.

Understanding the Crisis: Why are Doctors Quitting Medicine?

Several factors contribute to this departure, one of which is burnout.

One of the primary factors is the high levels of stress and pressure that doctors face, which play a crucial role in their decision to abandon medicine. The demanding nature of the profession, with long working hours, life-and-death decisions, and the emotional toll of dealing with patients' suffering, can lead to increased levels of stress and mental health issues.

There is an increasing administrative burden placed on physicians. With complex documentation requirements and regulations, doctors often spend more time on paperwork than patient care. The frustration stemming from this administrative overload can lead to burnout and a sense of disconnect from the core purpose of their profession.

Another contributing factor is the growing pressure to increase productivity and efficiency. Doctors are expected to see a more significant number of patients within a limited timeframe, resulting in rushed consultations and reduced personalized care. This constant demand to balance quality patient care with meeting productivity targets can lead to emotional exhaustion and a decline in job satisfaction.

Furthermore, the financial aspect of the profession must be considered. Many doctors report feeling undervalued and under-compensated, especially in rising healthcare costs and decreasing reimbursement rates. This perception of inadequate compensation can lead to dissatisfaction and even influence career choices for aspiring medical professionals.

The complex nature of healthcare delivery and the ever-changing dynamics of medical knowledge also contribute to doctor dissatisfaction. Physicians face the challenge of staying updated with the latest research and advancements in their field. The pressure to continually learn and adapt can be overwhelming, adding to the stress and dissatisfaction experienced by doctors.

Furthermore, the changing dynamics of the healthcare industry play a role in doctors leaving medicine. The shift towards corporate-owned practices and the influence of non-physician administrators on patient care decisions has diminished doctors' autonomy and professional satisfaction. A sense of loss of control over their practice can lead physicians to reconsider their career choices.

The Impact of Working Conditions on Doctor Satisfaction:

One of the critical factors that affect doctor satisfaction is their workload. As healthcare professionals, doctors work long hours in high-pressure environments, dealing with complex cases and making crucial decisions. This can lead to feelings of burnout and exhaustion, which can negatively impact their job satisfaction.

In addition to workload, the availability of essential resources also affects doctor satisfaction. Inadequate access to necessary equipment, medications, and support staff can create additional stress and frustration for doctors.

Moreover, the physical work environment can significantly influence doctor satisfaction. Factors such as the layout of the clinic or hospital, noise levels, and temperature can all contribute to the doctors' overall comfort and satisfaction.

Interpersonal dynamics in the workplace also play a significant role in doctor satisfaction. Supportive relationships with colleagues, nurses, and other staff members can positively impact job satisfaction. On the other hand, conflicts or poor communication can lead to dissatisfaction and stress.

Role of Patient Expectations in Doctor's Discontent:

Patient expectations play a significant role in contributing to a doctor's discontent. Patients with unrealistic expectations or demands can create a challenging environment for them. This phenomenon can lead to increased stress and job dissatisfaction and potentially compromise the quality of patient care.

One reason patient expectations can be a source of discontent is the influence of sensationalized medical shows and online resources. Many patients, influenced by the media, come into medical appointments with unrealistic expectations about treatment options, recovery time, and the ability to achieve a "perfect" outcome. This can put excessive pressure on doctors to meet these unrealistic demands, which may not align with the patient's medical condition or best practices in healthcare.

Moreover, the rise of internet-based health information has empowered patients with readily accessible medical knowledge. While patient education is crucial, it can sometimes lead patients to question their doctor's expertise or suggest alternative treatments. This can make it challenging for doctors to establish trust and a collaborative relationship with their patients, as their authority and medical decisions may be questioned or undermined.

Furthermore, the increasing demand for doctors to provide quick solutions or the desire for immediate relief further adds to the pressure. Patients may expect doctors to have all the answers or suggest a rapid fix to their health problems. Doctors who cannot fulfill these expectations may feel disheartened and depersonalized, as their expertise and efforts may not be appreciated.

Consequences of the Doctor Exodus:

There has been a troubling rise in doctors leaving the medical profession recently. In 2021, approximately 117,000 doctors exited the workforce, according to a report from Definitive Healthcare. This phenomenon, known as the "doctor exodus," raises significant concerns about the future of medicine and its consequences on healthcare delivery and patient outcomes. The ramifications of the doctor exodus are far-reaching. Projected doctor deficits ranging from approximately 37,800 to 124,000 by 2034 have been forecasted, affecting both general and specialized healthcare sectors, as indicated in a study by the Association of American Medical Colleges (AAMC).

First and foremost, it exacerbates the existing shortage of healthcare professionals, placing a strain on the already overwhelmed healthcare system. An analysis revealed that nearly 29% of hospitals in South Carolina were facing severe staffing deficits. Similarly, approximately one in five hospitals in Georgia, Vermont, Delaware, and Michigan reported significant shortages of essential staff during 2021. With fewer doctors available to tend to patients, the quality and accessibility of healthcare services are compromised. Longer wait times, limited appointment availability, and decreased continuity of care become more prevalent, negatively impacting patient outcomes.

Moreover, the doctor exodus also disrupts the physician-patient relationship, which is crucial for effective healthcare delivery. When patients lose their trusted healthcare providers, it becomes harder to establish rapport and trust with new physicians.

The consequences of the doctor exodus extend beyond immediate healthcare delivery. It also affects medical education and training. As experienced physicians retire early or leave the profession, the loss of their expertise and guidance affects the education and mentorship of future doctors. This burdens the remaining physicians and may impact the quality of teaching and patient care in the long run.

Finding Solutions: Retaining Skilled Doctors in the Medical Field:

As the demand for quality healthcare rises, the retention of skilled doctors in the medical field has become a pressing issue. Addressing this challenge is crucial to ensuring the continued delivery of optimal healthcare services. By brainstorming and implementing practical solutions, we can mitigate the problem of doctor turnover and improve the stability of the medical workforce.

1. **Work-Life Balance**: Policies promoting work-life balance, such as flexible schedules, reasonable workload distribution, and adequate time off, can help doctors maintain a healthier work-life equilibrium.

2. **Professional Development**: Doctors desire continuous growth and development like other professionals. Providing ongoing education, skill enhancement, and career advancement opportunities can motivate doctors to stay in the field. Offering mentorship programs, conducting regular workshops, and supporting research endeavors can foster professional growth and incentivize doctors to remain committed to their medical careers.

3. **Performance-Based Incentives**: Recognizing and rewarding doctors based on their performance and contribution can be a powerful retention tool. Designing an effective incentive system that considers quality patient outcomes, exceptional care, and patient satisfaction can boost doctors' morale and job satisfaction. Financial rewards, productivity-based bonuses, and non-monetary

incentives like professional recognition and awards can incentivize doctors to stay committed to their profession.

4. Supportive Work Environment: Creating a positive and supportive work environment is crucial for retaining skilled doctors. Encouraging collaborative teamwork and effective communication and fostering a culture that promotes camaraderie and respect can enhance job satisfaction and decrease the likelihood of doctors seeking alternative career paths.

5. Financial Assistance: The burden of medical school loans and financial constraints can influence doctors' career choices and their likelihood of remaining in the medical field. Implementing or expanding financial assistance programs and loan forgiveness initiatives can alleviate some of the economic pressures doctors face, making it more attractive for them to pursue and remain in medical careers.

6. Reducing the administrative burden: Healthcare organizations and policymakers should focus on reducing the administrative burden on physicians by streamlining documentation processes, simplifying reimbursement systems, and advocating for regulatory reforms.

7. Empowering doctors with autonomy:

Giving physicians more control and decision-making power can significantly improve their satisfaction. Healthcare organizations should involve doctors in developing policies and protocols, allowing them to have a say in decision-making processes. Additionally, fostering a culture that values and respects the expertise of healthcare professionals will enhance job satisfaction and motivation.

By combining these solutions, we can create a comprehensive approach to address the challenges of retaining skilled doctors in the medical field. Healthcare organizations, policymakers, and medical institutions must prioritize implementing these strategies to ensure a sustainable and highly trained medical workforce.

Learning from Other Countries: International Perspectives on Doctor Retention:

The scarcity of healthcare professionals, particularly doctors, poses a significant challenge for many countries worldwide. As countries continue to grapple with this issue, it is essential to explore and learn from the experiences and strategies implemented by other nations.

One country that has successfully addressed the problem of doctor retention is Australia. The Australian healthcare system has implemented various measures to attract and retain doctors. For instance, they have established financial incentives such as Medicare billing and rural and remote area incentives to encourage doctors to work in underserved regions.

The Netherlands has implemented innovative strategies to retain doctors in its healthcare system. They have introduced flexible working arrangements, allowing doctors to choose their working hours and better balance their professional and personal lives.

Canada has taken steps to retain doctors by providing career advancement and professional development opportunities. Their healthcare system offers various funding and support mechanisms for doctors to acquire additional skills and pursue specialized fields. This approach has increased doctor retention and positively impacted the quality of healthcare services in Canada.

These examples highlight the importance of studying and learning from other countries' experiences in addressing doctor retention. By examining successful strategies and implementing suitable measures, countries can work towards ensuring a sustainable and competent healthcare workforce.

Conclusion:

The issue of physicians leaving their professions is a pressing concern affecting the global healthcare system. This exodus of doctors is not only a personal decision prompted by stress, burnout, paperwork overload, and dissatisfaction with working conditions and compensation. It is a systemic issue reflecting the challenges inherent in current healthcare practice, including interpersonal dynamics, patient expectations, and changing dynamics in healthcare delivery. This phenomenon threatens the quality of healthcare delivery, patient outcomes, physician-patient relationships, and the education of future doctors. It is crucial to tackle this issue through comprehensive solutions, including work-life balance, continuous professional development, performance-based incentives, a supportive work environment, financial assistance, administrative reform, and empowering doctors with decision-making. Learning from other countries' successful strategies, such as Australia, the Netherlands, and Canada, can also offer valuable insights for addressing doctor retention. The collective efforts of healthcare organizations, policymakers, and medical institutions are imperative in creating a sustainable and resilient healthcare workforce.

Suggested Readings

• Peter Alperin, MD et al., 2020 Effectively Recruiting and Retaining Physicians: A Strategic Approach for 2020 | AAPL Publication

• Henry, T. A. (2022). Medicine's great resignation? 1 in 5 doctors plan exit in 2 years.

• DIVE BRIEF, Healthcare worker exodus continued through 2022; new data shows

• Shanafelt, T. D., Boone, S., Tan, L., Dyrbye, L. N., Sotile, W., Satele, D., West, C. P., Sloan, J., & Oreskovich, M. R. (2012). Burnout and satisfaction with work-life balance among US physicians relative to the general US population. Archives of Internal Medicine, 172(18).

• Maglalang, D. D., Sorensen, G., Hopcia, K., Hashimoto, D. M., Katigbak, C., Pandey, S., Takeuchi, D., & Sabbath, E. L. (2021). Job and family demands and burnout among healthcare workers: The moderating role of workplace flexibility. SSM - Population Health, 14.

• Browne, B. 2023. The great US doctor exodus.

• -ai -, P., & Bernard, R. (2023). Top 5 ways organizations can retain great physicians.

• Cohu, S., Lequet-Slama, D., & Volovitch, P. (2006). The Netherlands: reform of the health system based on competition and privatization. Revue Française Des Affaires Sociales, 6.

• Esmail et al., 2014 Esmail, N. (n.d.). Lessons from Abroad a Series on Health Care Reform Health Care Lessons from the Netherlands by Nadeem Esmail.

• (Vimal Sivakumar et al., 2024 Canada needs more immigrant doctors to support the national healthcare system _ CIC News. (n.d.).

Malpractice and Litigation: A Real Threat to Doctors

"They may forget your name, but they'll never forget how you made them feel."

- Maya Angelou

Overview:

The dynamics encompassing the medical profession are broader than diagnosing and treating diseases. Comprehensive healthcare delivery and patient safety also involve avoiding medical errors that can lead to malpractice allegations and litigation. Healthcare providers are perpetually at risk of being legally challenged. In the 12 months preceding 2022, 1.8 percent of physicians were subjected to legal claims. Throughout their careers, approximately 31 percent of doctors find themselves the subject of at least a single malpractice suit. On average, physicians work with the impending concern of unresolved malpractice litigation for about 4.4 years within a standard 40-year tenure in medicine. This text expounds on the contentious issue of "Malpractice and Litigation: A real threat to doctors," revealing its various challenges and implications for the medical profession.

Contending with patients' illnesses and disorders is a fundamental task of physicians. Nonetheless, beyond these clinical responsibilities arises a formidable concern: the threat of lawsuits following alleged medical malpractice. The following text aims to provide a profound exploration of this topic: how malpractice and litigation can potentially affect doctors, its impact on healthcare delivery, and how the risk can be mitigated. This is significant because, besides the possible financial repercussions, being sued could potentially cause emotional and psychological trauma that could drop a physician's enthusiasm and dedication toward their practice.

Alarming Rise in Medical Negligence Claims:

The number and associated expenses of medical malpractice lawsuits are rising worldwide. In the UK, the National Health Service (NHS) allocated £2.4 billion to cover these lawsuits in the fiscal year 2021-2022, which marks an 8.7% rise from the previous year, spurred by a 12.9% uptick in the frequency and expenses of these claims.

In Ireland, clinical claims surged by 46.7%, and related expenses soared by 297% from 2010 to 2020. Similar unsettling patterns are emerging throughout Europe. For example, in the Netherlands, the costs for settled claims increased fourfold from 2007 to 2021, while in Poland, the typical compensation payouts rose by 70% from 2014 to 2017.

In the US, the average payout for each claim has risen yearly, including those exceeding $1 million. According to the National Practitioner Data Bank, from 2017 to 2021, medical malpractice claims amounted to 36,050, with payouts totaling $17.19 billion. The American medical liability system is estimated to cost $55 billion annually.

In China, there has been a noticeable uptick in the number of medical malpractice claims filed against top-tier, grade-A hospitals since 2008, with a significant surge occurring from 2014 onwards, accompanied by a consistently escalating average settlement amount for each claim.

In the US, each year, roughly 9% of cancer specialists are subject to malpractice litigation, a figure that exceeds the physician average of 7.4%. This places them behind gastroenterologists and pulmonologists, both associated with procedure-oriented practices, in the hierarchy of legal challenges faced. Surgical oncology fields demonstrate substantial legal risks, as evidenced by 19.1% of neurosurgeons, 18.9% of cardiac and thoracic surgeons, and 15.3% of general surgeons encountering malpractice lawsuits annually.

The Legal Definition of Medical Malpractice:

The definition of medical malpractice varies across different states and jurisdictions. However, it is generally described as an act or omission by a healthcare provider that violates the standard of care required in a particular medical specialty. Medical malpractice arises when a healthcare provider fails their duty of care towards the patient, resulting in harm or injury. Medical malpractice is not limited to specific healthcare professionals but encompasses doctors, nurses, pharmacists, and other medical practitioners.

To establish medical malpractice, certain elements must be proven, including the following:

1. **Duty**: A healthcare provider must provide competent patient care.

2. **Breach of Duty**: The healthcare provider failed to provide competent care to the patient, breaching their duty of care.

3. **Causation**: The healthcare provider's breach of duty caused harm or injury to the patient.

4. **Damages**: Due to the healthcare provider's breach of duty, the patient suffered damages, such as physical or emotional pain, medical bills, and lost income.

If all these elements can be established, the patient may have a valid medical malpractice claim against the healthcare provider.

Common Types of Medical Malpractice:

Common types of medical malpractice include failure to obtain informed consent, Failure to diagnose, misdiagnosis, medication errors, and surgical errors.

Failure to obtain informed consent is a significant issue in medical ethics. It signifies a breach of trust in the doctor-patient relationship when a medical intervention or procedure is carried out without the patient understanding its nature, purpose, benefits, and potential risks. This violation can have severe legal and moral implications, emphasizing the significance of obtaining informed consent before any medical procedure.

Failure to diagnose: It's a severe mistake when a healthcare professional fails to notice the signs of an illness or doesn't order the proper tests to understand it. This oversight can lead to delayed treatment and harm the patient. In some cases, this kind of delay could even cause permanent damage to the patient.

Misdiagnosis: When a medical professional inaccurately identifies an ailment, it constitutes a grave error. Such a misstep can result in the postponement of proper care or the administration of incorrect therapies, possibly inflicting unnecessary damage on the treated individual.

Surgical errors can occur during any surgical procedure. However, standard errors include operating on the wrong body part, leaving surgical instruments inside the patient, and injuring a nearby organ or tissue during surgery. These mistakes can lead to significant harm, including prolonged hospital stays, additional surgeries, and long-term disability.

Medication errors are a serious concern that can result in adverse patient outcomes. These errors can occur in several ways, including prescribing the wrong medication, administering the wrong dosage, or failing to monitor the patient for adverse drug reactions. Such errors can harm patients, including causing severe side effects, complications, and even death.

Understanding the concept of Litigation:

Medical litigation refers to legal proceedings initiated against healthcare providers or institutions for alleged negligence or malpractice in the medical field. It encompasses a broad spectrum of issues, including medical malpractice, negligence, wrongful death, and other claims related to healthcare. Medical litigation statistics indicate that such cases are on the rise, causing significant impacts on both healthcare providers and patients.

One of the most significant aspects of medical litigation is medical malpractice.

Medical litigation encompasses a range of issues, including product liability. In such cases, pharmaceutical companies or medical device manufacturers may be held responsible for injuries caused by their products.

Similarly, healthcare facilities may face litigation related to premises liability, where patients suffer harm due to unsafe conditions or negligence within the facility.

Typically, medical litigation involves a team of legal and medical experts who review medical records, gather evidence, and provide testimonies to support the plaintiff's claim. Due to the intricacies of medical practices and legal frameworks, these cases often demand a significant investment of time and resources and can be complex to navigate.

The advantages of medical litigation are two-fold:

Firstly, it provides a recourse for patients and their families to pursue compensation and justice in cases where they have suffered harm due to inadequate medical care.

Secondly, it incentivizes healthcare providers to maintain a high standard of care and continually improve their practices to prevent future litigation.

Medical litigation is crucial in ensuring accountability in the healthcare industry and promoting quality care. Therefore, healthcare providers must adhere to high standards of practice and prioritize patient safety.

Impact of Malpractice and Litigation on the Healthcare Industry:

Medical malpractice can have a significant and long-lasting impact on patient care.

-Patients who suffer injury due to medical malpractice may lose their trust in healthcare providers, leading to decreased adherence to treatment plans, increased anxiety or depression, and ongoing physical or psychological damage.

-Additionally, medical professionals may be less willing to take on high-risk or complex cases due to concerns about potential malpractice lawsuits.

Medical litigation has significant impacts on multiple stakeholders within the healthcare system.

For healthcare providers, the apprehension of litigation can result in the adoption of defensive medicine practices, whereby physicians order unnecessary tests or procedures to guard themselves against potential legal action. This practice of defensive medicine not only increases healthcare costs but can also harm patient care by exposing them to needless risks and interventions.

Furthermore, medical litigation can have financial implications for healthcare providers and institutions. The costs associated with legal expenses, settlements, and increased malpractice insurance premiums can all contribute to higher healthcare costs. This financial burden can impact the availability and price of healthcare services, potentially leading to reduced patient care access.

Medical litigation can serve as a mechanism for patients to seek compensation for injuries or harm resulting from medical malpractice. However, the process can have unintended consequences, including prolonged legal proceedings, emotional distress, and a perception that healthcare professionals cannot be trusted.

The Psychological Toll of Litigation on Medical Professionals:

The process of litigation can inflict a significant psychological toll on medical professionals and lead to considerable stress, anxiety, and depression. Prolonged adversarial proceedings often exacerbate emotional exhaustion and pose mental health challenges for healthcare providers.

One of the primary reasons litigations can be psychologically distressing is the potential damage it can cause to the reputation and self-esteem of medical professionals. Being accused of malpractice or negligence can leave healthcare providers feeling personally attacked, questioning their abilities and competence. Consequently, they may experience feelings of shame, guilt, and decreased self-confidence, which can have long-lasting effects on their mental well-being.

The apprehension of facing litigation is a persistent concern among medical professionals that may foster an atmosphere of anxiety and hypervigilance. The awareness that any inadvertent error or unexpected outcome could result in legal action imposes enormous pressure on an already demanding occupation. This perpetual state of alertness can lead to burnout and even the development of anxiety disorders.

The emotional toll of litigation extends beyond the immediate effects on individual healthcare providers; it also impacts the entire healthcare team and the quality of patient care. When healthcare providers are preoccupied with the fear of litigation, it can compromise their ability to focus entirely on their patients. This, in turn, can lead to reduced empathy, communication breakdowns, and even medical errors, perpetuating the cycle of litigation and negatively affecting patient outcomes.

Ways to Mitigate Malpractice and Litigation Risks:

One of the most effective strategies is prioritizing patient safety by adhering to evidence-based guidelines, ensuring clear communication between healthcare providers, and promoting a culture of accountability and continuous improvement. Effective communication with patients is crucial to reducing the risk of legal action. Building a solid doctor-patient relationship based on trust and open dialogue can help prevent misunderstandings and dissatisfied patients. Doctors should take the time to explain medical procedures, diagnosis, potential risks, and treatment options in a language that patients can understand. Additionally, actively listening and addressing patient concerns can improve patient satisfaction and decrease the likelihood of patients resorting to legal action.

Mitigating litigation risks in the healthcare industry can be accomplished by strategically implementing technology. Electronic Health Records (EHRs) offer many benefits, including streamlining administrative processes, reducing errors, and enhancing communication among healthcare providers. Additionally, digital tools such as telemedicine or secure messaging platforms can facilitate timely and accessible medical consultations, effectively reducing the risk of miscommunication and patient dissatisfaction. By embracing technological advancements, healthcare providers can improve patient outcomes, safeguard their organizations against potential legal disputes, and promote efficiency and innovation.

Maintaining comprehensive documentation of all patient encounters and medical decisions is critical to the healthcare industry. Doctors rely on accurate and detailed record-keeping to defend themselves against malpractice claims. Proper documentation provides evidence of appropriate care, informed consent, and adherence to established medical standards. To ensure that medical records are complete, healthcare professionals must document all relevant information, including test results, treatment plans, follow-up discussions, and any deviations from the norm. By doing so, they can ensure that they provide the highest quality of care and mitigate potential legal repercussions.

In addition, it is crucial to promptly address any errors or complications that may arise during patient care. Documenting the measures taken to rectify such issues can significantly aid in mitigating the risk of litigation. Ensuring that such documentation is clear, concise, and accurate is imperative. This can help establish a record of due diligence in legal proceedings. It is also recommended that healthcare providers maintain open communication with patients and their families throughout the care process. By doing so, providers can demonstrate their commitment to patient safety and satisfaction and potentially avoid legal disputes altogether.

Medical professionals can benefit from implementing risk management strategies provided by professional liability insurers. These strategies typically include educational programs, publications, and guidelines that facilitate the identification of potential risks, adherence to best practices, and staying current with industry standards. By participating in these risk management initiatives, medical professionals can acquire valuable knowledge and skills to minimize the likelihood of malpractice claims.

Ultimately, preventing medical malpractice is a collective effort that requires the cooperation of healthcare providers and patients. By working together, healthcare providers can ensure they provide the highest quality of care possible while patients can actively engage in their healthcare and advocate for their well-being.

Legal Support for Doctors Facing Litigation:

Medical practitioners may face challenges when dealing with litigation, which can be a daunting and stressful experience for them. However, legal assistance is available to help navigate through this complex and multifaceted process. Doctors can explore various legal avenues to ensure they receive support and representation to protect their fundamental rights and interests. By seeking expert legal counsel, medical practitioners can alleviate some of the burdens associated with litigation and have the best chance of achieving a favorable outcome.

Professional liability insurance companies are a crucial source of legal support for healthcare professionals. These entities specialize in providing coverage and support to medical practitioners in the event of lawsuits or claims against them. In addition to financial coverage, these insurance companies often offer legal advice and representation for doctors. As such, they can assist doctors in understanding their legal rights and obligations, reviewing their insurance policies, and preparing a robust defense. By leveraging the expertise of professional liability insurance companies, doctors can navigate the complex landscape of legal claims with confidence and security.

Legal counsel specializing in medical malpractice defense is crucial for physicians facing litigation. Such attorneys possess a wealth of knowledge in healthcare law and comprehend the intricacies of safeguarding doctors against allegations of medical negligence. They can meticulously analyze the circumstances of the case, accumulate evidence, and collaborate with expert witnesses to establish a robust defense strategy. Legal counsel can also aid in negotiating settlements, representing physicians in court, and advocating for their best interests throughout the litigation process. These professionals play a vital role in ensuring that doctors receive fair and just treatment in the face of legal challenges.

Medical associations and professional societies are essential in supporting medical practitioners facing litigation. These organizations often maintain specialized legal departments or partner with law firms specializing in healthcare law. They provide expert guidance on legal matters, connect practitioners with experienced attorneys, and facilitate access to resources that can strengthen their defense. Additionally, they offer educational seminars and resources to help practitioners prevent future litigation risks.

Medical professionals need legal education to protect themselves and their patients in a litigious environment. Incorporating legal education into medical training programs can equip healthcare professionals with the necessary knowledge and skills to handle legal issues and minimize legal risks. Therefore, medical institutions should consider adding legal education to their training programs.

Healthcare institutions and hospitals can access legal departments or external law firms to help physicians during litigation. These legal practitioners have a profound knowledge of the particular challenges that healthcare providers encounter, and they can offer personalized legal advice and representation. They can examine documents, guide physicians in interacting with patients and legal entities, and help in case preparation and trial.

In addition to specific sources of legal support, doctors can also benefit from general legal knowledge and ongoing education on healthcare laws and regulations. Maintaining up-to-date information about legal requirements, best practices, and recent developments in the healthcare industry can aid doctors in reducing the risks of litigation and enable effective responses to legal challenges. Therefore, physicians must remain informed and aware of legal issues in healthcare, allowing them to provide optimal care while minimizing legal consequences.

Balancing Patient Rights and Doctor Protection:

In recent years, a debate has ensued concerning the delicate balance between patients' rights and the protection of doctors. It is critical to ensure that both parties are supported and their interests and well-being are considered. While patients have the right to receive high-quality healthcare and be informed about their treatment options, doctors also require protection to carry out their duties effectively without fear of unnecessary litigation.

Patients' rights are of paramount importance in any healthcare system. They should be entitled to receive accurate information about their medical condition, including the nature of their illness, available treatment options, and potential risks and benefits associated with each option. This information empowers patients to actively participate in shared decision-making with their healthcare provider, ultimately leading to more patient-centered care.

Furthermore, patients have the right to privacy, confidentiality, and informed consent. They should be able to trust that their personal medical information will not be disclosed without their permission, except in cases where it is necessary for their treatment or as required by law. Informed consent ensures that patients are adequately informed about the risks and benefits of a medical procedure or treatment before consenting. Upholding these rights is essential to ensuring patient satisfaction and trust in healthcare services.

On the other hand, it is essential to protect doctors from the risk of unwarranted legal actions hindering their ability to provide the best possible care. Physicians should be able to make well-informed medical decisions without fearing unnecessary lawsuits or repercussions. Frivolous malpractice suits not only put the doctor-patient relationship at risk but can also negatively impact the overall quality of healthcare by leading to defensive medicine practices.

Several measures can be implemented to balance patient rights and doctor protection. First, comprehensive and clear guidelines should be established to ensure patients' rights are respected, and doctors know their legal obligations. These guidelines should include protocols for informed consent, medical record privacy, and respectful communication between doctors and patients.

Secondly, medical professionals should receive adequate training and resources to improve communication skills and enhance patient-doctor relationships. By fostering open and honest dialogue, doctors can effectively address patients' concerns, explain treatment plans, and build trust and rapport.

Lastly, alternative dispute resolution mechanisms such as mediation and arbitration can be encouraged to resolve conflicts between doctors and patients outside the courtroom. These methods can facilitate open discussions, promote understanding, and potentially lead to mutually beneficial outcomes for both parties.

Conclusion:

Medical malpractice and litigation present significant challenges to the healthcare industry, contributing to increased healthcare costs and harmful psychological impacts on medical practitioners. Despite efforts to mitigate these issues, they remain substantial problems within the sector. Although the legal infrastructure successfully provides malpractice victims with recourse, the high frequency of malpractice cases signalizes the need for improvements within the healthcare system. Measures and strategies such as prioritizing patient safety, improving communication, employing technology, adhering to comprehensive documentation, and using risk management techniques can significantly mitigate the risks associated with malpractice and litigation. Furthermore, the availability of various sources of legal support, including professional liability insurance and specialized legal counsel, provides protection and guidance for medical professionals facing litigation. The delicate balance between protecting patients' rights and preserving the reputations and livelihoods of medical professionals is an ongoing challenge in the healthcare industry. To maintain this balance, it is crucial to ensure clear communication, thorough informed patient consent, and the implementation of alternative dispute resolution mechanisms. Ultimately, minimizing malpractice instances will require a collective effort from all stakeholders within the healthcare system.

Suggested Readings

• Baum, N. (2023). Suggestions for protecting your medical practice from litigation.

• Forrest, C., Madden, D., O'Sullivan, M. J., & O'Reilly, S. (2023). Learning From Medical Litigation. JCO Oncology Practice, 19(4).

• What Is Medical Malpractice_ Definition & Examples – Forbes Advisor. Bieber J.D. Christy.What is Malpractice_. ABPLA.

• Bal, B. S. (2009). An introduction to medical malpractice in the United States. Clinical Orthopaedics and Related Research, 467(2).

• Mackey, T. K., & Liang, B. A. (2011). The role of practice guidelines in medical malpractice litigation. Virtual Mentor, American Medical Association Journal of Ethics January 2011, Volume 13, Number 1: 36-41. 13(1).

• Jena, A. B., Chandra, A., Lakdawalla, D., & Seabury, S. (2012). Outcomes of medical malpractice litigation against US physicians. In Archives of Internal Medicine (Vol. 172, Issue 11).

• Miziara, I. D., & Miziara, C. S. M. G. (2022). Medical errors, medical negligence and defensive medicine: A narrative review. In Clinics (Vol. 77).

The Morality of Healing: Resolving Ethical Dilemmas in Medicine

"MEDICINE means Mercy - Empathy - Dare - Integrity - Care - Ingenuity - Nobility - and Ethics."

- Abhijit Naskar

Overview:

In healthcare, professionals often find themselves in complex situations that require a delicate balance of ethics, values, and responsibility towards their patients. To navigate these challenges, they rely on ethical frameworks and guidelines that provide a roadmap to make informed decisions. These principles include beneficence, which focuses on doing good and promoting the well-being of the patient; non-maleficence, which emphasizes the importance of avoiding harm; autonomy, which recognizes the patient's right to make decisions about their care; and justice, which advocates for fairness and equality in the distribution of healthcare resources. This chapter discusses some of the most common ethical issues and challenges healthcare professionals face. It also highlights the potential negative consequences of ethical dilemmas on patient care, the healthcare system, and medical professionals. The text emphasizes the importance of balancing patient rights and medical ethics, using numerous illustrative examples, and provides various strategies for resolving ethical dilemmas.

Common Ethical Dilemmas in Healthcare:

Informed consent

One of the most common ethical dilemmas in healthcare is related to informed consent. Healthcare providers are morally obligated to obtain informed consent from their patients before conducting any medical procedures or treatments. However, this can be a challenging task when patients have limited understanding of the treatment options, are mentally incapacitated, or are minors.

For example, A man suffering from a severe mental disorder needs a major surgical procedure. Despite multiple attempts, healthcare providers find it challenging to make him understand the process and its potential risks and benefits. In this case, the healthcare providers are morally and legally obliged to involve their guardian or caregiver for informed consent.

In these cases, healthcare professionals must balance patient autonomy and paternalism principles. They must ensure patients have all the necessary information and understanding to make informed decisions about their treatment while also considering their best interests. Navigating such ethical dilemmas requires careful consideration of all the factors involved and a commitment to upholding moral principles.

End-of-life decision

Healthcare professionals and families often face a challenging ethical dilemma when it comes to end-of-life decisions for terminally ill patients or those in a persistent vegetative state.

For example, A 65-year-old man is in the final stages of amyotrophic lateral sclerosis (ALS). His medical team and family must decide whether to continue with life-supporting treatments despite knowing the inevitable outcome. They are also tasked with considering his autonomy and previously stated end-of-life wishes.

In such cases, the decision-making process can be overwhelming. It involves complex considerations such as whether to continue or withdraw life-sustaining treatments, allocate limited resources, and respect the patient's autonomy. These debates can stir up intense emotions and ethical concerns, and navigating them requires careful consideration and a deep understanding of the patient's wishes and values.

Allocating scarce resources

In the healthcare industry, allocating scarce resources has always been a complex ethical issue that poses several challenges. The availability of limited resources such as organ transplants, vaccines during pandemics, or expensive medications puts healthcare professionals in a difficult position where they have to make tough decisions about who gets access to these resources.

The primary challenge lies in balancing the principles of distributive justice and prioritizing patients based on their clinical needs. This ethical dilemma requires careful consideration of various factors, such as the medical condition's urgency, the treatment's potential benefits, and the overall cost-effectiveness of the resource allocation.

For example, only a limited number of organs are available for organ transplantation compared to the many waiting patients. Healthcare professionals must decide who among these patients will receive the organ based on the severity of their medical condition, chances of survival post-transplant, co-existing medical conditions, and potential for quality-of-life improvement following the transplant.

Confidentiality breaches and conflicts of interest

Healthcare is an industry that deals with many ethical challenges beyond patient care. Healthcare professionals also face moral dilemmas in their practices. These challenges can range from confidentiality breaches and conflicts of interest to maintaining professional integrity. For instance, healthcare providers may face ethical complexities when balancing patient confidentiality and public health concerns during infectious disease outbreaks, such as contact tracing. For example, A doctor treating a patient for a sexually transmitted disease may face an ethical challenge regarding confidentiality. The doctor, at one point, might be in a dilemma about whether or not to notify the patient's partner about the condition, given the severe risk of the STD's transmission. This situation demonstrates the balance healthcare professionals strive to maintain between patient privacy and public health safety.

These moral dilemmas can be challenging, and healthcare professionals must navigate them with care and consideration for all parties involved.

Use of innovative technologies and techniques

The field of healthcare is continuously evolving with the use of innovative technologies and techniques. However, new ethical issues have also emerged with the rapid advancement in medical technologies. Using cutting-edge techniques such as gene editing, stem cell therapy, and artificial intelligence in patient care has raised concerns about safety, privacy, and consent. As such, healthcare professionals must navigate these ethical considerations by ensuring that technological advancements are ethically employed and weighing the potential benefits and risks to patients.

For example,

Hospitals using an artificial intelligence system to process patient data must be aware of privacy concerns. This technology should be accompanied by adequate data protection measures and informed patient consent to maintain an ethical practice.

Gene-editing technologies like CRISPR must be used under strict ethical guidelines. Medical professionals must guarantee its use is for beneficial purposes, like the prevention or treatment of severe genetic disorders, and avoid issues like "designer babies" that can infringe on ethical boundaries.

Impact of Ethical Dilemmas on Medical Practice:

One of the most significant impacts of ethical dilemmas is the potential harm they can cause to patients. When healthcare professionals face moral dilemmas, they may struggle to provide optimal care while respecting the autonomy and rights of their patients. For instance, a doctor may face a dilemma when a patient refuses a life-saving treatment due to personal beliefs. In such cases, healthcare professionals may feel caught between respecting patients' autonomy and ensuring their well-being.

Making morally challenging decisions can lead to moral distress, causing healthcare professionals to experience feelings of guilt, frustration, and burnout. These emotional burdens can ultimately impact the quality of patient care, potentially leading to adverse health outcomes.

Moreover, ethical dilemmas can also have broad implications for the healthcare system. When healthcare professionals face ethical conflicts, it can create tense and complex relationships within healthcare teams. Collaborative decision-making becomes challenging, decreasing efficiency and coordination in patient care. Additionally, if not handled appropriately, these dilemmas may lead to legal disputes and damage the reputation of healthcare institutions. Therefore, addressing ethical dilemmas promptly and appropriately is crucial to minimize their negative impact on healthcare professionals and the healthcare system.

Medical technology can also raise ethical concerns, such as genetic engineering, cloning, or experimental treatments. These practices may raise questions about the potential benefits, risks, and long-term consequences for patients, healthcare providers, and society.

Balancing Patient Rights and Medical Ethics:

Healthcare professionals encounter the complex process of understanding patient rights and medical ethics daily. Following are a few examples

1. A patient suffering from end-stage renal disease refuses to undergo hemodialysis due to personal beliefs. To resolve the ethical dilemma, the physician seeks to understand the patient's autonomy and respects his decision not to proceed with the treatment. However, he still strives to outline the

potential health consequences if the recommended treatment isn't followed.

2. A pediatrician is faced with a situation where parents refuse to have their child vaccinated due to personal beliefs that vaccines can cause more harm than good. The doctor engages in moral reasoning by respecting the parents' autonomy while educating them about the benefits and importance of vaccination for their child's health, demonstrating beneficence.

3. A pregnant woman, against her doctor's advice, wants to opt for a home birth instead of delivering her baby in a hospital. The healthcare providers need to ensure that the woman has complete information about the possible complications and risks associated with home birth for both the mother and the baby. In this case, the healthcare provider is tasked with balancing the woman's autonomy with her and her baby's safety.

4. An emergency physician is dealing with a critically ill patient without health insurance. The patient requires immediate surgery but can't afford it. The physician is moved by the principles of beneficence to provide the best possible care but is constrained by the economic realities of the healthcare system. He works with the hospital administration to formulate an acceptable payment plan, thus ensuring that the patient's access to care isn't compromised (justice).

5. The physician has a terminally ill cancer patient who is suffering intense pain. The patient's family asks the doctor to significantly increase pain medication, though this could hasten their loved one's death. By applying moral reasoning, the physician tries to balance the principle of non-

maleficence (not hastening death) against the principle of beneficence (relieving suffering). He discusses the potential outcomes with the family, helping them understand the implications of their request.

Strategies for Resolving Ethical Dilemmas in Medicine:

One of the most effective strategies for resolving ethical dilemmas is to engage in moral reasoning and analysis. This involves carefully evaluating a situation's moral principles and values, such as autonomy, beneficence, non-maleficence, and justice. Physicians can better understand the moral implications and make informed decisions by critically assessing the potential consequences of different courses of action. This approach ensures that physicians remain ethical while providing the best possible care to their patients.

Physicians often face ethical dilemmas in their practice, where they must make decisions that balance the best interest of their patients with other moral considerations. To navigate these complex situations, seeking ethical consultation and collaboration can be an effective strategy. This involves discussing with colleagues, ethics committees, or other healthcare professionals to gain different perspectives and moral insights. By doing so, physicians can explore alternative solutions, consider various ethical viewpoints, and ultimately reach a consensus on the best course of action.

In addition to consultations, ethical guidelines and codes of conduct can serve as valuable resources for physicians to resolve moral dilemmas. Professional organizations, such as the American Medical Association and the World Medical Association, provide ethical guidelines and principles that assist physicians in making ethical decisions. These guidelines prioritize respecting patient autonomy, maintaining confidentiality, obtaining informed consent, and acting in the patient's best interest. By adhering to these principles, physicians can ensure that their practice is grounded in ethical considerations and promotes the well-being of their patients.

Physicians must communicate clearly and concisely with patients and their families, providing them with all necessary information to make informed decisions. This includes explaining the situation and discussing all available treatment options in detail. By involving patients in the decision-making process, physicians can ensure that their values and preferences are respected, thus reducing the likelihood of ethical conflicts.

Moreover, establishing a trusting and open relationship with patients is essential in fostering shared decision-making. Patients are more likely to be satisfied with their care if their physician listens to their concerns and considers their input. This improves patient satisfaction and reduces the likelihood of ethical dilemmas arising.

Lastly, continuous professional education equips physicians with the skills and knowledge to handle ethical dilemmas effectively. By participating in ethics training programs and staying up-to-date with new ethical principles and guidelines, healthcare professionals can expand their ethical reasoning capabilities, enabling them to navigate complex situations with higher ethical competency. This ultimately leads to better patient care and outcomes.

Conclusion:

The medical profession frequently presents healthcare professionals with intricate ethical dilemmas that require careful consideration of justice, autonomy, non-maleficence, and beneficence. These issues can range from informed consent, end-of-life decisions, allocation of scarce resources, confidentiality breaches, and conflicts of interest to the use of innovative technologies and techniques. The impact of these dilemmas on patient care, the healthcare system, and medical professionals can be significant, potentially leading to compromising patient care and damaging professional relationships and reputations. Combating these challenges necessitates a delicate equilibrium between patients' rights and medical ethics, managed through effective communication, adherence to ethical guidelines, collaboration, and continuous education. These strategies equip healthcare professionals with the necessary insight to make informed, ethical decisions that prioritize patient well-being and maintain their integrity and the dignity of the healthcare field.

Suggested Readings

• Ewuoso, C., Hall, S., & Dierickx, K. (2021). How do healthcare professionals respond to ethical challenges regarding information management? A review of empirical studies. Global Bioethics, 32(1).

• Ethical dilemmas - an overview _ ScienceDirect, Stan Crowder, Brent E. Turvey, in Ethical Justice, 2013

• Kherbache, A., Mertens, E., & Denier, Y. (2022). Moral distress in medicine: An ethical analysis. Journal of Health Psychology, 27(8).

• Wiesen, J., Donatelli, C., Smith, M. L., Hyle, L., & Mireles-Cabodevila, E. (2021). Medical, ethical, and legal aspects of end-of-life dilemmas in the intensive care unit. In Cleveland Clinic Journal of Medicine (Vol. 88, Issue 9)

• Olejarczyk, J. P., & Young, M. (2021). Patient Rights and Ethics. The Journal of Law, Medicine & Ethics, 8(6) x.

•<u>CONFLICT RESOLUTION AND MANAGEMENT</u>, Striking a Balance: Managing Conflicts Between Patient Wishes and Medical Ethics, 2023

The Clash Between Pharmaceuticals and Ethics: Doctor's Dilemma

"Medicine is a compounded mixture of virtues, knowledge, and the ability to apply these to cure disease. Both doctors and pharmaceuticals must remember for whom they work – the patient."

- Dr. Edward Jenner

Overview:

Pharmaceuticals play a critical role in modern healthcare, offering solutions to a wide range of illnesses and improving the quality of life for millions of individuals. Doctors, playing a significant and indispensable role in patient care and treatment, interact with pharmaceutical companies that develop and market drugs to improve health outcomes. However, this relationship can raise ethical concerns regarding bias, influence, and potential conflicts of interest.

This narrative explores the intricate relationship between medical ethics, the objectives of the pharmaceutical industry, and the responsibilities health practitioners hold toward their patients. It delves into how physicians can uphold their moral convictions and prioritize their patient's needs in an era dominated by the robust pharmaceutical industry. Against the backdrop of a healthcare system where drug companies often sponsor the actions of medical professionals, this text questions the authenticity and autonomy of their decisions. "Doctor's Dilemma" is a must-read for those who wish to understand medical professionals' complex challenges. It offers as much insight as it does prompt deep reflection.

Friends or Enemies? Exploring the Pharmaceuticals Controversy:

Pharmaceuticals have undeniably made significant advancements in medical treatments, revolutionizing healthcare and extending human lifespan. Antibiotics, antiretrovirals for HIV, and cancer medications have all contributed to reducing mortality rates and improving the quality of life for countless individuals. These breakthroughs have put pharmaceuticals in the friend category, offering hope where there was once despair and suffering.

Moreover, pharmaceuticals play a crucial role in preventive medicine. Vaccines have been instrumental in eradicating or significantly reducing the prevalence of many diseases worldwide. They have saved countless lives and prevented suffering on a massive scale. For instance, developing and distributing vaccines like polio and coronavirus have significantly controlled and ultimately eradicated these once-devastating diseases.

However, the controversy surrounding pharmaceuticals stems from concerns about their potential harm. Many pharmaceuticals come with a variety of side effects that can range from mild discomfort to severe health risks. Additionally, the rising costs of prescription drugs pose a significant barrier to access for those without adequate healthcare coverage, exacerbating inequality in healthcare outcomes.

The greed-driven practices of some pharmaceutical companies, such as price gouging and unethical marketing strategies, have further fueled the negative perception of the industry. Several leading pharmaceutical companies have recently faced convictions for various unethical practices, such as incorrect branding, illegal advertising, misleading promotional strategies, unauthorized distribution, and providing physicians with incentives for prescribing their medications. They have also neglected to disclose safety information and misrepresented medication prices to decrease rebate payments. As a result, these companies had to resolve lawsuits that resulted in settlements costing them billions of dollars.

In short, the controversy surrounding pharmaceuticals as friends or enemies hinges on the balance between their potential to save lives and the concerns regarding their side effects, high costs, and ethical practices. Understanding this debate requires acknowledging pharmaceuticals' significant contributions to advancing medicine while addressing the challenges that arise from their potential drawbacks. Striving for transparency, affordability, and ethical standards is crucial to ensure that pharmaceuticals remain allies in the pursuit of improved health outcomes for all.

Analyzing the Ethical Implications for Pharmaceuticals:

One of the primary concerns is the high cost of pharmaceuticals. Many life-saving medications come with exorbitant price tags, often making them unaffordable for individuals without adequate healthcare coverage. This raises questions about access to essential medicines, especially for vulnerable populations who cannot afford them. The ethical dilemma lies in balancing companies' need for profit with the obligation to provide lifesaving medications to those in need.

Another ethical consideration is the promotion and marketing of pharmaceuticals. Pharmaceutical companies invest heavily in marketing strategies to increase the sales of their products. However, these marketing practices can sometimes blur the line between providing valuable information and influencing healthcare professionals to prescribe certain medications, even when more suitable options exist. Ensuring transparency and minimizing conflicts of interest between pharmaceutical companies and medical practitioners are essential for maintaining ethical standards.

In addition, pharmaceutical testing and development involve ethical concerns. Clinical trials play a crucial role in determining the safety and efficacy of new medications. However, ethical dilemmas arise when vulnerable populations, such as children or mentally impaired individuals, are involved in these trials. Balancing the potential benefits of advancing medical knowledge with protecting participants' rights and well-being is paramount.

Furthermore, intellectual property rights in the pharmaceutical industry present ethical challenges. Companies invest substantial resources in research and development, and patents provide a period of exclusivity to recover these costs and generate profits. However, these patents can limit access to affordable generic versions of medications, particularly in developing countries where healthcare resources are often scarce. A critical ethical consideration is balancing incentivizing innovation and ensuring more comprehensive access to essential medicines.

To navigate these ethical implications, various stakeholders play a crucial role. Policymakers must craft regulations that promote affordable access to medications while fostering innovation. Pharmaceutical companies must prioritize patient welfare and ethical marketing practices over profit-driven motives. Healthcare professionals should critically evaluate the medicines they prescribe, considering their patients' interests and the moral implications of their choices.

Understanding the Connection: Doctors and Pharmaceuticals:

There is ongoing debate about how pharmaceutical companies' influence on doctors impacts patient care. Critics argue that the relationship may lead to the overprescribing of expensive and potentially unnecessary drugs. On the contrary, proponents suggest that interactions between doctors and pharmaceutical companies are essential for medical education, research funding, and innovative drug development. Finding the right balance between these interests is crucial.

One aspect of the doctor-pharmaceutical relationship is providing information and education. Pharmaceutical companies often sponsor medical conferences, seminars, and educational programs for doctors. While such initiatives can be valuable for professional development, there is a concern that industry influence may influence doctors' prescribing behavior toward certain medications. However, these initiatives can improve patient care and treatment outcomes with proper regulation and transparency.

Some doctors receive payments, gifts, or other compensation from pharmaceutical companies for prescribing their products. Disclosure of these economic relationships has become increasingly emphasized in recent years to ensure transparency and prevent undue influence.

Many countries have implemented guidelines and codes of conduct that dictate the appropriate interactions between doctors and pharmaceutical companies. For instance, the United States has the Physician Payments Sunshine Act, which requires pharmaceutical companies to disclose any payments or value transfers made to physicians. The Sunshine Act has increased transparency and allowed patients to access information about their doctors' financial ties.

How To Achieve Doctor-Pharmaceutical Equilibrium?

In today's healthcare industry, finding a proper balance between doctors and pharmaceuticals is crucial for ensuring patients' well-being. While doctors play a central role in diagnosing and treating medical conditions, pharmaceuticals provide the necessary medications to alleviate symptoms and promote healing. However, an imbalance or misalignment of interests between these entities can lead to various ethical and practical concerns.

It is essential to recognize that doctors must prioritize the best interests of their patients. They are responsible for making informed treatment decisions, considering the patient's medical history, symptoms, and the most appropriate medication or therapy. Doctors must base their prescribing practices on evidence-based medicine and adhere to ethical guidelines to ensure the safety and effectiveness of drugs. Doing so contributes to patients' overall well-being and maintains their trust.

On the other hand, pharmaceutical companies are responsible for developing and providing safe and effective medications. They invest significant resources in research and development, clinical trials, and regulatory processes to bring new drugs to the market. However, the profit-driven nature of the pharmaceutical industry can sometimes conflict with patients' best interests. There have been instances where companies have engaged in unethical marketing practices, such as off-label promotion or concealing drug risks, to maximize profits. Such practices can compromise patient safety and undermine doctors' ability to make unbiased treatment decisions.

The following measures can be taken to find a balance between doctors and pharmaceuticals.

Transparency and regulation are essential. Governments and regulatory bodies should enforce stricter rules on the marketing and promotion of pharmaceutical products to ensure that they provide accurate and unbiased information to doctors and patients. This would prevent misleading claims and undue influence on prescription decisions.

Continuing medical education is crucial in empowering doctors to make informed decisions. Doctors should have access to unbiased, evidence-based information about medications, including their risks, benefits, and alternatives. Pharmaceutical companies can support educational initiatives that focus on improving doctors' knowledge and clinical decision-making skills, ensuring that they prioritize patient welfare over any external influences.

Open communication channels can also foster collaboration between doctors and pharmaceuticals. Regular meetings between medical professionals and pharmaceutical representatives can facilitate information exchanges about emerging therapies, scientific advancements, and patient needs. Such collaborations should be closely monitored to avoid conflicts of interest and ensure they genuinely benefit patient care.

To address these concerns, regulatory bodies and governments play a crucial role in ensuring pharmaceuticals' safety, affordability, and ethical standards. The establishment and enforcement of rigorous testing procedures, such as clinical trials, enable the identification of potential side effects and provide an opportunity for necessary adjustments or warnings. Additionally, initiatives such as generic drug availability and healthcare reforms aim to improve access to affordable medications and reduce the burden on individuals.

Conclusion:

The pharmaceutical industry is pivotal in enhancing global public health through innovative medicines. However, the industry is entangled in controversies and ethical implications concerning the high costs, side effects, and questionable marketing strategies. This necessitates striking a balance in the complex relationship between doctors and pharmaceutical companies, as both are vital in enhancing patient care. Ensuring transparency, affordability, and ethical marketing practices is paramount for the industry. Also, promoting access to unbiased, evidence-based information for doctors can foster informed decision-making. Policymakers, healthcare professionals, and pharmaceutical companies must work cohesively to navigate these issues, aiming to prioritize patient welfare and contribute positively to global health outcomes.

Suggested Readings

• Elliott, C. (2014). Relationships between physicians and Pharma: Why physicians should not accept money from the pharmaceutical industry. Neurology: Clinical Practice, 4(2).

• (Pitre Cotchet, et al., 2021.) Top Pharmaceutical Litigation Settlements of All Time_ Top National Trial Lawyers for the Underdog. (n.d.).

• Brax, H., Fadlallah, R., Al-Khaled, L., Kahale, L. A., Nas, H., El-Jardali, F., & Akl, E. A. (2017). Association between physicians' interaction with pharmaceutical companies and their clinical practices: A systematic review and meta-analysis. PLoS ONE, 12(4).

• Klugman, C. (2017). Shining Light on Conflicts of Interest. In American Journal of Bioethics (Vol. 17, Issue 6).

• Citrome, L. (2014). The sunshine act and transfers of value: Impact on non-industry authorship. Innovations in Clinical Neuroscience, 11(3–4).

• Niebyl, J. R. (2008). The pharmaceutical industry: friend or foe? In American Journal of Obstetrics and Gynecology (Vol. 198, Issue 4).

• Sillup, G. P., & Porth, S. J. (2008). Ethical issues in the pharmaceutical industry: An analysis of US newspapers. International Journal of Pharmaceutical and Healthcare Marketing, 2(3).

• Tabernero, P., Parker, M., Ravinetto, R., Phanouvong, S., Yeung, S., Kitutu, F. E., Cheah, P. Y., Mayxay, M., Guerin, P. J., & Newton, P. N. (2016). Ethical challenges in designing and conducting medicine quality surveys. Tropical Medicine and International Health, 21(6).

• Zarei, E., Ghaffari, A., Nikoobar, A., Bastami, S., & Hamdghaddari, H. (2023). Interaction between physicians and the pharmaceutical industry: A scoping review for developing a policy brief. In Frontiers in Public Health (Vol. 10).

Evolving with Technology: The Journey of Progress

"It is not the strongest of the species that survives, nor the most intelligent, but the one most responsive to change."

- Charles Darwin

Overview:

The medical profession has undergone significant changes due to technological advancements. Upon discovering that annually, 12 million individuals received incorrect diagnoses that could lead to harm, numerous physicians began to integrate technological solutions to enhance the precision of their diagnoses. To stay at the forefront, healthcare providers must continuously learn and adapt. This section reflects on historical milestones and emphasizes the necessity of navigating contemporary technological resources. The medical vocation's guiding principle remains the balance between embracing innovation and preserving the human touch that defines medicine. This article scrutinizes the various aspects of these advancements, from digitalizing patient records to expanding telehealth services, outlining the remarkable transition from traditional methods to the digital agora that frames modern healthcare. 'Evolving with Technology: The Journey of Progress' is a testament to the adaptive spirit and intellectual rigor that define and will continue to shape the medical profession.

Technological Advances: Transforming the Medical Sector

Electronic health records (EHRs)

Electronic health records transform patient medical records into digital formats, simplifying access for medical practitioners in various healthcare environments. The transition from paper records to electronic ones offers a fuller picture of a patient's health journey, enhancing decision-making and collaboration in patient care. Additionally, EHRs support the ability to monitor patients remotely, enabling timely interventions by healthcare providers and ultimately improving the quality of patient care outcomes.

Telemedicine

Telehealth allows individuals to engage with medical professionals via phone or video link-ups, eradicating the necessity for physical consultations and thereby diminishing patients' travel commitments and expenses. This method is especially advantageous for people living in remote or poorly served areas, providing access to expert healthcare without requiring extensive journeys. Furthermore, throughout the COVID-19 crisis, telehealth has been instrumental in maintaining consistent health services while simultaneously reducing the potential spread of the infection. Before the onset of the COVID-19 pandemic in early 2020, a mere 20% of American doctors were incorporating telehealth in their practices. However, as the pandemic took hold six months into the year, there was a significant surge, with virtually 95% of physicians adopting telehealth solutions.

Artificial intelligence (AI)

The advent of artificial intelligence has revolutionized healthcare, offering AI-driven tools that can evaluate enormous data sets to unearth patterns that may go unnoticed by human specialists.

This enables early disease detection, improved diagnostic accuracy, and personalized treatment plans. AI's effectiveness in diagnosing cancer surpasses 90%, indicating a substantial likelihood of its reliability. AI can also streamline administrative tasks, improving efficiency and reducing human error.

AI can also assist in robotic surgeries, where robotic systems controlled by skilled surgeons perform surgical procedures. This improves precision, minimizes invasiveness, and enhances patient safety.

Internet of Medical Things (IoMT)

Wearable devices and IoMT have also significantly impacted healthcare. By 2026, the IoMT market is estimated to reach $142.45 billion. Wearable devices such as smartwatches, fitness trackers, and biosensors can continuously monitor a person's health, such as heart rate, blood pressure, blood sugar, sleep patterns, and physical activity. These devices provide real-time data, allowing individuals to track their health progress and make informed lifestyle decisions. Additionally, the IoMT connects these wearable devices and medical equipment to a network, enabling seamless data transmission and analysis, further enhancing healthcare outcomes. Studies indicate that lifestyle enhancements occur in 10% of individuals using these gadgets, thanks to the insights gained from their data.

Recommending a Fitbit to a patient may increase their longevity.

Barcode Technology

In addition to technological advancements, innovation is vital in improving healthcare processes. By continuously evaluating and reengineering workflows, healthcare organizations can eliminate inefficiencies, reduce medical errors, and enhance patient safety. For instance, implementing barcode medication administration systems has significantly reduced medication errors by ensuring patients receive the correct medication and dosage.

Discovery of Novel Drugs

Furthermore, healthcare innovation extends to the development of new pharmaceuticals and treatments. Research and development efforts enable the discovery of novel drugs and therapies to combat diseases, improve patient outcomes, and extend life expectancy. Breakthroughs in personalized medicine, targeted therapies, and gene editing technologies are promising for treating previously incurable diseases or conditions.

Emerging Technologies: The Path Ahead for Healthcare Industry:

Blockchain technology

Blockchain technology will enhance data security, interoperability, and patient privacy. Utilizing blockchain technology guarantees a safe and open exchange of digital health records across medical practitioners, minimizing the replication of procedures and enhancing the integration of patient care. The decentralized nature of blockchain also reduces the risk of data breaches and ensures patient consent and control over their medical information.

Virtual Reality

Virtual reality (VR) technology can revolutionize patient care and training in healthcare. VR can help alleviate pain and anxiety in patients by immersing them in virtual environments and distracting them from medical procedures. It can also provide realistic simulations for medical training, allowing healthcare professionals to practice complex surgeries or emergency scenarios in a safe and controlled environment.

Genomics

Genomics, the study of an individual's genetic information, enables personalized medicine and targeted treatments. With advancements in DNA sequencing technology, genomics plays a crucial role in diagnosing and treating genetic disorders, predicting disease risks, and developing tailored therapies based on an individual's genetic makeup. This technology can potentially transform healthcare by providing more precise and effective treatments.

Nanotechnology

At the molecular and cellular levels, nanotechnology has immense potential in healthcare. Nanomaterials can be used for drug delivery, targeting specific cells or tissues, thereby increasing efficacy and minimizing side effects. Nanosensors can monitor patients in real-time, detecting abnormal biomarkers and alerting healthcare professionals for early intervention. Furthermore, nanorobots hold promise in performing targeted interventions, such as removing blood clots or delivering drugs to specific sites within the body.

These emerging technologies have already started impacting several healthcare areas, but their potential has yet to be fully realized. As with any advancement, there are challenges, such as regulatory concerns, data privacy, ethical considerations, and financial implications. However, the benefits they bring regarding improved patient care, enhanced diagnostics, personalized medicine, and increased efficiency are undeniable.

The Intersection of Healthcare and Artificial Intelligence (AI):

Artificial intelligence has advanced substantially, making notable impacts across different sectors, particularly in healthcare. The intersection of healthcare and AI is promising in revolutionizing patient care, improving diagnostics, and enhancing treatment options. From safeguarding patient data to optimizing clinical decision-making, AI can revolutionize the medical field.

AI has demonstrated remarkable capabilities in the field of medical imaging. The tedious and error-susceptible task of interpreting images like X-rays, MRIs, and CT scans, which take up much of radiologists' time, can be streamlined with AI-driven image analysis tools. These advanced algorithms expedite the review of copious amounts of imagery, highlighting potential irregularities and minimizing the chances of diagnostic mistakes. Research indicates that these AI systems can rival, or sometimes surpass, the proficiency of human radiologists in detecting certain medical conditions, thereby enhancing both precision and productivity in medical diagnostics.

Artificial intelligence is increasingly utilized to create predictive analytics models that can estimate the progression of illnesses and pinpoint patients at elevated risk. Machine learning algorithms digest extensive patient data, including medical records, genomic data, and behavioral patterns, to anticipate the trajectory of diseases. By enabling earlier intervention and crafting tailored treatment strategies, these models enhance patients' prognosis.

Moreover, artificial intelligence has become indispensable in pharmaceutical research and innovation. The conventional route to uncovering potential new medications is often drawn out and costly. However, AI systems can swiftly navigate through extensive collections of chemical substances and determine their likely effectiveness and safety characteristics, diminishing both the duration and expense of the exploration stage. Additionally, artificial intelligence can uncover alternative applications for current medications, proposing novel therapeutic approaches for various ailments.

While integrating AI into healthcare presents enormous opportunities, it raises concerns about patient privacy, ethical implications, and algorithmic biases. Safeguarding patient data and ensuring transparency in algorithmic decision-making is crucial to maintaining trust in these emerging technologies. Implementing robust governance frameworks and regulatory standards is necessary to address these concerns and provide the responsible use of AI in healthcare.

Innovation and Its Role in Defining a 'Great Doctor':

Innovation is crucial in defining what makes a 'great doctor' in today's ever-evolving healthcare landscape. As medical knowledge and technology advance at an unprecedented rate, doctors must embrace and harness innovation to provide the best possible care to their patients.

A key aspect of being a 'great doctor' is up-to-date with medical research and technological advancements. This requires doctors to be innovative in learning and adapting to new findings. By actively seeking and incorporating new knowledge into their practice, doctors can ensure they provide the most accurate and effective treatments for their patients. For instance, physicians who adopt electronic health records (EHRs) and utilize artificial intelligence (AI) in diagnosing and treating diseases can improve patient outcomes and enhance overall efficiency in healthcare delivery. Such innovative practices benefit individual patients and contribute to the advancement of medical science.

In addition to staying informed, great doctors are also proactive in seeking innovative ways to improve patient care and outcomes. They strive to identify and address gaps in the existing healthcare system while continuously improving the quality and efficiency of their practice. For example, the emergence of telemedicine has revolutionized how healthcare is delivered, allowing doctors to assess and treat patients remotely, particularly in underserved areas. By embracing this innovative approach, doctors can reach a broader population and provide timely medical care, ultimately improving patient satisfaction and access to healthcare services.

Furthermore, innovation extends beyond individual patient care to the collaboration among healthcare professionals. Great doctors engage in interdisciplinary teamwork, embracing innovative communication tools and approaches that foster effective collaboration and knowledge sharing. For instance, using secure messaging platforms and teleconferencing enables doctors to consult with colleagues and specialists, enhancing clinical decision-making and enabling a more comprehensive approach to patient care. By embracing these innovative practices, doctors can utilize the expertise of a diverse healthcare team, leading to improved diagnosis, treatment, and patient outcomes.

Conclusion:

As medical advancements evolve with technology, physicians must adapt and learn to navigate these contemporary technological resources. The medical field has benefited from innovations like electronic health records, telemedicine, artificial intelligence, and the Internet of Medical Things. Emerging technologies, such as virtual reality, genomics, nanotechnology, and blockchain, hold even more significant potential for the healthcare industry. However, the ethical considerations, data privacy, financial implications, and regulatory concerns cannot be ignored. Moving forward, innovation will continue to define what it means to be a great doctor, requiring a balance of up-to-date technological understanding and maintaining the human touch critical to patient care. Healthcare providers must stay informed, actively seek innovative practices, and engage in interdisciplinary collaboration to deliver the most accurate and effective treatments.

Suggested Readings

• Healthcare 16 Jaw-Dropping Medical Technology Statistics of 2022 Visitor Management Centralized Calendar Online booking pages. (n.d.).

• 55 Interesting Medical Technology Statistics: 2024 Data on Companies & Usage

• Tabche, C., Raheem, M., Alolaqi, A., & Rawaf, S. (2023). Effect of electronic health records on doctor-patient relationship in Arabian gulf countries: a systematic review. In Frontiers in Digital Health (Vol. 5). Frontiers Media SA.

• Bitkina, O. V., Park, J., & Kim, H. K. (2023). Application of artificial intelligence in medical technologies: A systematic review of main trends. In Digital Health (Vol. 9).

• Nagendran, M., Chen, Y., Lovejoy, C. A., Gordon, A. C., Komorowski, M., Harvey, H., Topol, E. J., Ioannidis, J. P. A., Collins, G. S., & Maruthappu, M. (2020). Artificial intelligence versus clinicians: Systematic review of design, reporting standards, and claims of deep learning studies in medical imaging. The BMJ, 368.

• Haleem, A., Javaid, M., Singh, R. P., & Suman, R. (2021). Telemedicine for healthcare: Capabilities, features, barriers, and applications. In Sensors International (Vol. 2).

• Hosny, A., Parmar, C., Quackenbush, J., Schwartz, L. H., & Aerts, H. J. W. L. (2018). Artificial intelligence in radiology. In Nature Reviews Cancer (Vol. 18, Issue 8).

• Mishra, P., & Singh, G. (2023). Internet of Medical Things Healthcare for Sustainable Smart Cities: Current Status and Future Prospects. Applied Sciences (Switzerland), 13(15).

• Haghi, M., Thurow, K., & Stoll, R. (2017). Wearable devices in medical internet of things: Scientific research and commercially available devices. Healthcare Informatics Research, 23(1).

• Spiegel, B., Fuller, G., Lopez, M., Dupuy, T., Noah, B., Howard, A., Albert, M., Tashjian, V., Lam, R., Ahn, J., Dailey, F., Rosen, B. T., Vrahas, M., Little, M., Garlich, J., Dzubur, E., IsHak, W., & Danovitch, I. (2019). Virtual reality for management of pain in hospitalized patients: A randomized comparative effectiveness trial. PLoS ONE, 14(8).

• Rickenbacher-Frey, S., Adam, S., Exadaktylos, A. K., Müller, M., Sauter, T. C., & Birrenbach, T. (2023). Development and evaluation of a virtual reality training for emergency treatment of shortness of breath based on frameworks for serious games. GMS Journal for Medical Education, 40(2).

• Jackson, M., Marks, L., May, G. H. W., & Wilson, J. B. (2018). The genetic basis of disease. In Essays in Biochemistry (Vol. 62, Issue 5).

• Malik, S., Muhammad, K., & Waheed, Y. (2023). Emerging Applications of Nanotechnology in Healthcare and Medicine. In Molecules (Vol. 28, Issue 18).

• Kuo, T. T., Kim, H. E., & Ohno-Machado, L. (2017). Blockchain distributed ledger technologies for biomedical and health care applications. In Journal of the American Medical Informatics Association (Vol. 24, Issue 6).

Enhancing Medical Care: Reflection and Self-Assessment Tools for Doctors

"To reflect is to grow. To assess oneself is the first step to becoming a better physician."

- Marie Curie

Overview:

Reflection is an essential aspect of medical practice that encourages doctors to think critically and analyze their feelings, experiences, and responses to improve patient care. Self-assessment is also necessary for doctors to actively evaluate their knowledge, attitudes, skills, and performance. High-quality patient care can be maintained by fostering a culture of reflection and self-assessment in healthcare institutions. This segment discusses innovative and efficient tools for medical professionals to aid self-assessment and reflection. These instruments assist doctors in evaluating their skills, performance, and knowledge while providing insights for personal growth and improved patient care. It also provides tips for effectively using these tools and tackles potential challenges that may be faced during their implementation. It concludes by highlighting the future potential of self-assessment tools with the adoption of cutting-edge technology like AI and machine learning. The importance of ethical considerations and data privacy in implementing these advancements is also emphasized.

Role of Self-Assessment in Improving Doctor's Professional Skills:

A critical aspect of self-assessment is evaluating clinical knowledge. Doctors must stay updated with the latest medical research, advancements, and guidelines to ensure they provide evidence-based care. By regularly assessing their knowledge base, doctors can identify gaps and take steps to fill them. This can be achieved through reading medical journals, attending conferences and workshops, participating in online courses, and engaging in discussions with colleagues.

Self-assessment also allows doctors to evaluate their clinical skills. This includes assessing their diagnostic abilities, procedural skills, and communication skills with patients. By reflecting on their clinical practice, doctors can identify weaknesses or areas for improvement. They can then seek additional training, shadow other experienced doctors, or utilize simulation-based learning to develop their skills further. Continuous self-assessment helps doctors stay updated with best practices and adapt to advancements in medical technology and treatment approaches.

Furthermore, self-assessment plays a vital role in improving doctors' interpersonal skills. Communication with colleagues and other healthcare professionals is crucial for optimal patient care. Doctors can use self-assessment to reflect on their communication style, empathy, and ability to build rapport with patients and colleagues. By identifying areas needing improvement, doctors can seek patient feedback, participate in communication skills workshops, or utilize role-playing exercises to enhance their interpersonal skills.

While regular self-assessment has numerous benefits, it also has challenges associated with its implementation. Doctors may face barriers such as lack of time, reluctance to reflect on their performance, or fear of discovering deficiencies. Overcoming these challenges requires a supportive environment that encourages and values self-assessment and effective strategies for integrating self-assessment into doctors' busy schedules.

Analyzing Different Reflection and Self-Assessment Tools for Doctors:

1. 360-Degree Feedback

This method allows doctors to receive constructive feedback from a circle of individuals around them, including their colleagues, subordinates, and patients. It provides a holistic viewpoint on physicians' medical skills, communication abilities, teamwork, and overall job performance. Doctors can focus on their strengths and weaknesses through this feedback system and continually improve their skills.

2. Self-Assessment Questionnaire (SAQ)

SAQ is a practical and widely used self-assessment tool in the medical field. It encourages doctors to evaluate their working experience, identify skills or knowledge gaps, and find effective ways to bridge them. The data from these quizzes can also support institutions in creating training and development programs tailored to the specific needs of clinicians.

3. Reflective Journals

Reflective journals are an essential self-assessment tool for physicians. They offer a platform to record and scrutinize their thoughts, emotions, and experiences over a period. Analyzing these records over time can reveal patterns, provide insights into decision-making processes, and highlight future learning and improvement areas.

4. Clinical Audit

Clinical audits systematically review care and treatment practices against specific criteria, evidenced through patient records. These audits can be seen as a valuable reflective tool for doctors, explicitly highlighting areas of practice needing improvement. Moreover, audits deliver feedback on the doctors' performance to review the clinical effectiveness of their practices.

5. Peer-Assessment

Peer assessment is a dynamic tool that allows physicians to evaluate each other's technical skills, patient management, and overall competence. The strength of peer assessment is that the reviewers understand the intricacies of clinical practice, and their feedback can be invaluable in improving professional competencies.

Tips for Doctors: How to Effectively Use Self-Assessment Tools:

To effectively use self-assessment tools, doctors should consider the following tips:

1. **Select the right tool**: Doctors have various self-assessment tools. It is essential to choose a tool that aligns with the specific needs and goals of the doctor. For example,

a doctor who wants to assess their communication skills might opt for a tool that includes patient feedback surveys.

2. **Establish clear objectives**: Doctors should set clear objectives and expectations before using a self-assessment tool. This will help them focus on specific areas they want to evaluate and improve. By defining goals, doctors can maximize their self-assessment experience and use the results to guide their professional development.

3. **Be honest and open-minded**: Self-assessment requires doctors to be honest and objective about their abilities and performance. Openness and willingness to acknowledge areas that need improvement are essential. By being self-reflective and unbiased, doctors can gain valuable insights and take appropriate actions to enhance their skills and knowledge.

4. **Seek feedback from multiple sources**: While self-assessment is primarily an internal process, doctors should also seek feedback from external sources to understand their performance comprehensively. This can include input from colleagues, supervisors, and patients. By garnering feedback from multiple perspectives, doctors can identify blind spots and address areas they may not have noticed during self-assessment.

5. **Develop an action plan**: Once doctors have completed a self-assessment and received feedback, it is crucial to develop an action plan based on identified areas for improvement. This plan should outline specific steps and strategies to enhance skills, close knowledge gaps, or modify behaviors. Regularly reviewing and revising the action plan will ensure continuous professional growth.

Potential Challenges in Implementing Reflection and Self-Assessment Tools:

One of the main challenges is resistance to change. When new tools or processes are introduced, individuals within the organization may resist adopting them. This resistance could stem from the fear of the unknown, the perception that the tools might be time-consuming, or doubtfulness about their effectiveness in improving performance. Overcoming this resistance requires effective communication, highlighting the potential benefits, and addressing concerns or misconceptions.

Another challenge is the lack of understanding or awareness of the benefits of reflection and self-assessment tools. Some individuals may not fully grasp the purpose or value of these tools in enhancing their personal or professional growth. Educating the employees about the advantages of self-reflection and self-assessment, such as identifying strengths and areas for improvement, setting goals, and enhancing self-awareness, is essential. This can be achieved through workshops, training sessions, or awareness campaigns.

Furthermore, implementing reflection and self-assessment tools also requires proper training and support. Individuals need to understand how to use the tools effectively and how to interpret the results. Providing comprehensive training sessions or resources can help employees develop the skills required to utilize the tools effectively. Additionally, ongoing support from managers or mentors can ensure employees receive guidance and feedback.

Ultimately, overcoming these challenges requires a proactive approach that involves clear communication, education, training, and support. By addressing the resistance to change, increasing awareness of the benefits, and providing the necessary tools and resources, organizations can successfully implement reflection and self-assessment processes and contribute to individual and organizational growth.

Creating a Culture of Reflection and Self-Assessment in Healthcare Institutions:

Creating a culture of reflection and self-assessment in healthcare institutions is not only beneficial for healthcare professionals but also for patients. By encouraging healthcare professionals to reflect on their practice, seek feedback, and engage in self-assessment, healthcare institutions can create an environment prioritizing quality care and patient safety.

One effective way to foster a culture of reflection is by implementing regular team meetings or case conferences. These sessions allow healthcare professionals to discuss and analyze their clinical experiences, patient outcomes, and any challenges faced. By engaging in open and honest discussions, healthcare professionals can gain valuable insights from their colleagues and learn from each other's experiences.

Healthcare organizations can introduce anonymous feedback mechanisms, such as surveys or suggestion boxes, where individuals can express their thoughts and opinions without fear of retribution. This allows healthcare professionals to receive feedback on their performance and identify areas for improvement.

Furthermore, implementing reflective practice tools can significantly facilitate self-assessment. Tools like the Gibbs' Reflective Cycle or the Johns' Model for Structured

Reflection provide a structured approach for healthcare professionals to assess their practice. These models guide individuals through questions and prompts, helping them critically analyze their decision-making, identify improvement areas, and set future practice goals.

In addition to these strategies, providing opportunities for professional development and continuing education is crucial. This enables healthcare professionals to stay updated with the latest advancements in their fields and promotes a mindset of lifelong learning and improvement. By investing in their growth, healthcare professionals can continuously enhance their skills and knowledge, improving patient care outcomes.

The Future of Self-Assessment Tools in the Medical Profession:

As technology advances, the future of self-assessment tools in the medical profession appears promising, offering numerous benefits for healthcare providers and patients.

As new technologies like artificial intelligence (AI) and machine learning (ML) further develop, self-assessment tools will become more sophisticated, providing even more accurate and tailored feedback to healthcare providers.

Additionally, self-assessment tools can facilitate the creation of virtual communities and discussion forums, allowing healthcare professionals from different locations to connect, share insights, and collaborate on research and development projects.

It is important to note that the implementation of self-assessment tools in the medical profession should be conducted with careful consideration for ethical and privacy concerns. The collection and analysis of personal data must adhere to strict confidentiality and security protocols, ensuring the privacy and trust of medical practitioners and patients.

Conclusion:

Self-assessment and reflection tools are vital to professional development in the medical field. The introduction of various self-assessment tools, such as 360-degree feedback, Self-Assessment Questionnaire (SAQ), reflective journals, clinical audits, and peer assessment, provide comprehensive, versatile ways for doctors to gain insights into their abilities and areas for improvement. Overcoming the challenges of implementing these tools, such as resistance to change, lack of understanding, and adequate training, requires a proactive, informed approach. New advancements like artificial intelligence and machine learning are set to further enhance these tools' effectiveness. However, careful handling of ethical and privacy concerns remains essential. By fostering a supportive culture of reflection and self-assessment, healthcare institutions can facilitate continuous professional growth, ultimately advancing patient care outcomes.

Suggested Readings

• Evans, A. W., McKenna, C., & Oliver, M. (2002). Self-assessment in medical practice. In Journal of the Royal Society of Medicine (Vol. 95, Issue 10).

• How to use the self-assessment tool. (2019).

• Mann, K., Gordon, J., & MacLeod, A. (2009). Reflection and reflective practice in health professions education: A systematic review. Advances in Health Sciences Education, 14(4).

• Norcini, J., & Burch, V. (2007). Workplace-based assessment as an educational tool: AMEE Guide No. 31. In Medical Teacher (Vol. 29, Issues 9–10).

• Davis, D. A., Mazmanian, P. E., Fordis, M., Van Harrison, R., Thorpe, K. E., & Perrier, L. (2006). Accuracy of physician self-assessment compared with observed measures of competence: A systematic review. In JAMA (Vol. 296, Issue 9).

• Stenov, V., Wind, G., Skinner, T., Reventlow, S., & Hempler, N. F. (2017). The potential of a self-assessment tool to identify healthcare professionals' strengths and areas in need of professional development to aid effective facilitation of group-based, person-centered diabetes education. BMC Medical Education, 17(1).

• Bose, S., Oliveras, E., & Edson, W. N. (n.d.). How Can Self-Assessment Improve the Quality of Healthcare?

• Baitha, U., Ranjan, P., Sarkar, S., Arora, C., Kumari, A., Dwivedi, S. N., Patil, A., & Jamshed, N. (2019). Development of a self-assessment tool for resident doctors' communication skills in India. Journal of Educational Evaluation for Health Professions, 16.

Securing Your Future: Retirement and Succession Plans for Medical Professionals

"Retirement is a blank sheet of paper. It is a chance to redesign your life into something new and different."

- Patrick Foley

Overview:

In the complex and demanding healthcare field, medical professionals dedicate most of their time to providing services and less time to considering what their future might look like post-retirement. This article addresses the crucial necessity of prospective planning for future security in the medical profession. It delves into the significance of retirement and succession planning, an often overlooked yet critical aspect directly impacting healthcare practitioners' long-term personal and professional stability. The text will explore various retirement and succession planning dimensions for medical professionals. This will include understanding the importance of such considerations, discussing the different elements that need to be factored into these plans, and offering practical advice to navigate through this process of planning successfully. Ultimately, the goal is to empower medical professionals to look beyond their immediate responsibilities and plan for a secure future.

Essential Tips for a Smooth Transition to Retirement:

Retirement is a significant milestone in one's life, marking the end of a professional career and the beginning of a new chapter. While it can be exciting, transitioning to retirement comes with challenges and adjustments. To ensure a smooth and successful transition, here are some essential tips to consider.

Adjust Your Lifestyle: Retirement brings a change in income, and it is essential to adjust your lifestyle accordingly. Review your current spending habits and identify areas where you can cut back or make cost-effective choices. This will help you maintain financial stability during your retirement.

Stay Active: Retirement often allows for more free time, but staying physically and mentally active is essential. Engage in regular exercise routines, join clubs or organizations, volunteer, or consider part-time work to keep yourself busy and maintain a sense of purpose.

Plan for Healthcare: As you approach retirement age, ensure that you have adequate health insurance coverage. Research and enroll in Medicare or consider supplementary health insurance plans. Additionally, uphold a balanced lifestyle and consistently schedule appointments with your medical professional to avoid potential health problems.

Socialize and Network: Retirement can sometimes lead to feelings of isolation. To combat this, make an effort to socialize and network with others. Join community groups, participate in hobbies or sports activities, or even consider taking classes to meet new people and maintain a solid social support system.

Set New Goals: Retirement doesn't mean you need to stop setting goals for yourself. Set new objectives for your retired life, whether learning a new skill, pursuing a passion, or planning a dream vacation. Having goals will give you a sense of purpose and fulfillment in your new phase of life.

Seek Emotional Support: Adjusting to retirement can be emotionally challenging for some individuals. If you struggle with the transition, don't hesitate to seek emotional support from friends, family, or professional counselors. Discussing your thoughts and concerns can help ease any anxiety and provide guidance during this significant life change.

Succession planning: Retirement in medicine is not merely the end of a career; it encompasses a complex process of transferring responsibilities, skills, and knowledge and ensuring the smooth handover of patient care. However, the absence of a proper succession plan can lead to disruptions in patient care, loss of expertise, and increased stress for patients and remaining staff. Succession planning plays a vital role in overcoming these challenges. It involves identifying potential successors and providing them with the necessary training and mentorship to ensure a seamless transition.

Additionally, organizations should prioritize creating a culture that values and supports retirement planning. This entails offering robust financial planning resources, retirement savings programs, and guidance on transitioning to the next phase of life. By encouraging open discussions about retirement, healthcare professionals are more likely to plan and make informed decisions about their future.

Exploring the Role of Financial Planning in Retirement:

Financial planning ensures a smooth and secure transition into retirement.

Strategic financial preparation is essential for a secure retirement, playing a vital role in evaluating and handling the expenses associated with healthcare. Medical expenses can quickly drain one's retirement savings, and it is essential to have a comprehensive understanding of healthcare options, insurance coverage, and potential out-of-pocket expenses. To make informed decisions and choose the most cost-effective options for their medical needs, retirees should explore various healthcare plans, including Medicare and supplemental insurance.

Another essential retirement planning consideration is evaluating and adjusting personal expenses and budgets. With a reduced income, it is necessary to review and potentially downsize one's lifestyle to align with the new financial circumstances. This may involve reassessing discretionary spending, reducing debt, and cutting unnecessary expenses.

As individuals age, the need for assistance with daily activities and healthcare increases. Long-term care insurance can help cover the costs associated with home healthcare, nursing homes, or assisted living facilities. Retirees should explore different long-term care options, understand the associated costs, and consider insurance coverage to give themselves a sense of security and alleviate potential financial burdens related to long-term care needs.

Furthermore, individuals should ensure that their financial planning includes strategies for maintaining an emergency fund and managing investments. Unexpected events can occur, and having a contingency fund can be essential in covering unforeseen expenses during medical retirement.

Consulting with a qualified financial planner or retirement specialist is highly recommended to navigate the complex world of financial planning in medical retirement. These professionals can provide personalized advice, develop customized strategies, and offer expertise in navigating the economic challenges associated with medical retirement.

Impacts of Retirement on Patient Care:

Retirement of healthcare professionals can significantly impact patient care in several ways. Firstly, their wealth of experience and expertise accumulated over years of service may need to be recovered. This loss can result in decreased quality and efficiency of healthcare services, as the retiring professionals possess valuable knowledge and skills that are not easily replaceable. Additionally, the departure of key personnel can disrupt established relationships between healthcare providers and their patients, leading to potential challenges in maintaining trust and understanding individual patient needs.

Several studies highlight the impact of retirement and succession on patient care. The studies found that patients who experienced the retirement of their primary care physician reported feelings of anxiety and uncertainty about the transition to a new doctor. They also expressed concerns about the potential changes in their treatment plans.

To mitigate these challenges, healthcare organizations must proactively manage the succession process. Planning for succession involves identifying potential candidates or developing strategies to attract new talent to fill the upcoming vacancies. Succession planning should include mentoring and training programs to ensure the transition of responsibilities and knowledge transfer from retiring professionals to their successors. Organizations can maintain high patient care while minimizing disruptions by investing in developing and retaining qualified healthcare professionals.

Future Prospects: The Changing Landscape of Retirement and Succession in Medicine:

Over the past few decades, medicine has significantly transformed retirement and succession practices. As the healthcare landscape continues to evolve, so do the expectations and aspirations of medical professionals. The traditional notion of retirement, characterized by a complete cessation of work and a leisurely lifestyle, is gradually replacing alternative models that promote a more gradual transition and ongoing involvement in the medical field.

One key factor driving this change is the increasing demand for healthcare services and a shortage of qualified physicians in many regions. According to new data published by the AAMC (Association of American Medical Colleges), the United States could see an estimated shortage of 37,800 and 124,000 physicians by 2034, including shortfalls in primary and specialty care. This shortage has compelled healthcare systems to explore innovative strategies to retain experienced physicians and ensure a smooth succession of their practices.

One approach gaining momentum is the concept of phased retirement, which allows physicians to gradually reduce their clinical workload while mentoring and training junior colleagues. This model not only preserves valuable expertise but also ensures continuity of care for patients. Phased retirement programs may include options for reduced work hours, part-time schedules, or even flexible arrangements such as telemedicine. These alternatives allow physicians to maintain professional fulfillment while transitioning into a more balanced personal life.

In addition to phased retirement, another emerging trend is the concept of Subsequent career or Career reinventions in later years in medicine. With a growing emphasis on work-life balance and a desire for continued intellectual stimulation, some retiring physicians are pursuing new avenues within the medical field. This may involve teaching at medical schools, researching, or contributing to healthcare policy development. By leveraging their extensive knowledge and experience, retired physicians can make valuable contributions to medical education and the advancement of healthcare as a whole.

To facilitate this changing landscape, healthcare institutions and professional organizations have started implementing support programs and resources for retiring physicians. These initiatives aim to assist physicians in navigating the retirement transition, exploring alternative career paths, and providing opportunities for continued professional growth. For example, the American Medical Association (AMA) offers resources such as retirement planning tools, mentorship programs, and opportunities for professional networking.

Conclusion:

Retirement for healthcare professionals marks the end of a career and the beginning of a new phase in life. A smooth transition into retirement requires careful financial planning, adjusting lifestyle habits, staying active, ensuring healthcare coverage, socializing and networking, setting new goals, seeking emotional support, and efficient succession planning. Emerging strategies, including graduated retirement and second-act professions, are gaining appeal due to projected physician shortages. These strategies provide avenues for retired experts to remain involved in healthcare. Ensuring a smooth handover by thoroughly planning for succession is equally important to continue providing high-quality patient care. The overall narrative suggests that healthcare professionals and institutions must prioritize and support retirement planning to maximize personal fulfillment and benefit patient care.

Suggested Readings

• Silver, M. P., Hamilton, A. D., Biswas, A., & Warrick, N. I. (2016). A systematic review of physician retirement planning. Human Resources for Health, 14(1).

• Ghadwan, A. S., Wan Ahmad, W. M., & Hisham Hanifa, M. (2023). Financial Planning for Retirement: The Moderating Role of Government Policy. SAGE Open, 13(2).

• Pannor, M., & Mpubpol, S. (n.d.). Critical reflection on physician retirement Work identity, personal identity, and physician health. Oct 2016

• AAMC Report Reinforces Mounting Physician Shortage _ AAMC. (n.d.). June 2021

• (Stuart Heiser et al., 2021. Discover more topics Blog Care Advocacy Care Navigation. (n.d.).

• Hernandez, N., & Article, F. (2022). Choose a Specialty Four tips for succession planning at your medical practice.

• Barnett, R., & Davis, S. (2008). Creating Greater Success in Succession Planning. Advances in Developing Human Resources, 10(5).

• Baldwin E D I T O R, R. G. (2018). NEW DIRECTIONS FOR HIGHER EDUCATION Reinventing Academic Retirement.

Evaluate Yourself and Decide:
Am I A Great Doctor?

"Go for greatness. Anything else is a waste of time."

- Marianne Williamson

Have you ever wondered if the person gazing back at you in the mirror is a competent, appreciated, and efficient medical professional? "Am I a Great Doctor?" This question often sticks in a doctor's mind.

Once you've happily explored each chapter in this book, you'll be ready and able to conduct a fair self-analysis and determine whether you're showcasing the qualities of a truly great doctor. Let's joyfully delve into the assessment process together, examining the diverse aspects that make an excellent medical expert.

"The Anatomy of a Great Doctor: Skills, Struggles, and Success in Modern Medicine" goes beyond quantifiable data or praises. The answer is perhaps buried deep within the compassionate hearts, versatile minds, and skillful hands of doctors who continue to strive for excellence amidst myriad challenges. They epitomize selfless dedication, ceaseless learning, and unwavering integrity - the heroes without capes. Indeed, the journey to becoming a great doctor lies in embracing this holistic approach to healthcare, celebrating each step of this lifelong journey toward excellence, compassion, and self-awareness. Reflecting upon the myriad dimensions of what it takes to become an extraordinary medical practitioner, it is evident that "The Anatomy of a Great Doctor: Skills, Struggles, and Success in Modern Medicine" is not merely one of professional identity but of personal commitment, ethical practice, and continuous transformation. It calls upon the healer's heart, the scholar's mind, and the sage's spirit—all fundamental facets intricately woven into the fabric of medical excellence.

To stand before the mirror and genuinely inquire if one meets the criteria of greatness in medicine is to engage in a profound act of reflection that touches upon the ability to juxtapose the idealism of expectations with the tangible grasp of reality. It is a manifestation of understanding that greatness is not solely found in the precision of a scalpel's edge or the accuracy of a diagnosis but rather in the calmness with which one navigates the unpredictable ebb and flow of human wellness and disease.

Greatness in this noble field requires more than clinical acumen; it calls for an unwavering dedication to the ethos of life-long learning, patient-centered care, and the well-being of the community at large. It is the art of empathetic communication, the humility to accept and learn from one's fallibilities, and the moral courage to admit uncertainty or error. A great doctor recognizes that brilliance in medicine is not just about battling diseases but fostering an environment of trust and understanding with patients, colleagues, and the society they diligently serve.

Each great doctor is a mosaic of multiple roles: a physician, a counselor, a mentor, a communicator, a learner, and a leader. They express charisma, kindness, and empathy, extending warmth and comfort to their patients. Yet, at the same time, they are not detached from their mental health, understanding the critical art of self-care and balancing empathy with professional boundaries.

Great doctors engage in critical self-assessment, continuous improvement, and learning from mistakes and feedback. They tread the fine line between knowledge acquisition and application, maintaining an up-to-date understanding of medical advancements yet ensuring their effective translation into patient care. They regard their weaknesses not as setbacks but as stepping stones, driving their journey towards professional excellence.

Moreover, they bridge the delicate equilibrium between treating ailments and understanding the human emotions accompanying them. They are not just remedy providers but emotionally wise figures who comfort their patients in their most vulnerable times, even when faced with drastic circumstances such as death and dying. They understand the value of building trust and transparency and nurturing a solid doctor-patient relationship.

Great doctors also grapple with the external pressures of the profession, including potential lawsuits, malpractice threats, balancing ethical concerns with pharmaceutical influences, and the challenge of technology. Beyond the confines of their clinics or hospitals, they are also influential leaders and mentors, fostering a culture of collaboration, understanding, and patient-focused care.

This profession demands the skill of balancing personal life and professional commitments, as doctors must tend not only to the needs of their patients but also to their well-being. They deal with life's fragility each day, knowing all too well the complexities of death and the importance of offering solace amidst sorrow. They hold the power to heal and alleviate pain; sometimes, they have the solemn duty to guide patients and families through life's final chapter with dignity and compassion.

Therefore, the accurate measure of a great doctor is not captured in accolades or the number of lives saved but in the quiet moments of patient gratitude, the relieved sighs of troubled minds, and the profound impact they make on the lives they touch. It is seen in their steadfast commitment to personal and professional integrity, their capacity for self-examination, and their relentless pursuit of improvement for those entrusted to their care.

In sum, the holistic approach to being a great doctor is far more than the sum of its parts. It is a seamless integration of skill, knowledge, compassion, and an unwavering oath to promote human health with every fiber of one's being. To any doctor pondering their place in this esteemed lineage, know this: your quest for greatness is an ongoing journey, a testament to the impact you make and the legacy you will leave in the hearts of your patients and the annals of medical history. A great doctor strives for medical mastery, flexibility, humility, and authentic compassion. Within this definition, if you find peace, ambition, and, most importantly, motivation, you are on the correct path to becoming a great doctor.